What a Girl Wants

DISCARDED
from the Nashville Public Library

What a Girl Wants

Liz Maverick

NEW AMERICAN LIBRARY

New American Library
Published by New American Library, a division of
Penguin Group (USA) Inc., 375 Hudson Street,
New York, New York 10014, U.S.A.
Penguin Books Ltd, 80 Strand,
London WC2R 0RL, England
Penguin Books Australia Ltd, 250 Camberwell Road,
Camberwell, Victoria 3124, Australia
Penguin Books Canada Ltd, 10 Alcorn Avenue,
Toronto, Ontario, Canada M4V 3B2
Penguin Books (N.Z.) Ltd, Cnr Rosedale and Airborne Roads,
Albany, Auckland 1310, New Zealand

Penguin Books Ltd, Registered Offices:
80 Strand, London WC2R 0RL, England

First published by New American Library,
a division of Penguin Group (USA) Inc.

First Printing, March 2004
10 9 8 7 6 5 4 3 2

Copyright © Elizabeth Ann Edelstein, 2004
All rights reserved

REGISTERED TRADEMARK—MARCA REGISTRADA

LIBRARY OF CONGRESS CATALOGING IN PUBLICATION DATA:

Maverick, Liz.
What a girl wants / Liz Maverick.
p. cm.
ISBN 0-451-21114-6
1. Young women—Fiction. 2. Female friendship—Fiction. 3. Unemployed women workers—Fiction. I. Title.
PS3613.A885W47 2004
813'.6—dc22 2003019337

Set in Centaur
Designed by Ginger Legato

Printed in the United States of America

Without limiting the rights under copyright reserved above, no part of this publication may be reproduced, stored in or introduced into a retrieval system, or transmitted, in any form, or by any means (electronic, mechanical, photocopying, recording, or otherwise), without the prior written permission of both the copyright owner and the above publisher of this book.

PUBLISHER'S NOTE
This is a work of fiction. Names, characters, places, and incidents either are the product of the author's imagination or are used fictitiously, and any resemblance to actual persons, living or dead, business establishments, events, or locales is entirely coincidental.

BOOKS ARE AVAILABLE AT QUANTITY DISCOUNTS WHEN USED TO PROMOTE PRODUCTS OR SERVICES. FOR INFORMATION PLEASE WRITE TO PREMIUM MARKETING DIVISION, PENGUIN GROUP (USA) INC., 375 HUDSON STREET, NEW YORK, NEW YORK 10014.

The scanning, uploading and distribution of this book via the Internet or via any other means without the permission of the publisher is illegal and punishable by law. Please purchase only authorized electronic editions, and do not participate in or encourage electronic piracy of copyrighted materials. Your support of the author's rights is appreciated.

To my family,

Mum, Daddy, and Bro.

Chapter One

In Hayley Jane Smith's defense, it should be noted that it was a record-breaking week during the hottest summer in ten years of San Francisco meteorological history.

And there's Hayley crammed into a tiny cubicle next to a bunch of other young New Economy professionals in one of those South of Market lofts. There's no air-conditioning, and the smell of leftover pizza and Chinese takeout is so pervasive, it's almost unnoticeable.

The point is that after a person's been there five minutes in the heat and the stink, she becomes one with the heat and the stink. Which is why it really pissed Hayley off when the investigating detective asked how it was possible to *not* smell Fred Leary's day-old decomposing body in the cubicle next to hers.

The tone the detective used suggested that while he could sympathize with her, he would have recognized Fred's predicament much earlier. Hayley didn't think that coming upon Fred on Thursday would have been any better than it was finding him on Friday.

All this is to say that finding Fred dead was an unusual incident in Hayley's relatively uncomplicated world.

• • •

Hayley pinged Fred with an instant message three times that morning, since that was his preferred mode of communication. When he didn't respond, she called his name over the cubicle wall. Still no answer.

With a huff she got up and went into his cube, only to find him slumped over his desk, obviously exhausted. Poor Fred. He probably hadn't even gone home last night. Hayley pushed the old pizza boxes off the guest chair and, holding one hand to her nose as casually as possible to ward off the surprisingly pungent stench of his cube without offending him, she tapped him on the shoulder. Nothing. No response.

She shook him slightly, and just like in the movies, Fred Leary's body fell backward in his chair and then just slid off the seat to the floor as the chair rolled to the other end of the cube. He posed there awkwardly, his legs straight out in front and the rest of his body doubled over at the waist.

Clearly in some sort of denial, Hayley called his name again and pushed at his shoulder, which caused his upper torso and head to slam backward to the floor with a sickening thud. And there was Fred's corpse, in a state of late-stage rigor mortis, staring up at her.

Hayley couldn't exactly remember the order of events after that. There was possibly some screaming. Most likely it was her screaming.

In any case, all hell broke loose, and twenty minutes later when the police detective caught up with her, she was in the employee kitchen, spread-eagled against the soda refrigerator with her palms and face pressed against the glass.

To put it another way, she wasn't at her best.

"Miss . . . Hayley Jane Smith?" a male voice asked.

"That's me," Hayley mumbled. She peeled herself off the glass and turned around.

He was attractive. Alarmingly so. A big guy, but quite well distributed. He obviously worked out, but she could tell he didn't take it too far. He wore a light blue oxford shirt rolled up at the elbows, and carried off his charcoal-gray dress pants verrry nicely.

Hayley swallowed and zoomed in a little further. An appealing little scarred area stood out on his left forearm . . . he had a bit of a tan going, dark brown hair cut short around the neck and sides but not too short on top. And he was sweating, of course, although in his case it didn't seem gross.

By the time Hayley looked up into his honey-colored . . . no, "honey-colored" was too feminine. They were closer to amber. By the time Hayley looked up into his amber-colored eyes, her only coherent thought was how glad she was that she'd opted for a dressier look today. She sported her new black strappy sandals, a delightful, flippy little black three-quarter-length skirt, and a black spaghetti-strap tank. And she'd had her faux-messy cropped haircut highlighted just last Saturday. It made her feel a little more confident.

"I'm Lt. Grant Hutchinson, a police detective with the San Francisco Police Department. I know this is a difficult time, but I need to ask you some questions about Fred Leary," he said. And then he looked down her body. Literally, his gaze moved straight down from head to toe.

Hayley leaned back against the refrigerator because she knew she was blushing and she needed something cool against her skin.

He looked away, apparently entranced by the espresso machine on the far counter, and repeated, "Um, Miss Smith?"

Nothing to be nervous about, Hayley. He's shy! How sweet. She could draw him from his shell, perhaps. "Call me Hayley."

"Um." He turned his face toward her again, looked her right in the eyes, and meaningfully lifted one gorgeous, perfect eyebrow.

Much later, Hayley would try to blame everything on this moment, that eyebrow. Or maybe it was the way he lifted his finger slightly and crooked it at her and quickly dropped his hand back down as if startled by his own boldness.

"Grant." Hayley said his name quietly. In a nice, encouraging sort of way. She didn't want to scare him or anything.

He looked confused. He raised his finger again with a little nod.

And with a kind of swamping horror, Hayley realized that it wasn't a beckoning sort of finger; it was a pointing sort of finger. Pointing downward. Specifically at her. She swallowed hard and looked down.

Her skirt was plastered up her thigh, the condensation from the refrigerator literally gluing the fabric partially above the waist. *How attractive. Not. I think I'm going to kill myself now. Fred and I can share a plot.*

"Right. Thanks." She shoved her skirt down and cleared her throat. Smiling brightly, she added, "I'll just be at my desk when you're ready with your questions." Then she ran past him out the door.

For the next ten minutes Hayley sat in her cube in semiparalysis, with her head in her hands. Eventually Grant came into the cube, slid the plastic door shut, and leaned against the desktop.

Since the cubes didn't have ceilings and Hayley could still hear everything going on with the medical examiner next door, it seemed like a funny thing to do.

To his credit, Grant made no mention of what had transpired. He reintroduced both himself and the concept of a police interview and went straight to the questions. "Can you describe your relationship to the deceased?"

"Fred was the senior copy editor. I write blurb copy and headlines for the Web site. He wasn't my boss, exactly, but he reviewed my material before it went live."

He nodded and openly surveyed her cube space. Hayley flushed. Had she known a handsome police detective would be questioning her about the corpse next door, she certainly would have made an effort to clean up. The layers upon layers of paperwork, candy-bar wrappers, and office supplies made the desk resemble an archeological dig. *Well, they say you take pride in what you care about, ha-ha. Heh.*

"And you worked with him on a weekly . . . daily basis?"

"Daily."

"Daily?" The eyebrow—the one Hayley had previously misinterpreted—shot up. Hayley stared at the eyebrow and sat back in her chair. Dubious, criticizing, evil eyebrow. *Cocky bastard.* Hayley narrowed her eyes in anticipation of his next question.

Grant opened his mouth to speak but was interrupted by a bead of sweat that rolled down the side of his chiseled face. Hayley forgot to be annoyed.

She watched, fascinated, as in what seemed like slow motion, he brought his blue oxford-clad upper arm to his face and swiped from one side to the other. It was the equivalent of a Pamela Anderson *Baywatch* hair flip. Hayley's mouth slowly dropped open as his arm fell away and he actually licked his lower lip. . . .

"Miss Smith?" He leaned down, picked up Hayley's trash can, and peered down into her face. "Do you need to vomit?"

Hardly. She shook her head.

He nodded and put the trash can down. Then he put his hand on her shoulder. Hayley turned her head and stared at his hand as he said, "I know this must be very difficult for you."

"I bet you say that to all the girls who find corpses."

He pulled his hand back. "Excuse me?"

Hayley cringed back into her chair. "Oh. That was out loud." She could have sworn the tiniest hint of a smile flashed across his face for a second. But she'd certainly been wrong before.

"Why don't we continue?" He picked up his notebook and cleared his throat. "So, let's see. It seems that Fred Leary has been deceased for at least a day and you didn't notice until approximately thirty minutes ago."

Hence the saying, "going for the jugular." "I don't think you understand. What with e-mail, instant messaging, and all that stuff, it's not like people here talk to each other face-to-face a lot."

Grant gave her a skeptical look and Hayley rushed to explain. "It's completely normal for entire weeks to go by without seeing certain people in the office. In fact, there are people here I work with I've never actually seen."

Grant studied her face. It made Hayley feel inexplicably guilty . . . and hot. "Did you think it was strange when you, what's the word, 'pinged' him three times and he didn't answer?" he asked.

"Well, after three times, I did think it was strange. No, that's not true. I thought it was inconvenient. I didn't think it was strange, per se. And it wasn't like it was a rush job or anything, so I didn't go and bug him about it immediately."

"And you didn't detect anything unusual until you went into his cube."

"You mean why didn't I smell anything." He just couldn't let it go, could he?

Something snapped. It just snapped.

Hayley slumped back in her chair, looked up at him, and waved her hands about in the air. "You think it's possible here to smell the difference between Fred's dead body on the right and the sweating engineer on the left?" She gestured with her head to the cube on the other side, then calmly stared at the detective for a beat before bursting into hysterical laughter.

As she laughed out of control for a solid minute, Grant Hutchinson didn't say a word. The look on his face went from incredulous to possibly amused—although it might have been disgust, actually—before it shut down completely into a blank facade.

Hayley stopped laughing immediately and jumped up from the chair, horrified. And then she burst into tears.

Through her tears, Hayley could see the detective take a deep breath and slowly exhale. He put down his notebook and came over to her, putting his arm loosely around her shoulders. With his other hand he pulled a travel-size Kleenex packet from his pocket and handed it to her.

Hayley dabbed at her eyes. The guy really was quite good-looking. He had a solid frame and good bone structure. He was polite enough to call her "Miss Smith" and Fred "deceased" instead of "dead," even if he was somewhat rude and condescending the rest of the time. So what if he'd pissed her off at least twice.

And now to top it all, here he was, totally prepared with a brand-new travel Kleenex packet, even.

Good-looking, polite but not so polite that it made you just want to be friends, and prepared.

Good-looking, fuckable, prepared.

Hayley leaned in, tucked her face into the crook of his neck, and sobbed a couple of times.

"That's all right. We'll take it slow," he said, and gave her shoulder an awkward squeeze. He cleared his throat. "We're almost finished with the questions anyway. In fact, I don't need to take notes. We'll just make it a little conversation. Okay?" He propped her back up and Hayley nodded, sniffling into her tissue.

She knew she was supposed to be thinking about Fred and the questions and what a tragedy it all was, but for some reason as she answered the detective's carefully worded questions, she kept focusing in on the oddest little non-Fred details. It was just that it was so difficult to concentrate, what with the cloying heat and the detective being so comforting and all.

The sweat at his hairline that was making the hair around his temples curl slightly. The mangled button third from the top that must have gotten melted when he'd last ironed his shirt. The scuffs on the toes of his dress shoes from chasing criminals (undoubtedly). And the fact that the guy was just massive compared to her.

She looked down at her own slight frame. And as she mentally calculated the width and breadth of the detective's chest, she started to think about the fact that this guy could suffocate her to death if, for some reason, he were ever to be lying prone on top of her.

And she contemplated this notion as he asked her casual questions and the sweat trickled down from his left temple, dampening his collar until he arrested it by wiping his forehead with his sleeve.

And the sweat would trickle. And he'd ask her a question. She'd answer the question. And he'd wipe his forehead. And somehow the grieving/comforting process went through some sort of high-speed metamorphosis, and Hayley found herself moving in for the kill.

She lunged at Grant, putting her arms around his neck. His first instinct must have been to grab a weapon, because his hand moved instantly toward what Hayley had to assume was a gun concealed under his pant leg.

But when Hayley pulled his head toward hers and started kissing him for all she was worth, he seemed to figure the scenario out pretty quickly.

His hands switched directions and went up instead of down, sliding under her shirt and skidding along her slippery, sweaty abdomen. But he didn't stop there. He was sliding his hands up her body, now, and—

Something thumped on the ground in the cube next door. "Damn. Here, can you take his arm a sec?" said one of the paramedics.

The delirious expression on Grant's face flickered a bit. It looked like his professionalism and common sense might be recovering from the assault. Like he might pull out of the gig. Not acceptable.

Hayley's hand went south on the detective so quickly that he flinched at first. But in that moment his brain obviously stopped communicating with the rest of his body, and she had him exactly where she wanted him. Which happened to be standing between her knees as she sat on the edge of the desk, grinding his business against the palm of her hand while he unhooked her bra and went for prime real estate.

Hayley had broken off the kiss a while back when things started to get interesting, because there wasn't a whole lot of oxygen in the workloft to begin with. But Grant was committed now, and he went back for more tongue, and, man, the guy was a pro.

Unless a guy was doing something really strange, Hayley couldn't really say that she noticed one guy's kissing technique being that much different from another guy's. But this was different, although her light-headedness might have had something to do with it.

Or maybe it was just because he was such a brilliant multitasker. Now he was full-throttle kissing her, had the one hand working pretty skillfully upstairs, and just skated the other one up under her skirt. Since Hayley was wearing a thong, she nearly jumped out of her skin when he grabbed a handful of bare ass.

Time to up the ante. She unzipped his fly and pulled him out. He seemed to like that, so she moved her hand on him, which he also liked, and he went to repay the favor, sliding his hand over her sweaty, sticky thigh and—

"Maggots. Uh-huh. This guy's been dead a little while. We've got maggots."

Grant's eyes opened. The foggy look cleared and he stepped backward, distancing himself from Hayley in one motion.

He looked stunned. He and Hayley locked eyes, panting. He put his business back in his pants and zipped up. He stared at Hayley. She stood up and stared back at him while she tried to snap her bra together with shaking hands behind her back.

He frowned, swallowed, turned her around without a word,

and rehooked her bra, then turned her around again to face him, straightened her shirt, and smoothed down her skirt.

Hayley just stood there like a rag doll, attempting to clear her throat, making more of a gargling sound.

He took a deep breath and slowly exhaled. "There's a deceased person approximately four feet from here." He took a business card out from his wallet, set it down on the counter, and walked out.

Chapter Two

After returning home early on Friday afternoon of the Unusual Incident and its accompanying Inappropriate Response, Hayley changed into an oversize T-shirt and crawled into bed. She stayed there for approximately thirty consecutive hours, rising only to pee and eat canned soup.

On Sunday morning, even knowing she had to get up and meet her friends for Girlie Brunch, she was still lying on her back, staring up at the ceiling.

When her alarm finally beeped, Hayley flung out an arm without even looking and slapped the off button with her palm. Resistance was futile. Not to mention she desperately needed a cup of coffee. She stood up, shuffled over to the closet, and squinted into the dim storage space. Then, to avoid unnecessary decision making, she simply picked Friday's clothes off the floor and put them on. She added a black baseball cap to bypass the hair issue, and finally got herself out the door.

Girlie Brunch started as a huge postcollege gathering of UC and Stanford alumnae and their friends. They'd promised to use the brunch as a vehicle to stay in touch. After a year of gradual attrition (read: those who found serious boyfriends stopped showing up), only Hayley and three others still attended. Now best friends, Hayley, Diane Gradenger, Audra Banks, and Suz Herrick never skipped a Sunday if it could be avoided.

Gerttie's Diner was walking distance from Hayley's tiny Bernal Heights apartment. It was the kind of breakfast place that didn't really deserve the classic interpretation of "diner," since the food bordered on gourmet and it served lattes. But the place still looked the part: red vinyl seat cushions, Formica tabletops, the works.

Hayley grabbed the usual window table and ordered breakfast; an oversize latte called "the Gigante" for herself, regular-size lattes for Diane and Audra, and the pancake special for Suz.

Minutes later, Diane arrived in her uniform of ripped jeans and an ancient UC Berkeley sweatshirt with a nasty blue ink stain on one cuff. Her wet, mousy-brown shoulder-length hair was soaking into her sweatshirt, but she didn't seem to notice. There were a lot of things Diane tended not to notice.

Scribbling furiously with a stylus into her Palm handheld, she never even looked at Hayley as she sat down. "I may end up failing my Human Sexuality elective if I don't get some sort of paper going here."

Hayley didn't take it personally. After all, Diane was known more for her extensive vocabulary and analytical mind than for her people skills. "I still don't get why an MBA student takes a class like Human Sexuality."

"It's supposed to be easy credits. As it stands, I'd rather do another excruciating round in the Stock Market Challenge than write this paper. All I have is a random accumulation of ideas that don't fit together into a coherent thesis whatsoever." She put down the handheld and pulled off her sweatshirt, used it to absorb the water at the ends of her hair, then tied it around her waist. "You know, it's too bad I'm not still seeing Bud. He would have been convenient subject matter."

"I don't think he would have hung around for that. He broke up with you because you kept overanalyzing his bedroom technique. If I recall, you likened him to a shar-pei."

"I never said that."

"You told him that his technique was cute and he obviously was trying to be cuddly, but after a certain point you just wanted him to get off you so you could get back to work."

"Oh, I did say that." Diane shrugged. "He *was* sort of like a lapdog. With an equally useless flapping tongue. He would have made a good subject for the paper, though." She finally glanced up at this point and did a double-take that must have seriously tweaked her neck. "Are you okay?"

Hayley obviously looked as glazed as she felt. "Well, actually it's like this. I found my copy editor dead at work on Friday, then lost control of myself somehow and followed it up with a sexual interlude in my cube with the investigating detective." It was odd the way it came out of her mouth so matter-of-factly. Made the whole thing seem even more disturbing than she'd originally thought. "I really think it speaks to larger issues. It's serious."

"What's serious?" Audra strolled up to the table decked out in full khaki and black Banana Republic regalia—her version of the weekend sloth look—and pulled a gorgeous silk scarf from her Kate Spade tote bag. She used it to wipe off her chair before sitting down.

"Hayley's got boy trouble."

Huh? "Wait, what?"

Audra patted Hayley's hand and drawled, "Lucky you! What a delicious mess. I wish *I* had boy trouble."

Hayley managed a weak smile. "No, you don't. You hate messes of any kind. Sometimes I think you hate men."

"I don't hate men. I love men. I just have a habit of loving the wrong ones. And nobody's even made the first cut in a while. I'm almost willing to go B-list, at this point. Almost."

Right. Audra rarely went less than A-list on anything. Of course with a six-figure salary from the city's most prestigious boutique venture capital firm, she could afford not to. But to her credit, Hayley had to admit that it was nothing less than sheer loyalty that kept Audra coming back week after week to a diner she referred to in exaggerated tones as "the palace of squalor."

"I'd be scared to be your boyfriend," Diane mumbled. "All that pressure."

"It's called standards, ladies. Being effectively high-maintenance is an art. Don't forget that. Anyway, Di, with your record, you're not one to talk. Hay, what kind of boy trouble are you in?"

"It's not boy trouble. It's bigger than that." She sighed. "Suz is going to want to hear all this, so I'm only giving you the digest. On Friday I found a corpse and fondled a police detective."

Audra gaped at Hayley, her expression equal parts disgust and admiration. Then she pulled back dramatically and flashed Hayley a sly look. "This is one of your exaggerated stories, isn't it? Naughty girl, I almost believed you this time."

Before Hayley could protest, Suz ran into the café, looked around wildly, and flew toward the table.

She sported a fitted pink and white V-neck baseball jersey with a shiny decal spelling out *Angel* across the chest and double-dyed denim jeans and Nikes. Her wavy red hair stuck out of a high ponytail.

"Sorry, couldn't find parking. Had to wedge the cruiser into an electric-car spot. Wasn't pretty. Christ, it's hot out there. What'd I miss?" Suz pulled a napkin out of the canister on the table and stuck it down her shirt.

Poor, poor Suz. Hayley looked jealously at her friend's rather spectacular endowments. All that cleavage—it must be like a wading pool in her bra. "Hey, Suz. We ordered your usual."

Audra cut to the chase. "Hayley's got quite the tale of murder and sexual intrigue."

"Experienced that myself last night. A thousand guys in a dark bar grabbing my ass and me wanting to kill them all." Suz jammed her fork into the pile of pancakes in front of her, ignoring Audra's wince when the fruit garnish skidded off her plate. Well, that was Suz, all right; she did just about everything with maximum . . . robustness.

Diane looked up. "I thought you were enjoying that gig as the Johnny Beer girl."

"Gig's fine," Suz said. "Just a little tired of the same guys week after week." Suz's original goals for putting her mass communications degree to good use had nothing to do with being able to flirt simultaneously with large groups of men in bars. However, over the past several years, she had turned the oft-disparaged occupation of "bar promotions girl" into an art form. In fact, she did so well on tips and commissions that she regularly forgot she was supposed to be looking for a "real" job.

Suz shoveled another bite into her mouth and chewed. "You know how it is. Guys are like glow sticks. Put the stick in your hand. Shake it just right. Light goes on. Everybody has fun. Then it's used up. Time to find new fun. Know what I mean?"

"Shar-peis and glow sticks." Hayley turned to Audra. "I can see why you're hesitant to stoop to the B-list. In any case, I think you should know that it wasn't a story. It's true what I said. I found the senior copy editor, Fred Leary, dead on Friday, and when the investigating detective came to question me, we ended up . . . you know . . . we ended up getting a little, uh, a little . . . 'personal' in my cube. We didn't actually do it, of course. But we got . . . how should I say this? We got 'close-ish.' "

Silence.

" 'Close-ish'? You and this policeman got 'close-ish' at your office . . . What exactly does that . . ." Diane paused and cocked her head. "Wait a minute. Doesn't Fred Leary sit right next to you?"

"Yes, as a matter of fact, he does. Did."

Audra leaned forward. "And you . . ." She wiggled her fingers suggestively. "Right next door? Good Lord. That's disgusting."

"Yeah, that is kind of disgusting." Actually, Suz looked impressed.

"This could be useful," Diane said. "By all means, keep going."

"It's just that the whole thing is really horrifying when you think about it. A man died. People walked around the cube in which his corpse lay for, like, a day, having one-sided conversations without realizing he was never going to answer."

She couldn't look at her friends. The whole thing was too terrible. "All of a sudden, Fred seemed . . . less important. Since he was already dead. I just kind of zeroed in on the detective." She cringed at the words and rubbed her eyes. "The key word being 'seemed.' At the time. I don't know why I did it."

Diane nodded sagely. "A spontaneous adrenaline burst of sexuality triggered by acute emotional upheaval." She turned and made a notation.

"So anyway, one moment I'm answering questions about Fred's decomposing body, and the next minute I'm grinding up against this very well built . . . big . . . beautiful detective man. And the thing is—"

"A *Big Dick!* Get it?" Suz blurted out. She then compounded the joke by asking about the length of his police baton, and after a few giggles muffled out of respect, the three girls just couldn't hold it in.

Hayley waited for the laughter to die down. "Seriously, though, the significance—"

"Did you exchange numbers?"

"Well, Audra, he left me his card, but I'm pretty sure it was for investigative purposes only. Ya know?"

Diane rapped her knuckles on the table. "Hey, does Big Dick have an actual name?"

"It's Grant Hutchinson, actually. A perfectly respectable name. So you can all stop calling him Big Dick right about now."

"No need to get testy. We're here to help. But we're curious about this business of 'close-ish.' Does that mean there was tongue?" This from Suz, of course.

"What?"

"Was there—"

"Oh, for cripes' sake!" But the girls were looking at her, waiting.

"Fine. He had his hands under my skirt on my thighs and ass; I had one hand inside his shirt and the other on his . . . big dick," Hayley explained, ticking the hand placements off like a shopping list. "Full-frontal grinding. It lasted for, like, a minute, tops."

"So was it in or was it out?" Suz asked.

Hayley put her hands on her hips. "You're totally missing the point. This isn't about sex. This is about a serious life crisis that I don't even fully understand yet."

Audra smiled sympathetically, but a telltale twitch at the corners of her mouth suggested something else. Suz was busy choking on her pancakes, so she couldn't toss out one of her zingers, and Diane just kept nodding and making notes in the damned Palm.

"What?" Hayley looked from one friend to the other. "What?"

The three girls looked at each other and seemed to realize that maybe this wasn't one of Hayley's exaggerations. Audra patted Hayley's hand again. "Okay. We hear you. But if we're going to understand exactly what we're dealing with here, you're going to have to give us a little more to go by."

Suz finally swallowed the clump of pancake, her eyes glittering with anticipation. "In other words, start from the beginning and don't leave anything out."

In spite of the depressing subtext of the story, Hayley was enjoying the attention. So she told them everything, every gory detail.

When she finished, Suz, Audra, and Diane just stared bug-eyed at Hayley with their chins resting on their hands. Absolutely riveted. Finally, Suz asked, "What did he say after that?"

Hayley stared morosely into her empty latte mug. "Nothing. It was just, 'There's a deceased person approximately four feet from here.' And then, like I said, he left."

"How rude," Audra sputtered.

"I don't think I follow his meaning," Diane said, scratching her nose thoughtfully with the stylus. "Why didn't he just say 'dead'? Why 'deceased'?"

"He didn't even *thank* you?" Suz asked.

Crushed, Hayley just looked at the girls and shook her head. They. Just. Didn't. Get. It. "This isn't a *guy* story. The issue is my totally inappropriate response! You've completely missed the point."

Audra kept her face hidden in her latte mug, but Suz let out an inelegant snort, which apparently gave Diane license to ask, "Fondling the policeman wasn't the point?"

"Okay, I get what's happening here," Hayley huffed. "You think I'm just being my usual alarmist self. You think this is just another one of my bush-league traumas. Uh-uh. Let me tell you. This was nothing less than a cry for help."

She leaned forward. "I found a coworker dead, decomposing after at least a day of going unnoticed, and apparently my strongest emotion was acute horniness. It's not the horniness itself that's an issue here. It's what's behind the horniness. I clearly have some sort of problem here. And I was hoping you could, you know, help me figure it out."

Suz raised her hand. "I have the answer to what's behind the horniness. It's called a failure to get laid."

Really, Hayley should have expected this. She was only getting as good as she gave on any other Sunday. And if it weren't her problem, she'd be laughing as hard as the rest of them.

"Oh, wow. Oh, man. I'm a genius. I can help. We can all help." They all looked over at Diane. She looked mighty pleased with herself. "Say you'll come over to the apartment on Thursday night."

"For what?" Suz asked.

Diane shook her head. "I don't want to spoil it."

Audra folded her arms across her chest. "Last quarter when you said that, you made us do an experiment for your biology elective that turned our fingernails green for three weeks."

"It's nothing like that. Just say you'll come. If you won't do it for me, do it for Hayley."

"I don't even know what you're talking about," Hayley grumbled. She had a bad feeling about this.

"It's not going to hurt you. But it could help. Come on, guys, say you'll do it."

"Oh, all right," Hayley finally said. Suz shrugged and Audra nodded reluctantly. After all, how bad could it possibly be?

Chapter Three

Hayley hid in Diane's tiny bathroom, listlessly rummaging through the contents of the medicine cabinet. Although she wasn't compulsive about it, Diane had obviously straightened up recently. Things were clean and white, including the towels. The whole place had a slightly antiseptic, two-star-hotel quality to it.

Hayley stared at Diane's lackluster collection of toiletries. Maybe she was just feeling resentful because Diane was a student and had spare time to do things like clean bathrooms. Lucky girl.

Of course, Hayley hadn't cleaned much of anything during the paid week of "mental health" time-off that New Economy Mouthpiece had provided, most likely to ward off one of those unpleasant emotional distress lawsuits. Granted she probably had enough evidence against the business even without the corpse, but free time-off was free time-off.

The sounds of Suz and Diane arguing about the DVD player filtered through the door. Those two seemed to be in cahoots about something. Audra was probably still in the kitchen arranging her signature crab puffs on a silver tray. With a shrug, Hayley closed the cabinet and delved into the top drawer under the sink.

Really, one would think with Diane's interest in analysis, she'd have some serious psychotropic drugs or something. Something mood-altering would be good. *Lithium, anyone? Heh. Oh, hello! Jumbo-size ridged condoms. Good girl, Diane. Ooh . . . expiration date: 2001. Not so good. I guess I'm not the only one—*

"Hay? Is everything okay in there? I made crab puffs. I know you like them." Pause. "Are you ever coming out?"

Hayley paused with her hand in the drawer. "Nope. I've got a clean bathroom and a closet full of blankets and towels. If you just leave the crab puffs outside the door and replenish every half hour, I see no reason to ever come out."

"Seriously, Hay. You're worrying me. Come out and let Diane do whatever it is she's going to do . . . Hey! What do you two think you're doing?"

Hayley heard Audra's footsteps retreat, followed by the sound of the microwave. Now Suz, Audra, and Diane were all arguing. She could hear the terms "crab puffs" and "popcorn" being discussed in angry tones. Well, she might as well go out there and get it over with.

Hayley closed the drawer and stepped out of the bathroom into the living room. Diane's studio apartment was that small—and very light-wood IKEA. Not that Hayley was judging, or anything, but although most of *her* apartment furniture was still black-metal IKEA, she'd at least managed to upgrade the bedding and such to Calvin Klein.

Audra sat hunched in the corner of the couch with her legs crossed and her nose in the air. Suz and Diane stood facing her with their backs to the television set. Diane tugged nervously at the hem of her oversize yellow-and-navy rugby shirt, while Suz kicked one of her pink flip-flop sandals into the carpet, trying to look innocent in spite of the fact that she was obviously concealing something behind her back.

Assuming her most morose expression, Hayley looked pointedly from one girl to the other, then sat down next to Audra. She plucked two crab puffs off the tray in quick succession and crammed them into her mouth.

Suz cleared her throat. Everybody looked at her. "Before we begin, I just want to say something." She cleared her throat again, which was unusual, because Suz generally leaped before looking. "Everyone should keep an open mind."

Audra and Hayley looked at each other in alarm, and Suz elbowed Diane.

"As you know," Diane said in that authoritative voice she often used when explaining esoteric concepts to idiots, "I've been taking an elective in human sexuality."

Audra and Hayley looked at each other again, and Audra started to get out of her seat, but Suz came forward and shoved her back into the couch.

"You don't need me. I'm delicate," Audra whispered through gritted teeth. But Suz gave her some special look and Audra sat back quietly, if not exactly calmly.

"Right. So . . ." Diane continued, speaking faster and faster, "we are going to test on Hayley the premise that adult films are useful for therapeutic purposes."

Suz whipped a DVD out from behind her back.

Audra gasped. "Hayley has mental problems. I don't see how that relates to adult films."

Hayley frowned. Sometime between Sunday brunch and Thursday she'd been downgraded from upset and confused to mental catastrophe. How nice. And these must be her three best friends from the asylum.

And that was when Hayley was struck by the delicious absurdity of the situation. Audra with her money issues and her ironic insistence on spending it all discussing said issues with pricey therapists, Diane racking up degrees in a prolonged campaign to use education to avoid the real working world, and Suz with her inability to function on anything other than a short-term physical level with a guy (although apparently she functioned in that capacity extremely well); these well-intentioned pals were just as mentally flawed as she was.

And these were the people who were going to help her through her crisis. Hayley gazed at her oblivious friends fondly, a bubble of hilarious laughter welling up in her throat.

I love you guys!

". . . and therein lies the question on which my thesis is based," Diane was saying, "which is: Have the therapeutic possibilities of adult films been underestimated?"

Suz knelt by the entertainment center, loading the disc into the DVD player. "This is some hard-core shit. I don't want to mess with their expectations by saying 'adult film.' This isn't E. M. Forster; it's porn. Can't we just say 'porn'?"

"I don't think we should," Diane said nervously.

"This is unbelievable." Audra appeared as incensed as Audra ever got. She was compulsively smoothing her mauve suede skirt, kneading it, actually, from thigh to knee. "First you trump my crab puffs with popcorn, and now you expect me to watch group porn. And this is supposed to result in some sort of personal epiphany for Hay?"

"I want you to know that my thesis is based on research findings in the *New England Journal of Psychiatric Studies*. And I know what you're thinking, so let it be known that I did not make this up. And it's not as if I'm using you as guinea pigs or anything." She coughed. "I will personally attest to the fact that adult films can be educational on many levels."

"Yeah, I've found them to be quite handy as reference material," Suz said.

Hayley giggled, and the girls all turned and looked at her, suspicious of her sudden mood change. "So, Diane, what you're saying is that I'm going to find self-understanding by watching... What's it called, Suz?"

"Bambi's Boobs."

"Oh. Well, that sounds delightful. See, Audra? It'll be just like watching Disney."

"Not funny."

Suz held the plastic DVD case out to Hayley for inspection, but Diane intercepted it. "You know, I have to admit," she grumbled, "how these people actually think they can build an entire story line around breasts is completely—"

Hayley stood up and grabbed the case from Diane and looked at the cover. "Look at the size of those things. They might actually be able to carry the picture." She started giggling again. She was feeling immensely better, and they hadn't even started the film.

Suz rolled her eyes and pointed sternly to the couch. Hayley took her seat again and Suz pushed play, then settled in beside Diane.

The opening credits began to roll along with a tinny synthesizer soundtrack. A muscular man with a face that looked like an unfortunate misunderstanding between his parents appeared on the scene in a white uniform and said, "My name is Thorne Savage. I'm here to . . . fix your copier."

Bambi, concealed behind a computer monitor, suddenly stood up from her desk and dramatically removed her suit coat, allowing her blouse to gape and reveal the largest set of breasts Hayley had ever seen in her life.

"I think I'm going to throw up," Audra choked out as Bambi led the ugly guy to the mailroom. Once there, the plot took a turn for the worse, and within five minutes Bambi and her copy-machine repairman were stripping down. The moment the guy removed his tiny briefs, multiple screams from all four women reverberated throughout Diane's apartment.

Thorne had a sort of a boomerang-shaped dick. As Diane hastened to remark, it bent at a forty-three-degree angle. And before anyone had time to calm herself from that shock alone, Bambi and her man got busy on the collating table, right between the paper cutter and the hole punch.

Audra shrieked and covered her face with a throw pillow. She'd look every once in a while and then scream at the top of her lungs before hiding behind the pillow again.

Suz sat forward, turbo-eating popcorn and pumping her fist in the air, yelling, "Yeah, baby, yeah! Give it to her! Yippee-ki-yaaay!" She jumped up and slapped her ass, then pantomimed roping a steer as the repairman flipped Bambi over and the two of them just kept going.

It was chaos. Popcorn flying everywhere. Audra screaming bloody murder. Suz hootin' and hollerin'. Diane waving the plastic disc case and ranting about the structural weaknesses of the plot.

Hayley sat very still on the couch in some kind of pseudocatatonic haze, a crab puff held frozen in midair between finger and thumb as she watched the movie. She tilted her head sideways to accommodate the horizontal nature of the scene before her, as she struggled to process the information.

Bambi's energy and drive were truly amazing. Of course, one had to factor in that these things probably weren't filmed in just one take, and it wasn't likely that Bambi had had all that sex in a single day. But she clearly had a tremendous amount of stamina and forward momentum.

Hayley put a puff in her mouth and slowly chewed as she sat back in despair. She had less momentum in her whole body than Bambi did in one boob.

And maybe that was the point. Hayley clearly suffered from some sort of urban malaise. And watching Bambi, she had a sense that the root of it was the total lack of momentum in her life. As an English major with no interest in teaching, she'd really just been drifting since college, simply taking whatever path the eager cold-calling head-hunters unfurled before her. Going from one dot-com to the next hoping to make it rich before everyone figured out the companies in question had no meaningful product or service.

But what an impossible task it seemed to change one's behavior and get out of the rut. She hadn't really thought about what she wanted, and for that matter, even if the desire was there, the drive certainly wasn't. Of course, her parents had thought quite a bit about all this. They'd relocated to the Midwest but phoned periodically to implore Hayley to seek stability. This translated roughly to 1. Go to work for a large, stable corporation, 2. Get married, and/or 3. Move to the Midwest. To Hayley, their notion of stability would merely be the exchange of one sort of rut for another.

In any case, Bambi's drive was clearly in high gear. She and Thorne had gone back to her place, ostensibly to fix her personal copy machine. Bambi was thrashing about enthusiastically on her pink satin bed like a giant spawning salmon with two bobbling fins.

Like a second wind, there was a sudden frenzy of movement and a tremendous amount of noise from both parties, and then it was over. Thorne put his tool belt back on and left. The movie faded to black with Bambi just lying there—finally sated, one would hope—staring up at the ceiling with an imbecilic smile on her face.

The four girls managed to sit in silence for a record forty-five seconds until Diane couldn't hold back any longer. Peering at the fine print on the compact-disc box, she said, "You know, I'm really disappointed with this production. I picked it out especially for this final paper. It says here that it's supposed to be a story fraught with tension and conflict."

"Tension and conflict?" Suz snorted. "That would be the moment where Thorne rolled over and his winkie got too close to the paper cutter."

Audra appeared to have recovered nicely and was now returning the throw pillows to their original locations. "In spite of the lowbrow quality and the lack of finesse by both parties, it was a little bit like primal-scream therapy for me. I feel quite refreshed, actually."

Diane looked at Hayley eagerly. "Well, you're my primary subject. What did you think?"

"You were right. This was a brilliant idea."

"Did Bambi speak to you in some way?" Diane asked.

Hayley nodded slowly, actually sort of enjoying making Diane wait for the Great Porn Epiphany. "Why, Diane, I believe Bambi *did* speak to me, in her own way. You see, it's like this. There's Bambi, lying in bed getting screwed, and it's her own doing."

She paused and looked meaningfully at the girls. Blank. "Think about it. She takes whatever comes, so to speak, and if she's not happy about what she gets, it's her own fault. But she seems perfectly happy with her situation. You can see that. Our Bambi's got energy, drive, momentum. She's a . . . she's a . . . a rolling stone not gathering any moss."

Suz and Audra snickered in the background. Diane whipped around to glare at them.

"The whole Fred/Grant thing. That was a signal that something needed to change. I'm suffering from inertia. The bad kind. I'm a motionless object with no hope of getting anything started. Inertia. I'm a motionless stone gathering moss."

"I think you just lost me," Suz said.

Hayley sighed heavily and slumped back into the couch. "Seriously. I need to . . . I need . . . I need to take a stand about something, anything, make some decisions, step out in the world."

She picked up the crab-puff tray and held it against her chest with one hand, dropping puffs into her mouth with the other. "I wothn't ethen thow ware t'thart."

"Well. All that from porn. I personally didn't pick up the same deep intellectual subtext, but that begs the question. What *are* your goals?" Audra asked.

Of course, she would ask. Hayley felt a deer-in-the-headlights expression come over her face.

"Geez, don't look so scared. Not everybody has to have them." This from Suz, currently employed as the Johnny Beer girl.

"I—I . . ."

"It's okay, Hayley," Diane said. "We're all friends. Go ahead."

Hayley swallowed hard. "I'm kind of a beginner here. They don't have to be really big goals, really big long-term goals, do they?"

Suz, Diane, and Audra scooched closer to Hayley on the couch. Audra shook her head. "They can be very small goals, very small. Why don't you just try saying one small goal really fast? Just say whatever comes to mind."

"We promise not to laugh," Diane said solemnly. Suz elbowed her.

"I want . . ."

They all leaned forward.

Hayley took a deep breath. "I want that raise they promised me over six months ago?"

"Excellent. More a question than a statement, but an excellent first attempt."

Audra nodded encouragingly. "Nicely done."

"You don't even like that job; you might as well get the most you can out of it. Especially if they owe it to you."

Hayley looked at Suz in surprise and bit her lip. "That's true. . . ."

"Anything else? Or should we just work with that?" Audra patted her hand.

"Um . . ." Hayley felt a little bit more confident now. Confident enough to take on two goals, actually. "Okay, I also want a fabulous, single, heterosexual boyfriend. As soon as possible."

Suz burst out laughing, Audra gasped and put her hand to her throat, and Diane just looked at her incredulously, her stylus twitching between her fingers.

"What?" Hayley asked. "What's so funny?"

"Maybe you'd better start with the raise," Diane said.

Hayley sighed and nodded. "You're right. Probably a lot easier to get in this town."

"I don't know about that," Suz said. "What about the policeman? Grant?"

"Oh, God, no! That was a onetime thing." Wasn't it?

"Well, he's the closest you've come to an eligible guy in some time," Audra pointed out. "Diane's right. I'm quite sure it's easier to get a raise than a man in this town."

Hayley considered that. At this point, in terms of instant gratification, a guy would definitely be preferable to increased wages. But one had to consider the time-cost trade-off. It would take her an insane amount of time to both locate and work up enough courage to actually ask out the kind of guy she'd actually want to date.

On the other hand, maybe she didn't have to start from scratch. Maybe Grant wasn't totally out of the picture. Maybe he was just holding back at a respectful distance, allowing her to grieve for her coworker before stepping in and making his next move.

Right.

Squaring her shoulders, Hayley looked up at her friends. "Let's go with the raise."

"Ladies, I do believe that's my cue." Audra assumed her game face, the one with the really calculating look around the eyes. "I'm sure we all agree that I'm best equipped to be Hay's career coach. Suzy will handle the relationship angle when it's time, and Di will . . . well, Di can document the progress in her research paper."

"If you guys can get me through this, I swear, I'll . . . I'll be insanely grateful. I don't know what I'd do without you." Hayley put her arms around Audra's and Suz's shoulders. Suz linked arms with Diane.

"Group hug, everybody," Diane said. "We'd better do it now before things start to get ugly and we end up not speaking to each other."

"Ha-ha," Hayley said. "I hardly think this is going to be quite that traumatic."

Diane looked at her and grinned. "Famous last words."

"Suzy, you and I have been through this sort of thing before. Whatever happens, friends. Right?"

"Absolutely, Audra. Friends. *Of course*, friends." Suz sounded like she was getting a little teary, but she apparently recovered in time and said, "But you do realize I'm going to beat you to the punch. Even with you getting a head start."

Audra sniffed disdainfully. "I find it hard to believe that you think Hayley will get a man before she gets a raise. Besides, this is hardly a competition, Suzy."

Suz cocked an eyebrow. She and Audra exchanged knowing smiles. They both loved to compete.

Diane said to Hayley, "Just remember, they have your best interests at heart. We all do."

"Yes, and I'm sure we can comport ourselves with the kind of respect and decency Hayley deserves," Audra said.

Hayley didn't know whether to laugh or cry. She'd seen Audra and Suz in the thick of competition before, and it wasn't pretty. Well, Diane would have to help referee. Frankly, Hayley wasn't about to turn down their help. These guys were pros. And she certainly couldn't do it alone.

Diane bent down and retrieved her handheld from where it had fallen on the floor during the chaos. She flipped the lid and turned it on. "Audra, if you're first, you might as well get started. It's still early."

Suz stood up and glanced at her watch. "Maybe I oughta make some more popcorn. Most of the first batch seems to be on the rug."

"Don't bother," Audra said. "This isn't going to take that long. Everything Hayley needs to know is condensed into three simple rules of salary negotiation." She smiled at Hayley. "If you memorize just these three rules, there's no way you can possibly fail."

Chapter Four

Hayley didn't hit the snooze button even once the following morning. She just popped out of bed like a true optimist. Today, she was going to ask for a raise, and she felt mighty fine about it. Mighty fine. She considered the contents of her closet carefully this morning, and selected, of all things, an electric-blue wool sweater.

She'd never actually worn the sweater before, but she selected it with great flair, whipping out the mothball-drenched sweater bag from the very back of the closet. She would wear it as a symbol. A symbol of a decision made and acted upon, a decision outside of the norm. Bright blue plucked out of a sea of endless black.

And so Hayley prepared herself for the big event, sallying forth on that promising June day in black canvas slip-ons, black skirt number four (A-line, again three-quarter-length but not so flippy, and this time with a tasteful slit over the left knee), a black baby tee with the New Economy Mouthpiece logo prominently displayed across the chest (to demonstrate employee loyalty), and the blue wool sweater tied around her waist (since it was too damn hot to actually wear).

She left the house feeling as ready as she'd ever be.

Unfortunately, the closer the bus traveled toward her stop near the office, the greater Hayley's urge to beat the driver unconscious with her purse, hijack the bus, and head over to Gerttie's for a hot breakfast became.

Why was it so hard for her to find the courage to step up and ask for what she wanted? It was bad enough it took three extra people and a skin flick to get to the point where she'd even identified what she wanted.

By the time she'd made it from the bus to the office elevator, she'd chipped the nail polish entirely off her left hand. Hayley stared at her decimated nails and just shook her head.

She'd been promised this raise. How hard could it be to ask for what she was due? Of course, once she had the raise, then what? Life was good? Hardly. Then she'd simply be making more money doing a job she didn't particularly like. Was that momentum? She wasn't so sure.

Settled in her cubicle, Hayley sighed and fished in her purse for a mirror. At least it was a step in the right direction. She checked her teeth and her hair, wiping under her eyes for any smudged mascara.

In a last-ditch effort to build confidence, she ran through Audra's three rules of negotiation one more time:

1. Don't let the bastards intimidate you; stand your ground.
2. Don't take no for an answer; suggest a creative compromise.
3. And whatever you do, don't get combative; be friendly but firm.

That was it. That was all she needed to know. She took a deep breath and stood up, retying the sleeves of her sweater around her waist with great ceremony as a sort of silent battle cry. And then she stepped out into the hall . . . looked left . . . looked right . . . and realized that she had no idea where her boss sat.

This should not have been surprising, given that it was Hayley's normal policy to stay as far away from the managing editor as possible, at all times. Oddly enough, she couldn't exactly remember why she'd made that decision. Come to think of it, her lack of visibility with the executive team probably had something to do with the fact that she never got the raise she was promised.

After returning to her cube and consulting the on-line floor map, Hayley made her way across the workloft to the designated cube and stood just outside her boss's doorway, psyching herself up for the big moment.

She peeked into the cube, then immediately pulled back out, flattening herself against the outer cube wall. That was her boss, Janice Rasler, all right. Now she remembered why she had initially decided to avoid her.

Janice wore huge Coke-bottle glasses that magnified her eyes about tenfold. Those eyes, coupled with a giant football-shaped head, gave one the uncomfortable sensation of being held under alien surveillance. In short, spending time with Janice was not conducive to the creative process.

Hayley took another deep breath and stepped into the open doorway. Janice didn't notice her at first, as she seemed absorbed in picking at the tail end of her lunch with both hands like an oversize pod creature, all ten fingers sort of mowing slowly through the remnants on her plate for a last tasty morsel. Hayley winced. Up until now Fred had made contact with Janice unnecessary in the big scheme of Hayley's daily working life. Poor Fred. Maybe he just couldn't take it anymore.

Janice suddenly looked up. "I'm done," she said, and pushed her lunch plate across the desk.

Hayley stared at the plate. "Um, hello, Janice. It's me, Hayley."

"Great. Tell them to send me the low-sodium lunch next time."

"I'm sorry?"

"You don't need to be sorry. Just make sure I get the low-sodium tomorrow."

"No, I mean . . . um. I'm not here about your lunch."

Janice pushed her glasses back against the bridge of her nose. "You're the new girl."

"Nooo, actually I'm not the new girl. I'm Hayley."

Blank expression.

"Hayley Jane Smith? The, uh, the 'old' girl. Heh. Blurbs and headlines? You're my boss." Okay, this had quickly surpassed embarrassing and was now entering the realm of excruciatingly painful. Hayley could feel that the area around her waist where the wool sweater was tied was already soaked with sweat. She took a deep breath and told herself not to panic.

She could now see that relying solely upon Fred to avoid Janice had been a fatal error. For the first time her life, Hayley understood the benefits of general office politics, backstabbing and ass kissing. They could be useful workplace tools and ought to be exercised on a regular basis, sort of like disaster training.

Janice squinted at her through her lenses. "Are you sure?"

"Um, yes, I'm sure."

"You work for me?" Janice closed one eye and gazed at Hayley out of the other. It was somewhat disconcerting.

Deep breath. "Yes, I do, and the reason—"

"Then you must be on deadline."

Negotiation rule number one: Don't let the bastards intimidate you.

Here goes. "Yes, and I can assure you that I will make the deadline. What I'd really like to talk to you about is . . . is . . . salary." God, with the exception of the pathetic stutter at the end, there, she sounded just like Audra. It was amazing.

Janice steepled her hands together. "We give raises on a meritorious basis after each six-month review."

"Perhaps I'm not communicating effectively, heh. . . . You see, when I was hired, the company didn't have all its funding, and I was promised a raise when it came through. And since it did, I figured—"

"Who promised?"

"Well, unfortunately, it was Fred. Fred Leary, the senior copy editor . . . he hired me. He was the senior person on my interview schedule."

"Ah, well, that explains it. That is unfortunate, since Fred doesn't work here anymore." Janice turned back to the papers that had been under her lunch plate, discussion over.

"Excuse me?" *Doesn't* work *here?* That was one way to put it.

"I'm saying, we can't ask him to confirm your statement because he left the company last week." Hayley sort of gaped until Janice added, "We'll have to table this until your next review."

"You think Fred—" *Wait a minute.* "The next review is months away. It will have been over a year since I was hired."

"Precisely."

Negotiation rule number two: Don't take no for an answer.

"I certainly see where you're coming from, Janice, but perhaps we can come to some sort of, uh, creative compromise?" Okay, that was good. That was really nice. Channeling Audra, now.

Janice sighed and put her pencil down. "One second." She rolled to the file cabinet against the back wall of her cube and fished around until she pulled out a folder.

"Aha. Mmm. I see. So *that's* you. Ahhh . . . I'm going to have to say this, aren't I?"

Hayley's stomach lurched and started to roil.

"The thing is . . . Hayley, is it? The thing is, Hayley, New Economy Mouthpiece is moving in a more professional, business-oriented direction. You haven't shown the ability to write material with that target in mind."

"It says that in my file?"

"Yes. Apparently your material is still struggling. It says, and I quote, 'Hayley's writing is still too snarky and not reflective of the serious nature of the business-oriented New Economy audience.' " She closed the file with a snap.

"I'm 'too snarky'?"

Janice smiled sadly and returned the file to the cabinet drawer.

"I'm 'too snarky.' "

Janice looked up with a frown.

Negotiation rule number three: Don't become combative, whatever you . . . Oh, shut up, Audra.

"Golly, Janice. Were we just going to wait and save the bad news for the review, at which point I would be denied a raise anyway? Was someone going to get around to telling me that I'm 'too snarky' and maybe I should start working on refining my writing style?"

Janice used her pinkie to fish a bit of lunch out of her front teeth. She made a repulsive smacking sound and said, "I believe Fred Leary was."

Hayley placed her palm down on Janice's desk and leaned forward. "Oh, I see, well, has anyone here on your side of the building noticed that Fred Leary is *dead*? No? Well, by all means, let me be the first to inform you that Fred Leary kicked the bucket last week. He's *no comprende.* Kaput. In other words, Fred Leary is physically unable to keep promises at this point, and he certainly hasn't been by my desk this morning to talk about excessive snarkiness."

Janice's skin turned a pasty white. In a low, threatening voice, she asked, "Was that an outburst?"

Hayley stared at her, numbly watching Janice's eyes bulge. Unnerved, she cleared her throat before answering, "It may have been an outburst." She had a bad feeling about this.

Janice leaned forward and slammed her palms flat on the desk. Hayley snatched her hand away and took a stumbling step backward.

"Too snarky," Janice hissed. Without a doubt, it was meant to be the final two words on the subject.

All at once Hayley deflated. Audra would have cringed if she'd heard the way Hayley simply squeaked, "Uh, never mind," then turned around and started to walk out of the cube.

"It's Hayley Jane Smith, right?"

How nice. Janice knew her name now.

Hayley didn't even look over her shoulder. Eyes on the exit, she just nodded and retreated to her own cube.

Yep, she was definitely roiling now. That combination feeling of helplessness, anger, and insecurity all rolled into one. She needed a good cry, that was for sure. But definitely not here.

She untied the sweater from her waist, slinging it over the armrest of her office chair. It immediately slithered to the floor.

Hayley glared at the pile of blue wool and then flung herself into the rickety chair, purposely sliding off the seat cushion until her ass was hanging in thin air and her elbows were hooked around the armrests.

With the one major exception surrounding the discovery of Fred's body, Hayley thought she normally handled stress pretty well. She'd been taking yoga once a week for three months now, and was starting to believe that total Zen was just around the corner.

Or at least, that was her justification for the ridiculous monthly fee she paid to have some guy who needed a shave and a pair of shorts with better coverage encourage her to place her legs in positions that she wasn't sure they really needed to go into.

But rather than invoking those special yoga swami breathing exercises, she kept replaying the Janice encounter over and over in her mind with variations on witty comebacks and snappy answers she wished she'd given.

So instead of feeling calmed and centered, she just sat there fuming, sprawled half-off her office chair with her arms and legs akimbo, and stared up at the hip industrial lighting system above her desk.

And after a little while the graphic designer's mutt, Ponzi, wandered into her cube and stuck his head up her skirt.

Hayley swallowed a bloodcurdling scream, maintaining enough presence of mind to recognize that this was not something she wanted anyone to witness.

In sheer terror, she pushed off the floor with her feet. With her arms completely stuck in the armrests due to the gripping tension in her muscles, she rolled the chair backward, pedaling desperately, trying anything to dislodge the dog's head from beneath her skirt.

It was obviously confused, its paws tangled in the blue sweater, struggling to find the light of day, and at this point, thoroughly uninterested (thank God) in what might be up there in the skirt.

After what seemed like a lifetime, the pooch finally popped loose.

Hayley scrambled into a wobbly standing position on the chair with her hands clenched in tight fists.

"Jesus! Fucking! Christ!"

She scared the little shit so badly it yipped and then peed on her sweater.

Every single person in the office gophered up out of the cubes, and a grim silence descended over the humid workspace.

Hayley looked out at the sea of faces and just smiled weakly at them all. It was all she could manage. "Heh. Ha-ha?" *Oh, boy.*

Behind her back she heard one of the engineers say to the other, "Did she just kick the dog? Man. Poor Ponzi."

Lovely. It was the last thought she had before the admin appeared and summoned her back to Janice's office. Really, Hayley didn't know what was worse, being offered head by the company mutt or . . . no, that was pretty bad.

On her way there, she decided to refuse to apologize for creating a ruckus, and within five minutes, she'd been fired. Just like that. The official grounds Janice cited were poor performance and irreconcilable incompatibility with the company mission statement.

Granted, "Jesus fucking Christ" wasn't the best thing to scream out in a crowded office, but it certainly wasn't the worst. Really, from a legal perspective, her behavior was probably good only for some sort of warning or probation, probably justifiable as a condition brought about by the emotional trauma of Fred's death.

But then Hayley inexplicably had gone on to dig her own grave with a diatribe about the fact that there was obviously no freedom of religious expression at this company, but the graphic designer's dog was allowed to run rampant and piss in people's workspaces, and what's more, she wasn't trying to convert anyone in the office, so what was the big deal. . . .

Within half an hour, a security guard from the lobby was summoned to Hayley's cube with three new packing boxes and two used ones with orange stickers pasted all around the sides.

Hayley stared in horror at the stickered boxes, at the bright orange stickers labeled "*Basura.*" Spanish for the word "trash." She could feel her face flaming, and of course her nose was running now. She swiped at it with the back of her hand and quickly sorted through the contents of her cube, placing things in the appropriate boxes. *Basura?* Or *casa?* It didn't take long to pack up.

She picked up the box and, after a stunned glance behind her, left the blue sweater crumpled and stained on the floor.

Back on the bus, Hayley stared unseeing at the box in her lap. The most feared and reviled of dot-com exit scenarios; she'd been unceremoniously "*basura*-ed" without the ego cover of an official layoff. It simply didn't get more humiliating than this.

After all, it was nearly impossible to lose your job from a technology company by actually getting fired for performance reasons. Even the biggest slacker, the most idiotic of employees could figure out ways to take advantage of the system or even appear productive.

So why then was Hayley sitting on the bus at ten o'clock in the morning with her personal effects in an open box on her lap and an urge to crawl into bed and assume the fetal position?

• • •

I'm eligible for the unemployment line. The economy's headed down the tubes, and I no longer have a job.

Hayley stared up at the ceiling, back in bed two hours after leaving her house on Friday morning. *I'm either a brilliant strategist with a trump move up my sleeve or a complete moron. . . .*

I must be a complete moron.

The phone rang. Hayley didn't move. It rang twice more before the answering machine kicked in. She cringed as the chipper recorded greeting played, then rolled over on her side just enough to get a good look at the black and white photographs of famous Parisian landmarks hanging on the wall, and wish herself anywhere but here.

"Get your ass out of bed and pick up the phone!" Suz. Word traveled fast. Hayley sighed and managed to knock over her lucky bamboo plant as she reached for the phone on the far nightstand.

She sat up properly, righted the bamboo with one hand and picked up the receiver with the other. " 'Lo."

"Are you in bed?"

Pause. "Yes."

"Are you dressed?"

Pause. "Yes."

"Excellent. I'm taking over."

"What? Oh. You talked to Audra about the, uh, the . . . job mishap, didn't you?"

"Yeah, you got fired. I love Audra, but I think it's time to try some new tactics. You should have called me immediately."

"It would have hurt her feelings if I'd called you first. She *is* my career coach."

"Well, she's doing a lousy job."

"Well, you're my relationship coach and I haven't had sex in over a year."

Silence.

"Suz?"

"Jesus. Don't know what to say. I had no idea you were in such dire straits."

"Don't rub it in."

"Well, considering that you've been exhibiting signs of sexual aggression toward the city's police force, I guess I shouldn't be surprised. You know, I could give you numbers for a couple of guys who could take care of that for—"

"Oh, for God's sake. One police detective. In unusual circumstances."

"Okay, okay. Anyway, I've got a plan."

Oh, God. "Thanks, Suz, but the job is already gone. There's no point."

"It's not about the job. It's about the guy."

"What guy? The policeman?"

"Any guy. I didn't want to say anything at the time, because I didn't want to make the girls feel bad. But it's way easier to get a guy than a raise. Trust me. You just need to understand how the male mind works. It's an incredibly simple instrument with one very basic underlying truth. Once you understand that, you'll feel much better about approaching the men you think have potential."

"I see. Well, I'm so glad. Um, are you going to tell me what this basic underlying truth is?"

"No. I'm going to show you. That's why I called. I want you to come meet me at the Beer Garden tonight at six. First we practice; then we execute. You just need a little education."

"Education?" Gulp. "Suz, does this involve intense personal

embarrassment on my part? You know I have a very low personal embarrassment threshold."

"Hayley, honey, I won't ask you to do anything I won't do myself."

How comforting. Suz really didn't have a personal embarrassment threshold at all.

Chapter Five

The minute Hayley followed Suz through the doorway of the Beer Garden, a sense of foreboding washed over her.

She couldn't put her finger on it exactly; she just knew it was more than the eerie combination of hunting-lodge kitsch bathed in the glow of giant red floor-standing lava lamps. More, even, than the sensation of being followed by the eyes of a large moosehead hung over the main bar with plastic flowers entwined in its antlers.

Although it was only a little after six o'clock, Hayley could see that the bar was picking up steam. "You know, just when things seem bleak, there's always a place like a crowded bar full of attractive people having a good time to make things seem even bleaker. Do you fully realize what happened to me yesterday? Do you realize the extent of my trauma? I failed."

Suz tugged on Hayley's hand and dragged her through the bar to the back room. "You didn't fail. The way I see it, you succeeded beautifully. Instead of a little change you made a big change. Listen, I'm sorry about the job screwup, but I can't help you with that.

That's Audra's domain." She gestured to the overdecorated dressing room. "But *this*... this is *my* domain. You just need to understand how the game is played. First we need to understand the principles. Tonight we understand the principles, and later we execute."

"Right. Well, I'll just watch and learn, I guess." Hayley'd seen Suz doing her thing before, and while it was impressive, it wasn't exactly enlightening. And she couldn't ever recall her own self-esteem improving as a result of watching Suz do anything. But she was making an effort to help, so Hayley kept her mouth shut.

Suz pulled her keys out of her bag and opened a tall gray locker backed up against one wall of the dressing room. After a couple of tugs, she managed to squeeze her elaborate green poofy Johnny Beer girl costume out of the narrow opening.

It was generically Germanic-looking, embroidered with multicolored thread and featuring an extremely short skirt. Well, it was more like a round piece of green fabric that stuck straight out from the waist with a radius of two feet held up by several layers of stiff white lacy petticoat ruffles.

Suz ran her palm down the fabric of her dress and nodded with satisfaction. "For me, being a Johnny Beer girl is the ultimate expression of feminist power."

Hayley reached up to the top shelf and pulled down a large blond wig with a long braid sticking out from either side. "I see. Sort of like being a stripper?" She grinned at Suz.

Suz didn't grin back. She was all business. "Well, no. Stripping is about showing. Providing. Giving. It involves direct commerce. Being a Johnny Beer girl is about power. Teasing. Toying. And ultimately denial. Unless, of course, you decide you really want him."

"Okay. I see." Well, not really.

"Your timing was perfect. Grace is on vacation." She opened

the locker next to hers, braced her foot on the edge of the metal, and pulled out a second dress.

That fuzzy foreboding sensation became clearer in Hayley's brain.

Suz tossed over the dress and Hayley reflexively caught it. "I e-mailed her about borrowing the costume. She's cool with it, so no problem."

Hayley held the dress out in front of her as if it were tainted meat. "No problem? No problem?"

"*Is* there a problem?"

"You're asking if there's a problem? You're expecting me to put this on? You're expecting me to put this on and go out there into the bar? *Yes,* there's a problem."

Suz put her dress on the makeup chair and took Grace's dress out of Hayley's arms and put that on the chair as well. "Let's sit down for a moment and calm ourselves."

Hayley refused to sit. "You can't lull me into sedation just by using the collective 'we.' I'm not a Moonie."

"A Moonie? Where is this coming from?" Suz shrieked with laughter.

Her laughter only made Hayley more stubborn. "I won't do it. I won't wear that dress. You wear the dress and tell me what happens."

"It's not the same. You have to wear the dress. You must experience the dress for yourself. Humor me for one second. Go stand over by the full-length mirror."

Jaw set, Hayley walked up to the full-length mirror. *God, I look unhappy. Why am I so unhappy?*

From behind, Suz plunked Grace's blond wig down on Hayley's head. The two girls stood there looking into the mirror in silence. On Grace's wig, the braids looped up in an arc from the sides of the head for a sort of virginal-milkmaid effect.

Hayley couldn't help but smile.

Suz put her arm around her shoulders and gave her a little squeeze. "It's not so bad, is it? Kind of fun, don't you think? What do you say?"

"They'll laugh at me. I can't pull this off. I don't have what it takes." Hayley choked back unexpected emotion.

"Not true," Suz said. "And that's just the kind of attitude we're here to tackle. This dress is going to show you that you don't have to sit around waiting for what you want."

Suz adjusted the braids so they weren't quite as U-turn-esque. "You'll practice tonight using the costume and you'll know that you are the same person, just in a large floofy green dress. And then when you're ready, you simply take the dress off and put all the same principles into motion the next time you see a guy you want."

Hayley didn't answer. It sounded completely ridiculous and totally plausible all at the same time. Finally she just shrugged. It wasn't likely things could get worse. Not to mention, it wasn't likely anyone would recognize her in the costume. She'd probably be the last person they'd expect to see.

Suz sensed that she'd won and leaped into action. "Let's get started. Remember, you're going to feel like it's because of the costume. But it's really not the costume. It's you. But we're just going to take it one step at a time. Okay, petticoats first."

Hayley stepped into the scratchy white stuff and held it by the waist. "Uh, your pal's a little bigger than me."

Suz handed her a safety pin and Hayley folded over the waist and pinned it together.

"Arms up; let's go," Suz barked. She dumped the green dress

over Hayley's head and pulled it down. The white underblouse portion sagged away from Hayley's chest.

Hayley rolled her eyes. Grace carried as much bust as Suz did, maybe more. "Look at this. Look! There's enough room in here to pack for a weekend. I wouldn't even have to take a carry-on."

She stuck her hand down the front and flapped it against the loose fabric. "In fact, I could probably add a croissant and a cup of coffee and avoid the airplane food. Of course, if I had bigger boobs I wouldn't need a cup holder. I could just shove the cup in my cleavage. And it could be my feed bag. I could just put my face down in my boobs and have a little snack—"

"Stop it." Suz slapped Hayley's hand away. "You're going to rip the lace. If you're done ranting, we can move on. I've come prepared." Suz fished around in her bag and pulled out what appeared to be a bra. "Here. Put this on."

An inflatable bra, actually. Closer inspection revealed it was constructed out of silver latex with a black velvet lining. Classy, for a plastic blowup bra.

"No way. No. Way. This is supposed to make things better?"

Suz put her hands on her hips and generated some serious attitude. "No, this is supposed to make things clearer. Look, if you want to do this, quit your bitching."

"I don't want to this. You want me to do this. And I'm willing to do this. But I don't want to do this. There's a difference."

"And the difference, my friend, is called inertia. This lack of momentum, the very thing you wish to be cured of, is what is responsible for putting you in an inflatable bra in a Johnny Beer girl dress in the first place." She thrust the bra under Hayley's nose. "Now, you're going to *put* this bra on and I'm going start *blowing* it up and you're going to *tell* me when the front of the dress looks right. You got that?"

Hayley swallowed hard, shrugged down the bodice and put the bra on, then slipped back into the top of the dress. Suz used the little side tube to blow air into the cups.

Entranced, Hayley stared in fascination at the mirror. "Hey, look, I'm a C! I'm a C! Now I'm a D. Look at that! Whoa, now I'm a double-D. Hold on. Too much! You'll stretch the dress. A little less . . . little less. Okay, plug it."

Suz pinched the air tube and tucked it into the dress. "Okay, now it needs just a little positioning."

Hayley started to bend over at the waist so she could sort of work the bra setup into place, but Suz grabbed her by the back of the dress. "Whoa! Whoa! Whoa! Hayley, didn't you study the principle of torque in high school?"

"I beg your pardon?"

"You bend over like that in that thing and at best you'll get a head rush like you've never had in your life, and at worst the weight imbalance will tip you over and you'll end up with a concussion."

"Wow. It's all so exciting," Hayley said in a deliberate monotone. "Fraught with danger and risk to life and limb."

Suz rolled her eyes. "Here, let me." She dived in with both hands and jostled things around for a few seconds while Hayley stared up at the ceiling trying not to think about being groped by one of her best friends.

"You know, the Beer Garden gets a lot of Financial District clientele. Some of Audra's friends could be here. What if they *do* recognize me? I might see these people again."

"They're going to *want* to see you again. Watch them fall all over you." Suz stepped back from Hayley, her hands up as if touched by angelic light. "Wear it and they will come," she said reverently.

"Yes, master."

Suz didn't crack a smile. "Remember. You have what they want. With or without the costume, you have what they want."

"I have what they want," Hayley intoned. She stepped forward, swaying slightly as she adjusted to the ballast of the petticoats. One boob seemed like it might be losing a little air, and her wig had slipped over one eye.

Suz impaled her with a couple of hairpins to stabilize the wig while Hayley awkwardly leaned down and pumped more air into her chest.

Then Suz quickly dressed herself in the matching costume and handed Hayley a pair of shoes. They were a half size off, but not too bad. Hayley stuffed a wad of tissue in each of the toes and slipped them on.

"Let's go," Suz said, and handed her a bag of Johnny Beer bottle-cap–opener promotional giveaways.

Hayley took the bag and gingerly stepped out of the dressing room into the hall. Peeking around the corner into the main room of the bar, she took a shaky breath.

"It's going to be fine. You'll love it," Suz whispered.

"Suz, what exactly am I supposed to do? Do I just hand these out?"

"Just pass out the swag," she said, pointing to the sack of bottle-cap openers. "You pass out the swag and party with the customers. Encourage them to drink Johnny Beer. That's all you need to do. Other than that, just have a good time."

"That seems doable."

"Oh, and if a customer wants to buy you a beer, no problem—as long as it's Johnny Beer you're drinking."

Hayley nodded, then expanded her stride and took a few experimental steps into the room. She felt like she was waddling, but she had to believe Suz wouldn't go so far as to make her waddle amongst strangers. It must look better than it felt.

She also had the urge to keep adjusting her chest. This was what it must feel like to have to keep moving your jock around to get it comfortable. Okay, well, that was an interesting takeaway.

And then suddenly, as she moved away from the door into the center of the room, it was as if a giant spotlight turned on her. People started cheering and waving their arms. "Over here!"

Over there? Me or Suz? She looked back at Suz, but her friend just stood back in the shadows of the door frame with her arms crossed, smiling.

Hayley turned her attention back to the loudest table, filled with guys who seemed tremendously happy to see her. It was a normal batch of guys. Some were quite disgusting, from a purely aesthetic perspective. Some were wildly attractive. Most, of course, just looked kind of nice. Acceptable.

Regardless of what they looked like, Hayley normally wouldn't have approached any of them. Certainly not the wildly attractive ones. Normally she would sit with her friends at a table, waiting for one of them to come up to her, hoping that it wasn't one of the really disgusting ones.

Or if her friends weren't around, for whatever reason, she'd be circling the room. Compulsively circling. Her fear of being mistaken for a wallflower was so great that she would traverse the confines of the party over and over, desperately hoping to see an acquaintance, at least, with whom to exchange fresh small talk.

Circling, circling . . . anything to avoid appearing alone (gasp) or uninteresting (horrors!) to her peers. But it wasn't like she'd ever just walk up to a guy she didn't know. She didn't have the guts. Stupid. Hayley knew this. She had many excellent qualities. Women much more annoying or unattractive than she did quite well at parties and bars.

Well, this time she had no choice but to enter the fray. And after all, she had armor. Hayley hoisted her boobs one last time, squared her shoulders, and walked up to the table. She offered a brilliant smile.

"Johnny Beer bottle-cap opener, anyone?"

Within seconds the men engulfed her in some sort of alternate universe. They ogled, flattered, bribed, begged, flirted, offered her an unlimited supply of free beer, and generally treated her like the most desirable woman on earth.

At the end of what seemed like several hours, Hayley detached herself from the mob to use the restroom. When she returned, a blond, heavily muscled blue-eyed hunk handed her a fresh beer and stepped directly in front of the sleek Asian fellow who'd been flirting with her last. "Do you have any idea how beautiful you are?" he asked.

He sounded drunk or stupid. Or maybe he was just from L.A. Hayley took a swig from the bottle and grinned. This was fun. "No. Why don't you tell me?"

He looked confused. As if he wasn't expecting to actually have to answer. "You're really, really beautiful." Hayley didn't say anything and he obviously got the impression he had to do a little better than that. "You're like a big yellow-and-green sunflower. Like a big yellow-and-green sunflower. Yeah."

Hayley shook her head and giggled before turning away. There really was something about the dress, the boobs, the commemorative bottle-cap openers, the act, the whole shebang, that attracted men like flies.

And the interesting part was that Hayley kind of got into it. She turned some of them away with a look or a word, insulted the ones who were too grabby, and flirted back with the ones she liked.

She was starting to understand just what Suz was talking about when someone tapped her on the shoulder. She turned around to find a gorgeous Latin-looking man dressed in Armani.

"My name ees Sergio Montoya-Azevedo." He put an arm around her waist and dipped her backward in a lover's swoon (she had to clap one hand over the wig to keep it from flying off), and then bent over her and lasered his passionate eyes into hers. "And now I am going to dance weeth you."

He lifted her up onto the bar, then, without looking, pointed with full arm extension behind him at the deejay station and cued Ricky Martin.

It wasn't like in the movies, where the bar being danced upon is miraculously free of drinks or other breakable objects. And it also wasn't like in the movies, where both parties coincidentally happen to know how to dance a decent salsa.

Hayley had no idea how to dance any kind of salsa, but since Sergio kept his body as close as he could get to her, what with the skirt smashed up between them, all she had to do was wriggle out a sort of bastardized version of dirty dancing and everyone was happy.

Her lack of dancing prowess didn't seem to matter much. Even as beer steins and martini glasses smashed to the ground and, in full view of the entire bar, Sergio's hands started to roam in places that had nothing to do with salsa dancing, nothing really seemed to matter. The bottom line was that a Latin hunk was dancing on the bar with Hayley Jane Smith trussed up as a buxom Bavarian virgin.

And what this told Hayley, as she leaped off the bar into Sergio's arms and headed with him to the coat closet, was that all men were ultimately the same.

Sergio pushed aside a wad of coats and moved Hayley into the back recesses of the closet, his hand wandering around her thighs searching for access. "*Querida, querida,*" he murmured as he pushed his knee between her legs and started to grind his hard-on into her pelvis while sucking on her neck.

Hayley really hadn't done the drunken snogging thing since college and was thoroughly enjoying that hazy, lusty, pit-of-the-stomach sensation. Since her inhibitions had pretty much disappeared several beers ago, she figured what the hell, maybe she could get an orgasm out of the evening. She reached down and flipped the skirt upward flat against her body to get better contact with Sergio's leg.

Unfortunately, his hands moved up her waist toward the boobs. Well, that was enough to break any woman's concentration. There was no way Hayley was traveling to the land of humiliation by letting him discover that her ample Bavarian bosom was a fake.

She pushed his hands down, hoping he'd pick a more southern destination to grope. Unfortunately, the train was an express. Blurting out a fervent prayer to Santa Maria, Sergio flailed out an arm for something else to hold on to, latched on to a coat, and yanked it off the hanger as he came into his perfect European trousers.

Hayley leaned against the closet wall as Sergio slobbered on the side of her neck in ecstasy.

Interesting.

Stripped down to their very essence, gorgeous or disgusting, men were all just a bunch of drooling horndogs. There was nothing discriminating or intimidating about them. That was Suz's basic underlying truth.

Once she could see that, Hayley realized there was really no point in waiting all her life to see which men would come to her. She might as well make a well-thought-out decision about which drooling horndog she really wanted and actively pursue him. Even if he was good-looking enough to give her a complex under normal circumstances. In fact, especially if he was good-looking. Because all she had to do was go up to one and ask.

It was a heady realization. Principle understood. Execution yet to come.

Suddenly the closet door opened. "Hayley, you done in there?"

Suz. "Yeah." Hayley eased away from Sergio and let him fall to the ground. Patting at her costume to straighten whatever might need straightening, she stepped through the wall of coats into the bar, ignoring Sergio's muffled cry of "*un momento!*"

Suz had changed back into her regular clothes and had her own bag and Hayley's bag with her. "I'm driving you home. We can pick up your car tomorrow." She put an arm around Hayley's waist and led her out the door and down the street. "I wasn't sure if you wanted to go home with him or not."

"Nah. We were kind of petering out anyway. There were too many things to deal with. I clearly wasn't going to get any satisfaction."

Suz propped her against a tree and opened the cruiser's door. Hayley winced at the sound of scraping metal, then rolled herself around the tree trunk and stumbled into the car.

She adjusted the seat into a reclining position and let her head loll to the side. Her head seemed somewhat large for the rest of her body. It was heavy. Heavy and stuffy was her head. "God, what's that smell? Is that me? Shit, Sergio couldn't have—"

"Nah. It's just some new species of fungus growing on the backseat upholstery. Don't worry about it. . . . So, from my side of the closet door I think I was hearing some satisfaction. Am I right?"

"It was only Sergio. I couldn't concentrate. The conditions weren't right. There was the bra issue. There was no way I was going to let him find out that there was no 'there' there." Man, her tongue was sort of thick as well. "There. There," she repeated experimentally. Was she starting to get bloated? Correct enunciation was clearly out of the question.

"Oh, right! Sorry about that. Kinda like wearing the wrong underwear."

"I don't know about that theory. If you wear sexy underwear, it makes it seem like you planned to have sex with him."

"So?"

"I prefer not to appear to be a slam-dunk. You really want to wear your middle-grade underwear. That's how I see it. And frankly, it was so dark in there, I don't think Sergio could have seen what I was wearing. Unfortunately, we didn't get to that point. But it was fun. He was a good kisser. Not as good as the policeman, but good. '*Querida, querida.*'" Hayley giggled. It sounded very loud in her ears.

"Maybe he'll go back to the bar tomorrow night."

"Who? Sergio? Can't say that I'm dying to see him again, in spite of his good looks. We really couldn't communicate."

Suz laughed. "Because your tongues were in each other's mouths?"

"No, because his English is terrible and my Spanish is worse. In any case, we didn't have that emotional bond."

"Well, you didn't exactly give it a chance."

"Well, I felt it right away with the policeman."

"You'd just discovered a dead man. You were upset."

"So." Hayley felt a breeze on her head and put her hand up to adjust the wig forward. "Hey, where's my wig?"

"Last time I saw it, the moose was wearing it. I'll get it down tomorrow night."

"My God, when did it fall off? How long was I wandering around without it? That's crazy! I thought I was unrecognizable."

Suz shrugged. "Sergio didn't seem to mind. And neither did anybody else."

"Well, that's another thing. What's with guys these days? Always looking for convenience. Sex isn't supposed to be about convenience. It's messy, embarrassing, and totally inconvenient." Hayley was starting to feel belligerent. "I'm tired of having all this foreplay standing up. It's so . . . noncommittal. I think I deserve a bed. I think I deserve a bed and some hot sex. I'm tired of excuses. Corpses, inflatable bras. It's always something. It's ridiculous. I'm ready."

"For what?"

"I'm ready to ask out a man. I'm ready to ask out a man of my own choosing. And I'm ready to proposition him. I'm ready, I say."

She belched and began to fade into a deep, alcoholic sleep as Suz whistled low and said, "Execution time. This will all be arranged."

"Just like you said. I wore it . . . and he *came.* Get it?" The last thing Hayley heard was her own slurred laughter ringing in her ears.

Chapter Six

"Let me get this straight. I only just scanned my e-mail. . . . So you went to ask for a raise and instead you lost your job?" Diane asked. When Hayley nodded, Diane's eyes narrowed. "Man, I disappear for two measly days for some hard-core studying and it's like Armageddon."

"Yeah, it's kind of embarrassing. And just to clarify, I didn't merely lose my job. . . ." Hayley paused dramatically, then hissed, "I got *basura*-ed."

"There was no way you could *possibly* have failed." Audra shook her head at Hayley, then sneezed and grabbed a couple of paper napkins from the canister to handle the result. She appeared to have cold symptoms in June. Failure had that effect on her. And Hayley's colossal raise disaster was a pretty big failure.

After Hayley'd e-mailed the girls detailed messages on Friday with the bad news, Audra had sent a reply—typed entirely in capital letters—that she'd gone home early from work, sick with "a blotchy swelling stuffiness." Now anyone could see that Audra's glossy bobbed haircut was in more than the usual disarray (the center part wasn't straight), and that, while swelling wasn't apparent, light pink blotchy patches did, indeed, blanket her face and arms—and she was clearly stuffy.

Hayley didn't want to think about what might happen to Audra if the whole Beer Garden episode came out right now. Cardiac arrest was not something she was prepared to deal with on a Sunday morning.

With one hand gripped around one of Gerttie's monster-sized orange juices, Audra railed on. "When we went home on Thursday night, you were all set. How could it all have escalated so quickly, with such nightmarish results? These things don't happen to me. And I coached you. I feel responsible."

"It was self-sabotage, really," Hayley explained, then took a fortifying swig of latte. "That's what it was. I was avoiding actually making a big decision for myself. I set things up so that I ended up with what I probably needed, but I made someone else do the dirty work. And it definitely wasn't a graceful exit. I don't blame *you*. If I'd just followed your—"

"So, Hayley," Suz interrupted. "Let's get to the good stuff. Tell me, when the dog went under your skirt . . . were you turned on at all?"

Three coffee spoons fell to the Formica tabletop with a clang. Hayley stared at Suz, her jaw practically in her lap.

"Not even just a teensy-weensy little bit?"

"No!"

"Ignore her," Audra said. "She's just trying to shock you."

Suz shrugged. "Just curious."

"Gross," Diane said, shuddering.

"Didn't Bud ever give you head?"

Poor Diane blushed scarlet.

Suz leaned forward with a wicked smile. "Well, you said he was like a shar-pei. . . ."

"Leave her alone," Audra said. "You're the one with a predilection for sleeping with dogs."

"Ha-ha. Ugly men can be excellent in bed. Overcompensation theory."

"Oh, shut up, Suz . . . you know, something's weird about all this." Diane looked Hayley over. "You're not acting like you normally do after this kind of catastrophe. Something's . . . off. It's not your mental state, is it?"

"What are you talking about?" Hayley asked in alarm.

Diane leaned in close and sniffed Hayley three times in quick succession. "It's physical. I smell alcohol."

Audra turned slightly puce. "I don't want to know. Don't tell me anything," she muttered, and then blew her nose into a paper napkin.

"You can't possibly smell alcohol on me. I showered this morning."

Diane sniffed some more. "Residual. You had a hangover yesterday, didn't you?"

Audra looked over at Suz in a daze as if she were trying to put pieces together but couldn't make them fit. Suz smiled cheerfully at her. Audra frowned back, suspicious.

The sound of Diane's persistent sniffing grew louder. Hayley put her hand on Diane's forehead and pushed her head away. "Stop smelling me. It's gross."

"It's objective analysis," Diane said, trying not to laugh. "Did you lose your job and get plastered as a way to forget your humiliation and despair?"

Suz snorted. It was a particularly gleeful snort, and if Audra hadn't been so sick, Hayley was sure her friend would have picked up on the nuances of Suz's behavior already.

"No, that's not what happened."

"By the way, that's a lovely little scarf you're wearing, Hay." Audra dabbed at her nose with a napkin. "I don't think I've seen it."

Hayley's hand flew up to her throat and she quickly fluffed the little black scarf she'd tied fifties-style around her neck. "Thanks, Audra. I really don't wear it too often."

"Yeah, *nice scarf*, Hayley." Suz overenunciated each word, and everybody turned and looked at her. "God, remind me not to wear shorts here on such a hot day. My thighs are sticking to the vinyl." With a rude squelching sound she detached herself and grinned broadly.

Audra rolled her eyes. "You're just happier and perkier than ever, aren't you?"

"Yes, I am. While I'm *extremely* saddened, of course, that your advice didn't work for Hayley, I am happier and perkier than ever . . . that *mine did*."

Audra gasped.

Hayley sighed. The writing was on the wall. The whole story was about to come out, and Suz was the only one who already knew everything. Hayley wished she'd called Diane and Audra before brunch to deescalate.

Diane sat forward. "This was after Hayley lost her job? You gave Hayley advice and it worked?"

Suz eased back in her chair rather smugly. "That's exactly what happened."

"Well, I don't know if I'd call it advice," Hayley said. "It was more of an experience. A real eye-opener, though."

Audra did her best to look blasé but she couldn't do much to hide the horror. "I can't imagine why Suzy's so smug," she muttered.

Suz produced a dazzling smile, then reached across the table and jerked down the scarf around Hayley's neck.

"Suz, you can't just—" Too late now. The three girls stared at her neck, at a nice medium-sized hickey.

Audra shrieked and looked at Suz with competitive ire.

"What on earth did you do to her?" Diane asked.

"Well, *I* certainly didn't give her the hickey," Suz said.

Hayley rolled her eyes. "I might as well go ahead and spell it out." And she did, right up through gorgeous Sergio's climax and rather anticlimactic collapse in the closet.

"Okay. Let me get this straight," Diane said, as she stole a piece of melon off Suz's pancake plate. "Suz dressed you up like a German prostitute, got you drunk, and then thrust you into the arms of a groping Spaniard." She popped the melon into her mouth and looked at Suz with exaggerated disbelief.

Suz deigned to lift an eyebrow. "The dress was Bavarian. Not German. There's a difference. And we don't know for sure if the guy was actually a Spaniard."

Audra shifted restlessly in her seat "This is outrageous. Absolutely outrageous. Poor Hayley."

"Poor Hayley, nothing." Suz tipped back her chair, balancing on the back two legs while she held on to the table with both hands. Her tank top slid up, exposing her belly button and a wide swath of skin. Hayley noted that Suz definitely had a little love-handle action going on, but she also noted that Suz somehow managed to get away with it. It was all about the attitude.

"Does she look poor to you?" Suz was saying. "Does she look

remotely unhappy about the events of Friday night? I think not. I think I see a shit-eating grin, that's what I think I see."

Hayley opened her mouth to speak. She did, in fact, have on a shit-eating grin. And she was in the mood to talk about it, but Diane cut in too fast.

"She looks like she's had a lobotomy."

"Yes, she does," Suz said. "And she didn't even get the orgasm."

Hold on just a minute. Hayley leaned in toward the middle of the table. "I'm right here, people. I'm sitting right here. No need to discuss my orgasms in third person."

"Do we need to discuss them at all?" Audra murmured, scratching the side of her face violently.

"Not having an orgasm is nothing to be embarrassed about," Diane said. "I'm not having any either."

"Oh, God," Audra said, looking around the diner.

Alarmed, Hayley put up a hand. "Wait a minute, I didn't say I'm not—"

"You haven't shown much interest in men or sex in quite some time now," Suz said to Diane. "Is there something you'd like to share? We're all progressive, you know."

"No. Nothing in particular." Diane shrugged. "It's true, I'm not concentrating on men right now. I'm developing my mind."

Suz rolled her eyes. "Well, there's an excuse."

Diane shot Suz a steely glare. "It's not an excuse. The only guys I have access to right now have bad skin and only want me for my note-taking prowess. It's not worth my time. I'm only twenty-five, I have a nonexistent sex drive, and I don't need to be bothered. You understand what I'm saying, don't you, Audra?"

Audra didn't answer. She was engrossed in viewing all possible angles of her face in the tiny mirror in her lipstick case. Little distressed moans and tongue clicks were all she was capable of at the moment.

"Why take a course in sex if you aren't interested in having any?" Hayley asked.

"Obviously I'm going to be having some at some point. And I might as well be prepared. I should have as much accumulated data as possible when that time comes. I just don't see the point of getting all worked up about it if I'm not going to enjoy it for another ten years or whatever. I'm waiting to peak." Diane leaned back and crossed her arms over her chest, completely unperturbed.

Suz, on the other hand, seemed bowled over by the idea. "You're planning to be celibate for *ten years*?"

"Well, I'm not really putting a time limit on it. I just figure I've been celibate by default for the last three. What's another ten or so? Besides, it's not like I'm taking a vow or anything." She shot Suz a meaningful glance and added, "I'm just not going to obsess about it. When I'm thirty-something and ready to go, it will all seem much more appealing. For now, if I want to, I can take care of business myself."

"Well, at least let me give you a couple of my *Cosmo* back issues," Suz said, shaking her head. "If you're going to do it that way, you might as well do it right."

Hayley almost laughed aloud when Audra looked up from her mirror, one eyebrow cocked, apparently at the ready lest anyone go into too much detail about "taking care of business" at the breakfast table.

In fact, she put the lipstick case down and quickly put the conversation back on course. "Honestly, Hay, was it just the fact that you got together with this Sergio person that's making you so upbeat, or did you really learn something from Suz's exercise?"

"You promise you won't laugh?" Hayley asked.

"Of course not."

"It made me put myself out there in a way I don't usually do, you know. I got a strange kind of confidence out of it." She blushed a little, because there was something embarrassing about admitting that you had low self-confidence to begin with, even to friends who knew you as well as you knew yourself. "I mean, it's true that most of the time I was in disguise, but—"

"Not the whole time," Suz noted. "In fact, not most of it. You just thought you were. You lost the wig about an hour in."

"Right. Well. Yeah, okay. Let's just say that I discovered what I'll refer to as the Drooling Horndog Theory."

"Drooling horndogs?" Diane hooted with laughter. "I'm definitely glad I wasn't there. What's the gist?"

"The bottom line of this theory is that men don't have to call as many shots as we seem to think they're entitled to. I think it's a fear thing."

"That's an interesting observation," Diane said. "As they say, 'Man has the advantage of choice, woman only the power of refusal'?"

"Exactly! Men just aren't as scary as we seem to think they are. We let them have this power over us and we shouldn't. They're all pretty much the same, with the same instincts and the same reflexes and the same tendencies. Even the good-looking ones."

Everyone digested that bit of news, Suz nodding in wizened agreement.

Finally, Audra begrudgingly said, "Well, that's more reasonable than I expected." But then she coughed, blew her nose, and scratched her neck vigorously.

"Jesus, Audra, are those turning into hives now? You're not getting hives just because of me, are you?"

Audra's eyes widened and she pulled a gold compact with a larger mirror out of her purse and moved it around. "Oh, God, you're right. The blotches are becoming hives. This is too much." She chewed on her lower lip and added, "I want you to see Bruno. Please, Hay. I really want to contribute."

"Who's Bruno again?" Hayley asked.

"Bruno Maffri. He's Audra's personal coach," Diane explained. "A specialist in success-visualization technique. He's quite good. Helped me pass the GMAT. It was actually much cheaper than taking a month's worth of study prep courses."

Suz rested her chin on her palm and watched Audra fuss with the hives. "You just can't stand it that I might have more to offer than you."

Audra glanced up at Suz, gave an exasperated squeak, and tossed the compact back into her purse in a gesture of surrender. She spread a napkin on the tabletop, then laid her head on top of her crossed arms. In a muffled voice she said, "I'm sorry, Suzy. I'm just jealous. You know I hate to lose."

"This isn't a competition, people." Hayley looked from one girl to the other. "This is my life. Look, Aud, you know I appreciate that you want to help me, but it looks like I'm getting things under control."

Audra blew her nose loudly in response.

Hayley cringed at the sound and said, "Maybe you should keep that appointment for yourself."

"I don't think Bruno's equipped to handle this. I need to see somebody else. Somebody who specializes in nervous tension. Please take the appointment."

But Hayley was feeling cocky this morning. She'd had a day to recover from her hangover and now she was fully able to appreciate Friday night's success. "Thanks, but I think I'll pass."

This triggered a rather alarming coughing fit. "Please take it, Hay. Consider it reinforcement. And even if you've got the personal part under control, you're going to need a new job."

Hayley shook her head and tossed her crumpled napkin on the table. "Thanks, but I'm going down to the Tech Job Fair at the Exploratorium. I'm sure I'll find something. Besides, to be totally honest, psychology mumbo jumbo really isn't my thing."

"No, but this is different. He's not a licensed psychologist," Diane explained.

"Oh, well, that makes me feel so much better." Hayley pushed her empty latte mug away. "Thanks—really, thanks—but no, thanks."

Suz slapped the table gleefully. "Sorry, Audra, but that settles it. Hayley's doing fine under *my* tutelage, and I think we'll stick with that. As a matter of fact, I've got phase two of my plan in the works already."

Chapter Seven

Indeed, there was no rest for the weary. Suz called a couple of days later. "It's time to execute. We're going to Fred Leary's memorial service."

"How depressing."

"It's not depressing. It's an opportunity to turn the Beer Garden triumph into lasting results. It will do you good."

"I'm not seeing how that's the case. It's a funeral, not a morning jog."

"Good things always happen to me at funerals. There are lots of single men who need comforting. We can practice what we learned on Friday night."

"You've got to be kidding me."

"Did I steer you wrong before?"

Hayley didn't answer. The truth was, she did feel anxious to get out of the house. She'd spent the day slumped on her black IKEA couch wrapped in her charcoal-gray, pin-striped Calvin Klein comforter watching her black television. The grayscale environment was beginning to depress even her.

"Look, the paper says Fred's thing starts in an hour. I'll come pick you up. Oh, and put on some cute high heels. You'll need something that really shows off your calves. 'Kay? Oh, and see if you can find something black to wear." Suz laughed and hung up.

Hayley managed to find a halter dress in black cotton eyelet that was summery yet respectful, which she paired with a black straw purse and black platform espadrille sandals. She had just enough time left to create her signature bedhead look and slap on some makeup before Suz arrived, screeching up to the curb outside the apartment building in that giant metallic green boat of a seventies Chevrolet she called "the cruiser."

When she opened the car door, Hayley instantly recognized the smell from Friday night, even though she couldn't actually remember riding in the cruiser at all. She peered into the backseat. It looked fuzzier than usual, but she didn't say anything, since it was a free ride.

Audra called the cruiser "a cesspool on wheels." Diane used "the rolling petri dish." Hayley just called it better than nothing, since she hated to drive in the city.

There was nothing about it that was remotely appealing. It wasn't so bad that it was cool . . . it was just plain bad. It disturbed all five senses. You didn't want to be seen in this thing. Ever. Not only that, but the thing could not be parked.

After a harrowing ride through the streets of San Francisco, which involved being unable to turn off Market Street for a solid fifteen minutes, going down not one but two one-way streets the wrong way, and nearly mowing down an entire eight-person Chinese family at Broadway and Columbus, Suz whipped the cruiser into a spot next to a fire hydrant. She noted that they'd be okay because of Hayley's new "connections" with San Francisco law enforcement.

They climbed out of the car and walked half a block before escaping from the fiery outdoor heat into the somewhat more humid but no less fiery indoor heat of St. Elton's Church of Divine Oneness and Heavenly Togetherness.

Suz fanned herself with her hand. "If there is a God, you'd think He'd have enough pull to wire His home for air-conditioning."

"Suz, St. Elton's is a gay, Catholic, New Age San Francisco church with a cross-dressing priestess. It's probably not at the top of His/Her maintenance list."

Hayley looked around. The tiny church was absolutely packed with people, which was odd because of Fred's fairly antisocial behavior. She was the only person from work she could see, but maybe he just didn't like people from work. Couldn't really blame him.

Instead, there were about forty other people at the service that Hayley had never seen before. Most of them seemed to be holding . . . were those what she thought they were? Yup. Forty people holding tiny origami designs in their hands.

Origami? Suz and Hayley looked at each other. "I'm having a *Twilight Zone* moment, how 'bout you?" Suz asked.

Hayley just nodded. Then, "Oh, my God. Look at that woman's tote bag."

"The Northern California Paper Folding Society? Well, that's different." Suz grimaced and slid into the nearest open pew. "Say, do you think there'll be a fruit platter or something afterward?" She reduced her voice to a loud whisper. "Funerals make me hungry. Do they make you hungry?"

"Oh, my God . . . oh, my God."

"They're getting started," Suz said. "Looks like there's gonna be some praying."

"Suz . . . Suz."

Suz picked up the prayer book and opened it to shield her mouth. "What is *wrong* with you?"

Hayley tried to swallow but her mouth had gone completely dry. "Oh. My. God." It was all she could muster up.

"What?"

"Shh!" Hayley scrunched down in the pew.

Quieter. "What?"

"It's him. I think it's him." Suz looked puzzled until Hayley added, "The investigating detective. The one I . . . you know. But I'm not sure. No. Noooo . . . nope. Wait! Oh, my God, it *is* him. I think. Okay, I'm going to indicate his general direction, but don't look now." Hayley bobbed her head up from behind the prayer book in the direction of a man sitting slightly to the left, two pews up.

"Suz! I said don't look now. Could you be a little more subtle?"

"You want *me* to be subtle. You look like you've got Tourette's." Suz craned her neck. "Anyway, I don't know who you're talking about. That woman's hat is the size of a small child. Can't see a goddamn thing. You're telling me the Big Dick is here?"

"I'm not positive, but I think so. That guy. The one with the white shirt . . . and I guess he's wearing a tie . . . from this angle, his upper-body measurements seem about right." Hayley held up her hands, trying to estimate in the air what she could remember of his size and shape. The woman in the pew next to her gave her a dirty look.

"Hey! Here's your chance." Suz dug her elbow into Hayley's side. "People are already getting up to pay their respects. You can check out the guy while you go up and tell Fred how sorry you are for disrespecting him."

Hayley pointedly ignored her and murmured, "I wonder why he's here. . . ."

"Probably to tell Fred how sorry he is for disrespecting him."

"Shut up. You're supposed to be supporting me in my time of need."

"I am. I'm going to walk you through this. Now I want you to just slip into the line. You're gonna go up there and give Fred his moment. And on the way up, verrrry casually I want you to tilt your head and maybe make like you're wiping away a tear." Suz demonstrated the technique. "As you do so, you can look at the guy's face and see if it's him. Once we've established it's him, we'll figure out the next best move. Got that?"

"Wipe away a tear?" Hayley grimaced. "Jesus, Suz, you're cold. Poor Fred."

"What's the problem? It's very simple. It's not like Fred is here to judge. I'd be more concerned about how many times you've taken the Lord's name in vain in the last thirty minutes, not to mention the last three days alone. What could possibly go wrong?"

Indeed. What could possibly go wrong? "Wait. I don't have a paper thingy to put by Fred's casket."

"What?"

"All these people have cute little origami animals and stuff. I can't go up there without an offering."

Impatiently Suz unfolded Hayley's four-panel memorial service program, smoothed it flat, and with astonishing speed produced a surprisingly realistic miniature F-16 Falcon. "Here."

"Wow. My own personal MacGyver." Hayley took the airplane and scootched forward in the pew to get up, but at the last minute she turned to Suz. "What do I do if it's him?" she blurted out.

"We'll deal with that when you get back." Suz put her hand on Hayley's back and shoved. Hayley lurched forward and stood up, then stumbled her way to the center aisle, silently cursing the espadrilles.

She smiled politely but not too cheerfully, as would befit the funereal circumstances, and wedged herself into the line between a very handsome man holding an intricate Roman-chariot origami and a woman with a less decorative but no less poignant teddy bear origami. Hayley sheepishly concealed her paper airplane with her hand.

As the line inched its way up toward Fred's casket, there was a point at which Hayley was directly parallel to the mystery man's pew. She glanced back at Suz who egged her on with a wave of her hand.

As a compromise, Hayley tilted her head and sort of wiped under her eye, more like she was wiping mascara than tears because it seemed at least incrementally less offensive.

And even though it seemed as though her glance was the subtlest thing in the world, eye contact was definitely made. It was without a doubt Grant Hutchinson. Her heart lurched and she just stared at him.

She'd turned the corner around the long end of Fred's casket now. It was a closed casket and Fred's picture was propped up on an easel as a substitute.

A very distraught short man just in front of the Roman chariot guy was taking his time speaking with Fred's image, so Hayley had a bit of spare time for analysis. She used it to stare directly at Grant staring back at her, trying to gauge what he might be thinking.

She hoped she was mistaken, because in the final interpretation, he seemed to be looking at her the way a guy looks when the most unpopular girl in junior high is crossing the gym floor to propose a slow dance in front of all his friends. It was somewhat discouraging in the big picture.

The line inched closer to Fred, and as Hayley stepped forward, still staring at Grant, her feet hit a footstool but her torso kept moving.

To prevent herself from falling, she had to fling her arms out and grab on to a combination handful of lily arrangement and casket cover, both of which were draped over the top of Fred's casket.

The sound of memorial service programs fluttering in the air stopped short as Hayley's yelp echoed throughout the cavernous space.

A single chord hummed, held by the organist's paralyzed hands. Everybody looked up and followed the paper airplane as it lurched out of Hayley's grasp and floated lopsidedly to the back of the church.

Not surprisingly, Hayley was expecting the worst. What she got was the entire forty-person membership of the Northern California Paper Folding Society bursting into spontaneous applause.

Maybe there was something to the whole God concept, because it would have been a complete disaster at just about any other funeral. Hard to believe, but she was at a funeral with the only people who could possibly construe her mishap as some sort of tribute.

As they clapped, Hayley released her death grip from the side of the casket and slowly stood upright. She managed a weak smile for her fellow mourners, then turned and straightened the casket cover and prettied up the loose lilies as best she could.

She looked at Suz for a clue, but her friend's face was now entirely hidden by her program, so Hayley swallowed and turned back toward Fred.

And nearly knocked his portrait off the easel. *Whoa.* Hayley took a step back and squinted. The picture didn't look anything like Fred. Probably because it was one of those heinous high school yearbook pictures. Hayley flicked a bit of lily pollen off the glossy and tried to compose her thoughts.

Okay. Uh, hello, Fred. Gosh, um, I've never seen you in a coat and tie before. You look great, and I'm not just saying that. . . . Okay. So I just wanted to say that I hope you didn't think that I was disrespecting you when you were dead and the policeman and I were . . . well, you know. Really, it was just one of those things. Has no bearing on our friendship. Er, had *no bearing. Right. Well, I guess we're squared away now.*

She put her fingers to her lips, then touched them to Fred's glossy high school forehead.

Hayley quickly made her way to the steps from the casket, and continued back down the aisle. She couldn't resist taking a peek at Grant.

And maybe it had nothing to do with God or no God. Maybe it was just Fred's way of telling her he knew no disrespect was intended. But things started to look really good right about then, because not only did Hayley just manage to avoid almost certain widespread public humiliation, but Grant Hutchinson was looking right at her with both eyebrows up and a huge smile.

So what if it could be interpreted as a smile of disbelief.

When Hayley finally reached the safety of her pew, she slid in again next to Suz to wait for the remaining guests to pay their respects to Fred. "It's definitely him. Did you notice we made eye contact? I think he wants me."

Suz didn't answer. She seemed to be scanning the crowd for something . . . or someone. "The guy with the Roman chariot. He was standing in front of you in line. Did you see where he went?"

Hayley ignored her question in turn. "Do you think Grant's here to see *me*?"

Suz unfolded her memorial service program and proceeded to wipe her underarms with it before crumpling it up and tossing it in her purse. "Could be."

"I knew I should have worked on the relationship goal first. You were so right. This is a lot easier. And it's obviously some kind of a sign that he's here. I'm going to ask him out." Hayley looked curiously at Suz. "Seriously, did you know?"

"Did I know what?" Suz answered absently, still scanning the church.

"Did you know he would be here when you took me to the Beer Garden? You said good things always happen to you at funerals. Was this a setup?"

Suz stood up in the pew. "That was a very nice service." She looked around and brushed off the butt of her tight snakeskin-patterned jeans. "What makes you think his being here is a good thing? Maybe he's still investigating Fred's death."

Hayley laughed, but Suz shrugged, and her laugh trailed off. "You're not suggesting this is part of his investigation?"

"Why don't you just go ahead and ask him? You already committed to asking him out." With that, Suz stepped deftly into the aisle and walked toward the back of the church.

She stopped next to the last pew and leaned down, murmuring something in the Roman-chariot-origami guy's ear. He got up and followed her into the nearest confessional, ostensibly for some sort of impromptu paper-folding lessons.

Hayley swallowed, half-impressed, half-daunted. Suz made these male-female things look so easy.

Remember, Hayley, inside they're all just drooling horndogs, there for the choosing. Nothing to be intimidated by. He wants you. He just may not realize it quite this minute.

People were already heading for the church courtyard. Hayley was tempted to stand up on the pew and look for Grant, but it seemed sort of inappropriate. Instead she followed the mass of people outside, and decided to wait for him to leave.

He appeared in the church doorway a few moments later. Hayley caught her breath. There he was, Lt. Grant Hutchinson, looking right at her. Not unlike the way he had in the soda room—Wait a minute. . . . Hayley took stock of her appearance this time, but everything checked out okay. She seemed to be wearing her dress properly and nothing unusual was stuck to the eyelet. And when she looked up again, he was coming right toward her.

Hayley stared in fascination as that sense of slow motion came into being again and the crowd of mourners seemed to separate in his path as he came at her like a linebacker . . . no, that wasn't quite it. Maybe like a linebacker who'd once had ballet lessons.

Wait. Wait a minute! I'm supposed to ask you out. I'm supposed to approach you. Hayley looked around wildly, disoriented, hoping to see Suz. Maybe Suz's offhand comment about his being here on behalf of the investigation was right on the money.

In all honesty, the guy hadn't exactly begged for Hayley's home phone number last time she saw him. Come to think of it, he hadn't asked for any personal information at all, and since she didn't work at New Economy Mouthpiece anymore, Fred could very well be the reason he was here.

Suddenly Hayley transcended nervous and went straight to panic. Panic in the way a person might get panicky when they know they haven't done anything wrong, but also know that it could be perceived that they have. She reflexively backed up a few steps and bumped her heels against the courtyard wall as Grant continued on his warpath, looking about as hot as it was possible to look at a funeral.

Well, if he wasn't going to arrest her, she was definitely going to ask him out.

Chapter Eight

"I just want to make one thing clear," Hayley blurted out, blushing like a love-struck idiot. "I did not murder Fred."

Grant shaded his eyes against the sun and said, "I'm happy to hear that, believe me."

There was an awkward little silence, which Hayley felt responsible for filling. "Right. Well, I just thought it best to get it out in the open. Neither I nor anyone else I know of would have wanted to see Fred dead. I mean suicide, I can see. I know tons of people working in startups who'd like to kill themselves. . . ."

Grant smiled, and Hayley almost expected to hear a little toothpaste-commercial sparkle chime.

Nervously she took a step backward, forgetting about the courtyard wall. Her heel slammed against the concrete and she almost fell, but Grant steadied her by her elbow.

Hayley flushed and tried to play the whole awkward scenario off by picking up the thread and continuing the conversation. "Well. So, as I was saying, the thing was, Fred, well, he was a *total* stickler for the AP style guide. Personally, I'm of the mind that a little creative license never hurt anyone, but Fred, nope, he didn't want any extraneous hyphens. I mean, this was something he was willing to go to violence over. I'm not kidding. I could tell he had it in him when he'd send me one of those e-mails written in all caps. So it wouldn't surprise me if he couldn't take it anymore, what with everybody's constant use of split infinitives and sentence fragments. . . . He really was an unusual guy. . . ."

Grant just stood there listening to her talk, with his head cocked and his arms crossed, and finally she clued in to the fact that she was totally babbling. Time to wind it down gracefully.

"I mean, I always knew he liked paper, but I had no idea he was part of this vast origami subculture. Well, that's not entirely true. There was that crane mobile he gave me last Christmas. But I didn't realize he was a professional . . . origamist. Really, it's amazing the things you learn about a person after they're, you know . . . dead. . . ."

Just as she said the word "amazing," Grant's arm started forward in a Heisman, and by the time the word "dead" came out of her mouth, his palm was firmly planted against the wall next to her ear. He leaned down and looked into her face with about six inches between them.

"You're saying that Fred Leary may have killed himself over grammar?" The corner of his mouth twitched.

Hayley swallowed and finished weakly. "Or maybe it was just natural causes?" *God. How lame.*

"You seem nervous. I don't mean to make you nervous."

He thinks I seem nervous. Yes, I'm nervous, you big idiot. My insides feel like smashed atom particles stuck in the Stanford Linear Accelerator supercollider. Not to mention there's serious personal-space violation going on here.

With his free hand, Grant suddenly raked his fingers lightly through Hayley's hair. It took him right up close to her to do it. "Fluff."

Fluff is right. My brain is fluff. Hayley noticed that he didn't back away once he'd rubbed his fingers together and disposed of this mystery fluff. Hayley wiped her sweaty palms against the fabric of her skirt.

God, how did one reel in a guy like that without appearing obvious? She definitely wanted him. Of course, she'd just proved to herself a few days ago that being obvious wasn't necessarily a problem. If only she had that green dress . . . or not even the dress. She'd settle for the wig. Or the boobs—she'd even wear the boobs again. *I can't do this on my own. Oh, stop it. Yes, you can. Get a hold of yourself.*

She released a breath of air she'd been holding for way longer than was healthy, and said, "Well. It's nice to see you again."

"Yeah, I'm actually here on official business." He winked.

Why the wink? Why the wink! Suz, where are you . . . what does he mean by the wink?

He seemed to be waiting for her to say or do something—Confess? What?—and the silence stretched out.

Grant pushed off the wall and put his hand on her shoulder, pressing down gently. It was nonthreatening but definitely controlling. She could feel herself moving into that space—that space where hormones meet heat and ridiculous and humiliating things occur. It was not a space that she really wanted to be in. Because there would either be a bed and hot sex or forget it.

There was not going to be any random, noncommittal groping taking place in the church confessional or any other vertically oriented casual space, no, sir.

He cleared his throat. "I wanted to apologize to you for my unprofessional behavior last week. You were clearly in emotional distress, and I probably took advantage of the situation. My behavior reflects on the entire San Francisco detective squad, and I stepped over the line."

Awwwww. Hayley melted a little. How sweet was that? "I'm not going to be arrested then."

"No." He laughed.

Hayley bit her lower lip and looked up at Grant. "Not questioned in any way about Fred's death?"

"Not right now, anyway." He smiled. "I don't have enough time."

"The point, then, is that you're apologizing."

"That's right."

She should ask him out. Right now. Immediately. This was too good to be true. A man who wasn't afraid to say "I'm sorry." It was like finding the Holy Grail.

"Apology accepted." Hayley smiled back at him. "Not to mention, it wasn't all your fault." She thought she'd just about found the courage to get on with it and ask him out when he derailed the whole notion by tilting his head slightly and moistening his lips.

Hayley's eyes flew open wide. *Oh, my God, he's going to kiss me. He's looking at my mouth. That's a classic indicator. Jesus . . . wait a minute. You can't French-kiss a person at a funeral. You just can't. In fact, I don't want to go out with a guy who would try to French-kiss a girl at a funeral. It's remarkably inappropriate. I don't care what Suz thinks.*

But then Grant pulled away slightly and looked at his watch. He frowned and stepped back. "Damn."

Hey! Wait a minute. What's up with that? Flooded with disappointment, Hayley narrowed her eyes and gazed at him suspiciously. If she hadn't already made it to third base with him, she'd have to accuse him of being a tease.

Grant didn't seem to be put off by her expression. He pulled his wallet out of his back pocket and removed two business cards. Handing them both to her he said, "I have to go. Can I get a contact number?"

Can I get a contact number? Could he possibly have picked a more unromantic way to ask for her phone number?

Hayley fished around in the bottom of her purse and pulled out a pencil. She wrote her phone number on one of the cards and handed it back to him without a word.

"I'm glad we cleared everything up. I'll see you around." Then he turned and walked out of the courtyard to the street.

Hayley watched him leave and then pressed two fingers to her forehead above her right eye, where a throbbing pain was just now gaining some steam. If she weren't so confused, she'd be certain she was supposed to feel pathetic.

Somebody's elbow dug into her side. Hayley turned and could only roll her eyes at the sight of Suz tucking her shirt back into her jeans.

"That looked promising," Suz said enthusiastically.

Hayley shook her head, miserable. "Mistakes were made. I'm not exactly sure what happened, but I have reason to believe that, between our first meeting and just now, he thinks I'm a politely deranged nymphomaniac with murderous instincts." She ran her fingers through the choppy strands of hair he'd ruffled up. "It wasn't the effect I was going for. I don't know if he wants my phone number for a date or for a future police interview."

Suz grinned. "Just like Audra said, 'murder and sexual intrigue.' I'm impressed."

Hayley groaned. "Be serious. I needed you. I really needed you.

I didn't ask him out and I got nervous and I looked for you but you weren't there and I started babbling and now I don't know if he's attracted to me or what."

Suz looked at Hayley askance and put her arm around her friend's shoulders. "You're serious, aren't you? You didn't ask him?"

Hayley shrugged and kicked the toe of her shoe against the ground.

Hands on her hips, Suz gaped at Hayley. "But you said you were ready. We went to the Beer Garden, you came out all empowered and stuff, and you said you were ready! And he asked for your phone number."

She snatched the business card from Hayley's hand and peered at it. "Oh, geez. *And* he gave you *his* phone number. How much more obvious did you want the poor guy to be?"

"It wasn't obvious," Hayley said sullenly. "He said 'contact number,' not 'phone number.' And that's his office contact number, not his personal phone number on his business card, and since I haven't the faintest idea as to whether he gave it to me for business or personal reasons, it's not going to do me any good."

"Audra's going to have a field day with this." Suz sighed. "Let's just look on the bright side. He gave you his card and if you want, you can use Fred as an excuse to go down to the police station and talk to him."

"Are you nuts? I can't just prance into the police station and proposition him. There's no way I would do that. No possible way."

In a strained voice that sounded suspiciously like she was trying not to laugh, Suz said, "Okay, but think about it this way. You just go in there asking about Fred, and if you get positive vibes that he seems interested in you, you can still ask him out."

• • •

To avoid wallowing in misery, the minute Hayley returned home from the memorial service she called Audra to set up an appointment with Bruno Maffri.

She was pretty happy with herself for taking the initiative on that matter. Free therapy, free lunch, and plenty of free time sans gainful employment; what excuse could there possibly be for turning it down? She'd run out of ideas. Or rather, she'd run out of her friends' ideas save for this one.

And so it was a day later she found herself eating Chinese food in Audra's swanky office. The Humbert & Quigley building was located in downtown San Francisco in the prestigious Spear Street Tower complex by the waterfront.

It would make the girls feel much better if they could attribute Audra's meteoric rise at such a young age to the fact that she'd had a head start by graduating a couple of years earlier than the rest of them. But Audra could smell money about to happen from miles away, and she'd had the smarts to put herself in the right place at the right time, when venture capital companies couldn't hire people fast enough to handle all the money flowing in and out of the economy.

Which explained why Audra occupied a large office on the thirty-second floor with a window overlooking the Bay Bridge. She sat behind her giant mahogany desk eating the last third of a carton of chow mein with personalized red-lacquered chopsticks.

She was looking much better, in spite of the thicker-than-normal layer of foundation on her face. Hayley assumed the hives had mostly gone away, and Audra didn't say anything about it. She was her normal self-satisfied self, actually, which meant she'd been feeling much better lately, too.

Hayley shoveled more broccoli beef into her mouth with a plastic fork and looked around the office while she chewed.

It was hard to tell which was more impressive, the pricey digs or the fact that Audra was able to wield chopsticks so vigorously without damaging her fabulous suit. Audra's Donna Karan charcoal-gray crepe pantsuit was severe, masculine even. But those stiletto death heels and the perfectly crisp white shirt opened deep at the neck just short of "wow" . . . well, she was truly magnificent, in her element. A true queen of kick-ass.

Why can't I be like that?

"I really don't think you should be taking advice from Suz. You know I love her, but really, Hayley. Let's be honest." Audra tapped her temple with two fingers and mouthed, *Not quite all there.*

"I don't know." Hayley sighed. "I can't seem to get things on track. I thought all I had to do was decide to change my life and give it a go, and things would get better. But I've been giving it a go, and in spite of what feels like a yeoman's effort, things seem to be degrading rapidly."

"That's not true. Well, I guess losing your job was a decidedly inferior outcome, but the situation with the policeman, in all honesty, I don't think we've seen the end of that story yet. There's potential there."

Hayley peered into her take-out carton and pushed the contents around to find the good stuff. "You don't understand; I was supposed to take a stand and ask him out. I'd been trained less than twenty-four hours earlier for just such a scenario, and I copped out."

Audra let out a short laugh. "No pun intended."

"Ha-ha. I just don't seem to have what it takes. I established these two goals. I decided I wanted a raise and a guy, and the best I can do is to keep the one goal afloat—barely—while the other tanks. That's not progress."

"Well, we'll just see what we can do about that." She laid the chopsticks carefully on a napkin spread out on her desk, closed the carton, and tossed it back in the takeout delivery bag. Then she passed it to Hayley, who did the same with hers.

Audra's assistant knocked on the glass pane of the office wall and opened the door. "Diane Gradenger." She ushered Diane into the room and removed the Chinese-food garbage.

Hayley did a double take. "What are you doing here? Don't you have class?"

"Nope. I usually have a team project meeting but I switched it so I could be here." Diane slid her backpack off and set it on the ground. She shrugged her wrinkled tan linen shirt down her arms and tied it around the waist of her jeans, then flapped the collar of her T-shirt to circulate a little air. "Okay, I'm ready."

Audra turned back to her computer. "I'm sorry, Hayley, but I have to get some work done, so I asked Diane to take you to Bruno."

Something was up. "Why do I need Diane to take me? The guy works five floors up. I've got legs."

"I'm just here to, uh, be here for you," Diane said. She and Audra exchanged glances over Hayley's head.

They were so obvious. Hayley crossed her arms. "I'm not budging until someone tells me what's going on."

"You're totally overreacting."

Hayley glared at Diane until her friend finally sighed and said,

"Okay, look. I'm here to make sure you give it a fair shake. That's all."

"What makes you think I wouldn't? Audra didn't force me to come here. I asked her."

"Right, but you've never had any kind of therapy or analysis whatsoever."

Hayley snorted. "I'm not sure that's actually a strike against me."

Audra looked up from the monitor. "We're just going to have to say it, Diane."

"You say it."

"Fine." Audra swiveled her chair around and looked Hayley right in the eye. "Hayley, the real reason is that you have a tendency to get hostile."

Hayley made a disgusted sound and put her hands on her hips. "Hostile. I have a tendency to get hostile? I see."

"Yes, you *do*," Audra said. "This could be just the sort of situation that might set off an already loaded gun."

"You're making me sound like an unstable mental patient with hostages."

"Don't be ridiculous." Audra looked at her watch.

"I'm not being ridiculous. I'm one of the most passive people I know. That's what this exercise is all about, isn't it? How can a passive person be hostile?"

Diane cut in. "You're a passive person with a low tolerance threshold. When you're bugged, it's 'kaboom.' Major hostility. I can't believe you don't see this in yourself."

Hayley grimaced. "Maybe I *am* like an unstable mental patient."

"It's not such a big deal. I've simply asked Diane to go along and make sure you don't hurt Bruno's feelings," Audra said. "He can be very sensitive."

"*Bruno's* feelings? Isn't he the shrink? This is *crazy*."

Audra stood up, her eyes narrow slits. "Crazy is inflatable breasts, an ugly dress, and a bad wig." She put her palms flat on her desk and leaned over it. "Bruno Maffri is an internationally recognized professional. He counts numerous celebrities amongst his clients. The *Chronicle* ran an article about him just last month. In fact, Oprah's people are looking at him. Not to mention, I can personally attest to Bruno's ability to help his clients achieve their goals. . . ."

Within two minutes, Diane and Hayley were in the elevator on their way to the thirty-ninth floor.

They stepped out into the entryway facing two enormous brass doors. Hayley took a deep breath and reminded herself not to make any snap judgments based on the pink-tinged walls and matching set of extravagant artificial flower arrangements.

Diane pressed the intercom doorbell and the doors swung open. While Diane checked in with the front-desk receptionist, Hayley hung back, staring at the pictures covering the walls.

The pictures were color glossies: eight-by-tens framed in black matte with the words "I did it!!!" embossed in gold at the bottom. She wasn't sure she trusted anything involving the excessive use of exclamation points, but if that were the worst of it, she'd probably be fine.

Each picture featured two people with their arms around each other's shoulders, one of whom could only have been Bruno Maffri, personal coach to the stars . . . and apparently a bunch of other suckers in San Francisco.

He wasn't at all what she'd expected. Especially for someone Audra would admit to being associated with, but since he was some sort of *celebrity* personal coach, Hayley figured the standards were different.

In each picture Bruno held the same pose, clad in navy-blue nylon Adidas sweatpants and a white muscle-T that said "Visualize Success!" Hayley noted that the very same shirt could be hers in white or black with gold script for a mere twenty-five dollars, according to a placard next to the leather-bound sign-in book.

She looked back up at the pictures. In each one Bruno's arm was raised in a jubilant fisted salute, positioned just right so that the diamonds encrusted on his thick gold watch reflected the flash of the camera. He looked like a cross between Tony Robbins and a *Sopranos* cast member.

Hayley glanced behind her and started calculating the likelihood of escape without Diane noticing. Thirty-nine sets of stairs were a lot if one couldn't afford to wait for the elevator.

"Hayley Jane Smith?"

Hayley turned back to the front desk. Diane was gone, replaced by a tiny woman with librarian glasses and a clipboard.

She was wearing a pink lab coat.

Hayley swallowed. "Yes?"

The woman peered over her glasses and smiled. "Follow me, please."

Hayley took one last, longing glance behind her, then followed the woman into a spacious changing room. She immediately honed in on a vase of pink tulips atop a tiny pink-painted coffee table, a pair of pink fuzzy slippers, and a pink dressing gown hanging on a brass hook.

She looked back over her shoulder at Lab Coat Woman. "Um, could you get my friend over here for a sec?" The woman pursed her lips and answered with a curt nod before walking out.

A minute or so later, part of the dressing room wall opened

and Diane came through the fake doorway with two steaming mugs. "Okay, what's wrong?"

What wasn't wrong? Hayley stared into the secret passage, then back at the fuzzy slippers. "Um, what is all this?" She gestured to the pink. "I'm not here for the mani-pedi."

"Now, don't start getting excited."

"And what's this about?" She pointed back toward the open door through which Diane had just arrived. "Am I being observed? Is there something sinister afoot? Does some security guy want to watch me take my clothes off?"

Diane kicked the door closed with her foot. She took a sip from the mug in her right hand and held the other one out to Hayley. "It's just the kitchen, Hayley. Cool, huh?" Hayley didn't take her mug, so Diane put it down on the mini–coffee table.

Instead Hayley picked up a throw pillow and ran a hand along the seam of the sofa, vigilant for any hidden recording equipment. She gave up and tossed the pillow back on the couch, then looked at Diane, who was obviously not amused. "Hey, don't look at me like that."

Diane rolled her eyes and took the dressing gown off the hook, laying it over her arm.

Hayley grabbed the mug from the table and sniffed. "And what's this?"

"Chamomile."

Hayley held the mug back out to Diane. "I drink coffee."

Diane pushed it back. "You can't have coffee. Coffee invigorates. You need to be calmed."

"Is this the part where my friends trick me into drinking a sedative, and I wake up as an inpatient at the asylum on the edge of town, unable to convince the evil nurse who resembles a small pink rat that I'm not crazy and end up spending the rest of my life in fuzzy slippers and a dressing gown?"

"Okay, this is why I'm here."

"I'm simply tense. I'm not hostile."

"That's debatable. Have some tea."

Hayley took a sip. It wasn't bad. She took another sip. Actually it was quite tasty, in a New Age sort of way. She tipped her head toward the garments. "You know I can't wear that stuff. It's pink. I'll break out with welts all over my body. It's like Audra and failure. I haven't worn pink since I was two."

She poked at the dressing gown on Diane's arm as if it were a dead animal. "This is why I don't go to fancy salons. There's always a pink smock to be worn. And I never know how I'm supposed to put the thing on. And what items of clothing I'm supposed to take off and what I should leave on. Like at the doctor's. They tell you to take all your clothes off but you can actually leave your socks on. If you leave your socks on before you get in the stirrups, it's not like they're going to tell you to take them off."

"What's with all this about taking off clothes? Jesus Christ, this isn't a haircut or a Pap smear."

Hayley gulped down some tea. "Well, you just don't know, you know?"

"This is definitely not a Pap smear." Diane started tapping her foot.

"I mean, you just don't know about the protocol. The salon protocol. It frightens me. I wasn't raised properly or something."

"What do I know? I go to Fast Cuts and get the nine-dollar special."

Hayley noticed Diane's voice was developing an edge, but she chose to ignore it. "No, really, can you imagine the horror of walking out of the dressing room with your smock tied in the back, only to find a salon full of women with their smocks tied in front pointing and laughing at you?"

Diane didn't say anything for a moment. "I'm thinking you had some bad high school locker-room experience that is still with you. Maybe you should save this for Bruno."

As if on cue, there was a knock at the door. Lab Coat Woman looked in. "Oh. We're not quite ready, are we? Well, a few more minutes. But Bruno's waiting for us."

Hayley elbowed Diane. "She's doing that collective 'we' thing. I can't stand that."

"You're stalling."

"You know, Suz said that to me just the other day."

"There's nothing to be nervous about."

"I'm merely tense."

"You've been babbling since you got here. Come on. You don't have to take your clothes off." Diane took the mug out of Hayley's hands and set it back down on the coffee table. "Just put the robe on over the clothes. . . ."

"Why the robe? Can you just explain that to me? I can kind of see slippers, although these particular slippers—"

"Bruno likes all of his clients to be as relaxed as possible. It's part of his strategy to have the professional experience simulate relaxing in the home." Diane pulled a couple of disposable "peds" from a pink cardboard box sitting next to the tulips, took the slippers out of Hayley's hands, and got on her hands and knees. She pulled Hayley's black loafers off and tried to force the fuzzy slippers over her feet.

Steadying herself with a hand on Diane's shoulder and not helping at all, Hayley said, "I don't think I've ever been this tense in my own home. . . ."

Suddenly Hayley jerked upright and Diane grabbed her around the knees to keep her from falling. "What am I doing? What. Am. I. Doing?" Hayley asked.

"Um . . ." Diane let go and rocked back on her heels, chewing her lip. "I'm not sure what you mean."

"I did the same thing when Suz was trying to help me. I bitched and I moaned and I made her know that I wasn't happy about it. Why? I actually volunteered for this. And I'm not even paying. Why am I being so difficult?"

"Because you're just being you?" Diane guessed.

Hayley frowned. "Not this time. I'm going to embrace this. Yes, I am." She struggled to slip her other arm into the pink smock. "I am going to embrace this fluffy slipper therapy and work on improving my inner self so that jobs and men will fall at my pink-clad feet. There's absolutely nothing wrong with chamomile tea. In fact, it's delicious. And they say pink makes your skin look smoother." She wiggled her feet deeper into the slippers. "Okay, now. Are you sure I don't need to take more clothes off?"

Diane stuck out her hands defensively. "No, really. You can leave your clothes on. Please."

"In that case, I'm ready. Wait, let me get my tea. Don't want to leave my yummy chamomile tea."

Hayley ignored Diane's suspicious look as they left the changing room and approached the door to an adjoining room in the suite.

Diane knocked, and a man who was unmistakably Bruno Maffri opened the door. It was a surreal moment, particularly when Diane, of all people, did the East Coast socialite kiss-kiss thing.

Hayley really hoped Bruno wouldn't feel compelled to kiss-kiss her, at least not this first time out. Instead he took both her hands in his, which was disconcerting enough.

"Audra tells me you're experiencing an inability to make decisions and improve your life."

He had a very thick accent—the kind a person from San Francisco would think of as Long Island. *Just go with it.* Hayley cleared her throat. "Yes. That sounds pretty close."

"Mmm. You're working on a couple of different things. Career and love. But you find yourself stymied."

Hayley was already beginning to feel a little antsy and they hadn't even started yet. "Uh, that's right."

"Mmm." He clicked his tongue and, still holding her hands, moved her arms outward and looked her up and down. "Why don't you make yourself comfortable on the chaise, and we'll begin."

With her arms held out away from her sides, Hayley felt exposed, not comfortable. And he still hadn't let go—just held her hands and looked at her. As politely as she could, Hayley pulled away and went over to the . . .

. . . *What the hell is this thing and how are you supposed sit on it?*

Hayley perched awkwardly on the oh-so-modern mutated couch-bed combo furniture thing and arranged her robe around her.

Bruno made himself comfortable in a lavender velour club chair. Diane chose a similar chair in robin's-egg blue and sat down next to him. She pulled out her Palm and the two of them sat there in pastel velour hell just staring at her.

Hayley swallowed hard. This was going to take serious effort.

Diane looked at Bruno and said, "Why don't we start with that exercise you do?"

Hold everything. Hayley sat up. "I'm sorry, Bruno, could you give me just a minute? I just need to ask Diane something."

Bruno looked at his watch and shrugged.

Hayley tried to lean over to the side, so Bruno couldn't hear. "Diane, what are you doing?"

"Sorry?"

"I thought you were just here . . . for me." Hayley didn't actually want to say the word "hostile" in front of Bruno. Didn't want to give him any ideas.

She had a suspicion he was like one of those TV psychics who used anything you said as a clue to guess the details of your problem, and then gave you some generic predictions that could apply to just about anyone. If he were really as good as Audra said, he wouldn't need any hints.

Meanwhile, Diane was fumbling for some sort of explanation. "Oh. Right. Well, I'm also using you as the subject of my paper. I've decided to expand the scope and follow your journey." She coughed. "Didn't I tell you?"

Hayley sat up as straight as she could in the "chaise." "Uh, no, you didn't. What do you mean by 'my journey'? I thought you were just writing about porn?"

The corner of Bruno's left eye twitched.

"I'm not writing about porn, per se. I'm writing about sexuality. It just so happens it's your sexuality. Your 'sexual journey,' if you will. In the context of larger goals. The porn epiphany is only one small part of that."

"Whoa. My sexuality? That would be one short paper, since I haven't managed to scrounge up even a bad date since you started working on this thing. Believe me, as much as I'd like to pretend otherwise, two dry-humping incidents do not a sexual journey make. And as it just so happens, I don't much like the idea of being your sexual subject matter."

Bruno's eye twitched again and he pressed down on the spot with his fingers. Diane glanced at him, frustration starting to break through her usually neutral surface.

"Look," Hayley said, "I understand you're getting a little desperate about this paper, but I don't feel too positive about seeing my name and the words 'porn' and 'sex' used together in hard copy for public distribution."

"You'll be anonymous, I promise. And it's an honor, really. It's an academic paper. Come on, Hayley, I need this." She leaned forward and whispered, "It's not just the paper. I'm thinking of becoming Bruno's protégé. I graduate in one year and I have no idea what the hell I'm supposed to do with an MBA. I don't even balance my checkbook. Just let me do this, please?"

Hayley rolled her eyes. This was no time for Diane to start having a crisis, for God's sake. Hayley wasn't even close to being finished with her own. Better give her what she wanted. "Fine. Whatever."

Bruno adjusted his jock and tapped his watch. "Ladies, I beg your pardon, but the session only lasts thirty minutes. If we could get started, please?" He leaned forward and put his hand on Hayley's shoulder, pressing her down on the chaise to a prone position.

"Let's begin the exercise. Hayley, I'd like you to please close your eyes and relax." He masterfully altered his voice from Long Island to a deep, calming swamilike incarnation. "We're going to begin with an exercise called 'daydream projection.' Breathe in deeply . . . breathe out deeply . . . in . . . out . . . in . . . out . . . okay, now, Hayley, I want you to put yourself in a place of perfection. Youuu aaaarrre perfectionnnnn. . . ."

Perfection? No wonder Audra liked this guy. Hayley opened one eye. "I'm sorry. Do you mean that I'm supposed to pretend that I'm actually perfect or is it that I'm supposed to pretend that I'm perfect but I'm actually somebody else?"

Bruno looked at Diane, concerned. "What are these questions?"

"She's new."

Bruno massaged the diamonds on his watch thoughtfully, then turned back to Hayley. "Okay, what I'm asking is for you to tell me what a perfect you would be like . . . perfect on the inside and outside. With no insecurities, no jealousies, no demands. Let your mind go free and think about it for a few moments . . . then tell me what kind of you, you see."

No insecurities, no jealousies, no demands. That would really be something. Hayley closed her eyes again and tried her best to let her mind go free. "I'm not sure . . . okay . . . it's a little hazy. Okay. I think I see some sort of foliage . . . yeah, jungle foliage . . ."

"I need you to concentrate."

She could hear the impatience in his voice. What was he getting so worked up about? She was the one with the problems. "I *am* concentrating."

"And what is it you see?"

"I'm tall . . . I'm blond yet extremely intelligent . . . I have a great body . . . I have weaponry skills. I think I'm French—"

"Hold it."

Hayley opened her eyes to find Bruno staring at her like a scientist who'd just discovered an astonishing new specimen of idiot. His jaw was clenched, and she could see a vein twitching in the side of his neck.

Bruno looked at Diane. "Ms. Gradenger, may I see you privately for a moment?"

Hayley figured it must be bad if he was using her last name like that. And sure enough, Diane frowned at Hayley, then stood up and followed Bruno into the corner for an animated discussion.

They returned and sat down. Diane gave her one of those wide-eyed warning looks. Composed again, Bruno smiled and said, "Let's try something more traditional. Why do you think you got fired from your job?"

Okay, this was the odd thing about therapists or analysts or coaches or whatever he was: You tell strangers personal information. That was just a really odd concept for Hayley to deal with. Of course, the more problems you had, or the more serious the problems, the more you needed to see a therapist, and the less he would seem like a stranger.

But, as much as Hayley wanted to give it an honest go, for her friend's sake if for no other reason, she didn't think there was too much progress to be made in the remaining fifteen minutes during a one-time-only session.

That was becoming patently obvious.

"I think I got fired because I wanted to get fired. I didn't want to do what I was doing anymore."

"Why didn't you simply find another job you wanted to do and then quit the one you disliked?"

"Because I obviously have a very serious problem committing to change."

"Mmm. Ahh."

Hayley looked at Bruno. He looked quite pleased. What, did the guy think he earned a gold star for that? She just told him what the problem was. He hadn't uncovered anything new.

"And you put on a degrading costume in a bar because . . . because why?"

Degrading? What kind of uplifting personal coach sort of adjective was that? Hayley sat up. "Hey, buddy, don't knock the dress. It looks stupid, but the minute you put it on—"

"Hayley, let the man do his job," Diane pleaded.

"I'm not hearing any revelations, here." Hayley could feel it coming—she could feel it, even as Diane gave her the most begging, pleading look she was capable of. But Hayley couldn't stop herself. Or wouldn't.

Pure sarcasm dripped from her voice as she looked at Bruno down her nose and said, "I seem to be figuring it all out for both of us. How much is he charging, Diane? Because I'm actually kind of good at this."

Bruno crossed his arms over his chest. "Interesting reaction, Hayley. Why do you think you're so hostile?"

"Okay, that's it, Diane. I'm done."

Bruno just looked at her indulgently and smiled. "You're not even close to done."

Hayley flicked her ankle and sent one fuzzy slipper flying over Diane's and Bruno's heads smack against the pink-tinged wall.

Chapter Nine

"Well, how did it go?" Audra asked. "Isn't Bruno fabulous?"

Hayley leaned against Audra's desk. "Let's just say that he didn't make me feel better and he didn't make me feel worse. But I really appreciate the gesture."

Audra gazed at her for a moment and then said, "You must be one of those delayed-reaction people."

"What you mean?" Hayley froze. "Do they put something in that tea?"

Her friend laughed. "Don't be silly. That's not what I meant. . . . Did Diane leave?"

"Yeah, she seemed really tired by the time the whole Bruno thing was done. And I think she's starting to get really nervous again about graduating."

"Well, if she didn't insist on taking summer school, she wouldn't graduate so quickly. And I'm so tired of all those ceremonies, anyway. They're incredibly boring, those huge public-university graduations. I don't understand why they don't have everybody wait in a bar. They could just page you when it's time for your friend to claim her diploma." Audra shook her head. "Diane won't be able to avoid working forever."

Audra's assistant knocked again and opened the door. "Nanette from Neiman Marcus Union Square is here." She stepped aside and ushered in an impeccably made-up brunette wearing a light yellow-and-black Chanel summer suit.

Nanette looked wispy but she walked like a tank, and behind her she pulled a mobile garment rack three times her size. It was crammed with clothes and featured a built-in top shelf packed with shoeboxes.

"You'll need to remove your shoes and step up on the coffee table," she said curtly. She went over to the coffee table and began pushing it to the center of the room.

Hayley looked at Audra and grinned. "So this is how rich people shop."

"She's talking to you, Hay."

Hayley's smile vanished. "No way. She's talking to you."

Nanette marched up to Hayley. "I'm talking to you."

"Nanette is my personal shopper. She's here to take care of you." Audra put her arms behind her head and leaned back in her leather executive chair to watch.

Hayley held up her hands in protest. "Believe me, I'd love for Nanette to take care of me in the manner to which you've become accustomed, but there is no way I can afford your personal shopper. If you want to call the Gap personal shopper, I'll start stripping down immediately."

"Nonsense," Audra said, looking horrified. "You're going to try for a job today and we need you to look the part."

"That's really sweet of you, but the thing is that you don't generally wear supernice clothes to techie job events. It's a dead give-away that you don't have any experience in the industry."

"Nonsense," Audra repeated dismissively. "You can never look too good for this sort of thing."

There was really no point in trying to explain. Audra would never understand that worn-out cargo pants and blue hair were considered indicators of likely technical genius. "Well, the thing is, I need to leave in, like, half an hour."

"Fine. Half an hour. Nanette, we're ready for you."

Hayley shrank back as Nanette marched up to her and started giving her a pat-down, a technique she seemed to be using to assess Hayley's physical build.

Hayley politely batted Nanette's hands away and asked, "Is all this some sort of massive overcompensation for the raise mixup? I want you to know I don't blame you for that whatsoever."

"Absolutely not. No point in looking back," Audra said, waving her index finger in the air. "We must go forward!"

Right. Hayley had to wonder just how many sessions with Bruno Audra paid for each week.

Immune to Hayley's skeptical expression, Audra stood up and came around her desk to the opposite side of the garment rack to meet with Nanette.

Hayley couldn't quite make out what the two women were saying, but after quite a bit of rustling, Nanette reappeared with an outfit protected by white plastic.

She dramatically whipped the plastic cover off and held out a black suit for Hayley's inspection. "This says 'power.' " She put her hand on her hip and waited for Hayley to gush.

It was a great suit, Hayley had to admit. Nanette obviously knew her stuff. Terrific styling and the perfect color. Hayley lifted the sleeve and peered at the tag. *Hello.* "This says Michael Kors—seven hundred and ten dollars." She dropped the sleeve and sadly shook her head.

Audra hurried forward and put the sleeve back in Hayley's hand. "Consider it an early birthday present."

"No way. I gave you a wool scarf for your birthday. There's a huge difference there."

"But it was Ralph Lauren."

"Yeah, but I got it at Ross."

"Oh!" Audra looked momentarily disconcerted. "Well, just humor me, okay? Just try a couple of things on. Then we'll see."

Hayley supposed she could at least let Audra do her thing, if she was so determined. "Look, I'll try them on if you want me to, but I'm telling you, I'm not buying. I just can't spend that kind of money, and I won't let you spend that kind of money on me, either."

"Up, please." Nanette stood in the center of the office next to the coffee table with a tape measure hanging from her neck and a pincushion Velcroed around her wrist.

Hayley shook her head, but she removed her loafers and stepped up onto the table anyway. Nanette pushed her arms up to full span and began to take measurements.

Suddenly Audra looked up from her desk toward the door. "Oh, I need to take care of this."

Hayley followed her glance and saw two giant blond specimens of manhood waiting patiently behind the glass. "Nanette, turn around, turn around... check these guys out." They looked like the Abercrombie & Fitch representatives except they had all their clothes on.

Nanette looked over her shoulder and then turned back with her eyebrows raised. "Ooh-la-la," she murmured.

Hayley started to blush, partially because they were so good-looking and partially because she was standing in bare feet on a coffee table in an upright spread-eagle position.

But as stupid as that felt, she felt even more stupid when Audra waved the men into the office and they walked around the coffee table without even looking at her. To her even greater dismay, Nanette took the opportunity to start in on the inseam measurements.

One of the men handed Audra a manila folder while the other said something about a net loss of profits. It sounded banal enough to Hayley, but for Audra it was like being struck by lightning. She stood up slowly and just laid into these guys.

Hayley had no idea what Audra was talking about with all that financial mumbo jumbo, but without ever raising her voice, her friend expressed her displeasure so eloquently and so forcefully, even Hayley felt compelled to apologize for whatever it was the men had done.

Iron fist, velvet glove, indeed.

Sure, she could be a high-maintenance pain in the ass at times, but to see Audra like this, a fabulous corporate dominatrix with more charisma and presence in her baby finger than in both those two blond gods combined . . . well, it was an incredible display of . . . of . . .

Hayley couldn't think of the word. It was just that Audra knew what she wanted and she knew how to make it happen. Audra was a woman with a plan and the wherewithal to carry it out.

Maybe Bruno wasn't so full of crap after all. Or maybe Hayley just needed one of those suits. Well, the suit was out of the question, but . . .

Hayley bent down and whispered to Nanette, "Look, I don't want to waste your time, since I'm not going to be buying clothes from you today, but if you can dig up a pair of shoes like Audra's I'd be interested. Seven and a half."

Nanette nodded and went over to the garment rack and started rummaging through the shoeboxes. By the time she fitted Hayley into a pair of black stilettos, Audra had dismissed the blonds.

They got out of the office pretty fast, and Audra tossed the file into one of her leather in-boxes. "Men," she said, rolling her eyes. "Men can be such . . . slow creatures. Or maybe everyone just got a little stupid today because their minds are on the bonus meeting." She rubbed her hands together a little nervously. "Today we're going to find out if we're on target for the big money at year-end."

Hayley sat down on the edge of the coffee table and admired her new shoes. "If I hadn't already known you before you became so impressive, I'd probably never know you."

"Don't be silly. Are you and Nanette done?" She looked suspicious, so Hayley quickly said, "Yeah, we agreed on a pair of shoes. That was incredible, by the way. You were great. The whole performance."

Audra just looked at Hayley woefully. "No suit, huh? Well, the shirt you're wearing is kind of cute. I'm sure it won't work against you."

Hayley grinned. "Gee, thanks. I'm just praying I'll make it to the job fair before I start getting sweat circles."

"You know, Hay, I have at least a dozen contacts who would love to hire you. Why don't you let me make some phone calls? It would be much more efficient than this job-fair thing." Audra shivered with obvious disgust. "Job fairs are for people without a good network. You have a good network. You have me."

But Hayley had been relying on her friends to help her solve her problems since the moment they'd all figured out exactly what those problems were. Of course, they'd all said they *wanted* to help.

In fact, they were falling over themselves and each other for a chance to help her.

But the point was that she needed to go to the job fair for the very purpose of doing something on her own.

Audra wasn't ready to give up. She sat on the coffee table next to Hayley. "Look, let me just describe this one opportunity. All the other on-line women's mags are either dead or dying, but this one still has solid financial backing. And you have the perfect qualifications. It's called Mouth-to-Mouth Recitation. Charming name, isn't it? And not only that, but—"

"Charming," Hayley said. "I agree. The name is absolutely charming. Charming and oddly familiar."

"Well, there's not a whole lot of creativity left in the Silicon Valley scene," Audra admitted.

"And you are a true friend for offering but . . . thanks, but no, thanks. Maybe Bruno didn't have an effect on me, but I guess I did realize one thing while I was up there: If I'm serious about making changes, I can't be so resistant to the process of figuring out what those changes need to be."

"Well, that's something," Audra said, doubtfully.

"So I need to go the tech fair and explore my options and meet some people, really think about what kind of job I want." It felt good to say that. It made things seem possible. Doable.

Hayley smiled and added, "And then I'm going to set up some interviews and make a good long-term decision based on my future career goals. It's important that I learn to do this."

Audra looked at Hayley in silence for a moment, then said, "Well, that's fine. But before you go, I want you to go outside and come in and introduce yourself as if you were at an interview. The least we can do is make sure you've got the basics down."

Hayley looked at her watch. "You know, maybe I should get going. I don't want to miss out on all the good jobs. Ha-ha."

"Don't worry, the bonus meeting is in fifteen minutes, and I certainly don't want to be late for that. Seriously, this job crisis of yours could be over so easily. If you'd just let me call Mouth-to-Mouth, I could have you a job in the next five minutes."

"No!" Hayley yelped in horror. "That's how I got my last job. I'm going to do this on my own. And I want to get the job because I want the job and they want me."

Audra huffed, but said, "Fine. I get it. Now go outside and then come back in and introduce yourself."

Hayley rolled her eyes, then walked out into the hall, turned around, and walked back inside. "Uh, hi. I'm Hayley Jane Smith." She stuck out her arm at Audra.

Audra stared at her. "An arm is not a foreign object without relationship to the rest of the body. You do have control over it, you know. Seriously. Do it like you were really in an interview situation."

What the hell was she talking about? "I just did."

"You're kidding. That was it?"

"Yeah. That was it."

Audra shook her head and motioned for Hayley to sit down again. "You've got to understand that image is everything. You've got to ooze perfection."

"Ooze. You want me to ooze."

"You're purposely misunderstanding me to be difficult. I'm trying to help. You can be so frustrating." Audra swung her hair back from her face, then composed herself by taking a deep breath. "I mean that from the moment you walk in the door, it must be clear to the interviewer that you are perfect for the position; there is no other person who should have that job."

"Okay. I see where you're going with this."

"I know you don't have a lot of time, but let's just work on the opening. First impressions are everything, and I can't let you go before you're ready. At least give me that."

"Fine." Hayley stood up. "Here goes: Hello. My name is Hayley Jane Smi—"

"No, no, no. I want you to lean forward slightly, bending almost imperceptibly from the upper body. You need to smile, but it must be a confident smile, not giddy, not too many teeth. And don't bobble when you walk. You do that. It makes you seem nervous."

"I am nervous."

"Well, if you seem as nervous as you feel, they will assume you are underprepared. Let's do it again." Audra crossed her arms over her chest. "You enter, close the door behind you firmly, turn, walk purposely forward, bend slightly, smile confidently, shake hands with a firm grip by pumping two and only two quick times but not so roughly that it draws attention, and then introduce yourself. And don't slur or say your first and second name too quickly."

"Hayley Jane?"

"Right. Don't do it like that. It makes you sound like something from *Petticoat Junction*."

"Audra, have you ever watched *Petticoat Junction*?"

"No, but it sounds just dreadful, doesn't it?"

Hayley sighed. "You have no idea how ludicrous this all sounds, do you?"

Audra smiled her cat-in-the-cream smile. "I'm here, aren't I?" Framed by her waterfront view, she lifted her Donna Karan-clad arms and gestured to her million-dollar office.

She had a point.

Chapter Ten

So Hayley left Audra's office with the clothes she'd arrived in, plus a pair of brand-new black Calvin Klein alligator stilettos that she'd paid for herself.

She wouldn't be able to eat out for a month or two, but they looked really great and did actually make her feel substantially kick-ass. Just the right attitude to have before being forced to beg for a job.

Unfortunately, Hayley hadn't considered the fact that Audra never drove herself to work. She used a car service. Which meant that Audra never had to worry about trying to drive a stick shift on the hills of San Francisco in a 1989 Honda Civic with dysfunctional air-conditioning while wearing four-inch stiletto heels.

The experience was flustering, to say the least, and to avoid thinking about the cramps in her calves and the sweat circles that had, indeed, formed after all under the arms of the shirt Audra deemed barely passable to begin with, Hayley concentrated on practicing her introduction in the rearview mirror. She tried out several variants.

Plain: "Hello, I'm Hayley Jane Smith." *Petticoat Junction*-style: "Howdy, Ahm Hayley Jane." Audra-style: "Hallo, dahling. My name is Hayley. Jane. Smith!" Enthusiastic: "Hi! I'm Hayley Jane." Jaded and depressed: " 'Lo, I'm Hayley." Of course, that was how she normally sounded, which made her laugh. One more street variation: "Yo! I'm Hayley Jane . . ." *Shit!* Nearly missed the turn off Lombard.

By the time she arrived at the Tech Job Fair site at the Exploratorium in the Marina, she was a nervous, cramping, limping, sweating, multiple-personality wreck.

Luckily she knew the layout because she'd been to the Exploratorium before. It was essentially a giant hands-on science museum often used in the tech industry as a job fair or party venue.

This was really a great idea, particularly for the tech industry. Invariably the museum was more interesting than the attendees, so when you got tired of listening to someone talk about the value (or the lack thereof, as was increasingly becoming the case) of their company's stock options, or how cool it was to be able to work at a company that didn't care if you dressed like a slob, you could always try out one of the interactive exhibits.

In fact, if it happened to be a product-launch party, after two or three rum-and-Cokes, swinging in a chair attached to a giant pen was just about the most amusing thing ever.

Two huge groups of people were lined up behind the two doors, and Hayley stepped up to the back of the line on the left, just as the Tech Fair reps in their yellow polo shirts were unlocking everything.

Unfortunately the lock on the right door was jammed, and as the door on her side opened, Hayley got squashed in the middle between the people in front of her and the anxious people from the other side who came up behind her.

It was a sea of humanity in the worst possible sense.

Hayley didn't know what was scarier: the fact that all of these people really thought they wanted one of these jobs, or the physical sensation of being trapped in the middle of hundreds of laid-off dot-com dweebs frothing at the mouth as they jockeyed for position near the best job booths set up between the exhibit for cow's-eye dissection and the Make a Rainbow project.

Hard to say. The teeming mass lurched forward, and someone stuffed a plastic goody bag into Hayley's hand, and then for a moment Hayley found herself heading straight for the Amazing Sound and Light Tree, which apparently flashed different-colored lights depending on the volume of sound. At that moment, it was going berserk with the combined decibel level of hundreds of people enamored by the sounds of their own voices.

Unable to do anything to change course, Hayley was starting to come to terms with how being rendered deaf and blind might affect her job prospects, when suddenly she was jostled off to the left and swept farther into the depths of the building.

Hayley couldn't actually see which company booth she was lined up for, but she could see that it would take a while before she ever reached the front. There was nothing to do but pass the time in line by checking out the contents of her goody bag.

Whatever disparaging remarks there were to be made about her peer group, you had to admit that techie freebies could be pretty good. And Hayley certainly wasn't above admitting that free stuff was cool.

Enthusiastically she opened the bag to find a limp neon-orange dog Frisbee and three ballpoint pens lying in the bottom of the sack.

All four items were embossed with the names of defunct startups.

And then once again she was thrust forward, nearly winding herself against a glass counter, her résumé portfolio squashed in front of her.

Hayley regained her balance and found herself pressed up against a poster sporting a ten-stage drawing of the intricate features of a cow's eye.

Even better, this remarkable example of bovine anatomy was actually being displayed in the refrigerated glass section under her right elbow.

A stack of brochures on the counter said, *Go to www.exploratorium.edu to find out how you can make cow's-eye dissection more exciting!*

More exciting? Could it *be* more exciting? Would you *want* it to be more exciting?

Hayley swallowed and wiped her sweaty forehead with one of the brochures. She'd give a lot for a bottled water right now.

When a faint chemical smell reminiscent of formaldehyde wafted upward, Hayley's stomach lurched. The only saving grace was that the crowd finally shifted, and she landed in front of a recruiter at her first job booth.

He was a doughy fellow wearing bad pants and a bright green trade-show polo from 1998. Hayley remembered that that particular trade show didn't exist anymore.

Well, here goes nothing. Lean. Smile. Extend arm. "Hi. I'm—"

"I'm sorry, I can't hear you!"

"Hi. I'm—"

"What? Can't hear you!"

"Hayley! Jane! Smith!" she yelled. She leaned and was slowly raising her arm up just like Audra showed her, when he reached out and grabbed her hand in two sweaty palms and pumped so hard Hayley made a mental promise not to skip yoga again this week, or if she did, to call a chiropractor.

"Nice to meet you, Jane!"

"No, it's . . . Whatever."

He really wasn't too concerned with her first name, as it turned out, because Hayley wasn't the only one who'd practiced before the job fair. This fellow apparently practiced delivering some sort of epic saga, and he was determined to recite it in its entirety.

He droned on ad nauseam, managing to use an ungodly number of techie buzzwords and catchphrases in complete sentences. Continuum, bandwidth, ping, mindshare, B2B . . . they were all there. From a vocabulary point of view, Diane would have been quite impressed.

Since she couldn't actually move anyway, Hayley fixed an interested expression on her face, and killed time by counting the number of words he used and cataloging them by their parts of speech. Finally he took a breath and asked, "So what kind of engineer are you?"

Hayley smiled gamely. "Actually, I'm not an engineer. I'm content. Editorial."

His lip actually curled before he said, "Oh. Sorry. No one's hiring editorial anymore. We're looking for engineers."

"Who does your content, then?" Hayley asked.

"Nobody. Nobody does content anymore. All the companies I know just pipe the stories in from this central repository owned by one of the media conglomerates."

She must have looked pretty shocked, because he obviously felt the need to rub it in, just to make sure she understood him.

Very slowly, as if he realized she'd forgotten one half of her brain at home, he clearly and distinctly repeated, "No one does original content anymore. It's too expensive." And with that he turned and began his performance all over again with the unfortunate person on Hayley's left.

The thing was, Hayley couldn't move.

This sucks. This sucks really badly.

She had to just stand there, seething from a rejection she really didn't care about as the sweat circles expanded in radius and the shooting pain in her feet crept up her legs.

And the guy the recruiter was now talking to, who was apparently lucky enough to be an engineer, kept pressing against her with the side of his body to give himself more space.

Hayley could feel herself being pressed closer and closer back toward the cow's-eye exhibit. She inhaled a shaky breath, praying she wouldn't embarrass herself by hyperventilating.

And that was when the phone rang.

The high-pitched trill sounded like an angel singing. It really did. The sacred notes of her cell phone ringing reminded Hayley of cool running water and the prix fixe menu at Gary Danko. Pure heaven.

Hayley hit the talk button and prayed for deliverance. " 'Lo?"

"It's Audra. How is it going?"

For some strange reason, Hayley wasn't surprised it was Audra. At this point all she felt was relief. She plugged her free ear with her finger and said, "You're going to have to talk louder. Sorry."

"How are you doing?"

"It's . . . fine."

"Good. Just checking in."

"Audra, could I call you back in, like, one minute? I just need one minute here." Hayley pressed the off button, flipped the lid down, and just stared at the phone.

She could smell it.

Hayley could smell deliverance coming out of the seemingly innocuous form of a small black Motorola. And she was thankful deliverance didn't smell anything like sweaty engineers and cow parts.

All she had to do was reach out and take it.

Audra had the power to hand deliverance to her on a silver platter. Hayley could either stick to her guns and get a job on her own terms with the requisite suffering it was obviously going to entail, or just let Audra do what Audra was best at, with a minimum of trauma for everyone involved.

I need a sign. That's what I need right now. Some sign to tell me what to do.

Hayley wiped her sweaty forehead with the back of her hand and looked up reflexively for a tissue or napkin or something. Her eye caught on . . . a sign.

Literally, a sign. It was hanging from the rafters at the far end of the room. *Data Entry Jockeys/Telemarketing Here!*

She had her answer. As cold sweat suddenly poured down her back into her waistband, Hayley flipped back the lid on her cell phone and pushed the memory selector for Audra's phone number.

"Audra, it's me. I lied. It's not fine. I don't want to be anybody's jockey."

"Excuse me?"

"This is a nightmare. I swear to God, I just want to crawl under a rock." Hayley stood up on her toes. "Luckily I can see some sort of prehistoric Stone Age exhibit across the room. Oh, and then there's another one, something about a tactile approach to the Jurassic Age."

In her best take-charge voice, Audra said, "Don't worry. Just get out of there. You have an interview with Mouth-to-Mouth Recitation. It's in SOMA near your old job. Details later."

Hayley closed her eyes. "You already set up the interview for me? When did you do this?"

"The minute you left my office. I figured I could cancel it if you didn't need it, but I figured you'd probably—"

"Need it," Hayley echoed. Some beefy guy jostled Hayley for the umpteenth time. She opened her eyes too late, as a hand slithered into her plastic freebie bag and swiped her dog Frisbee.

It was the last straw. You didn't steal someone else's swag. You just didn't. No matter how pathetic it was.

"I'll take it. I don't want to be anybody's jockey," Hayley repeated, her voice cracking. "It's just an interview, anyway."

"Well, it's all set up." Audra sounded just delighted. "You're good to go."

"Thanks, Aud . . . Ow!" Hayley gritted her teeth as an eager job searcher lifted his combat boot off her foot. "I promise I won't embarrass you."

Hayley dropped the phone into her goody bag without stopping to disconnect the call and scooched around to face the exit.

She took a deep breath, set her jaw, and used the stilettos for what they were best suited for until she'd made it out of the building.

Chapter Eleven

"That's hilarious." Suz slapped her thigh, laughing. "Cow's-eye dissection?"

"Disgusting," Audra choked out. "We're eating here. We don't need to be discussing this right now."

"I'm the only one *eating,* unless you want some." Suz picked up her plate of pancakes and thrust it in Audra's direction.

Audra turned away abruptly, pulled out her compact, and applied powder over the traces of last week's hive breakout.

"I think it's hilarious!" Suz said. "*Cow's-eye* dissection," she repeated, obviously just to be annoying.

"Reminds me I need to pick up an application for medical school," Diane said.

Suz couldn't quite stop laughing.

"Did you hear what I said?" Diane asked loudly. "Cow's-eye dissection reminds me that I need to pick up an application for medical school."

The table remained silent for a moment. Then Suz took the

bait. "And why would you be picking up an application for medical school, oh woman of three majors, four minors, and half an MBA?"

"I'm thinking of studying to become a doctor." Diane ran a hand through her hair, which was beginning to resemble a bird's nest this morning.

"Do you want to be a doctor now?" Hayley asked.

"No. Maybe I should go to law school. I could do law school."

"Do you want to be a lawyer?"

"No."

Diane really looked miserable. "Maybe you should become Bruno's protégé," Hayley said, forgetting that Suz didn't know she'd been to see Audra's shrink. "You seemed very comfortable in his job environment."

Diane crumpled a bit and sighed. "I wouldn't be surprised if he refused to see even Audra again after what happened."

Suz frowned in confusion. "Wait a minute. . . ."

Audra gasped and set down the compact. "Did he say that? Thank God I have his emergency line." She immediately pulled out her cell phone and dialed. "This has been *such* a week of ups and downs; I'm beginning to wonder if I'm becoming a manic-depressive . . . Hello, Bruno? It's Audra . . ."

She leaned away from the table as if doing so would somehow make it a more private conversation, gushed an apology into the phone, and then hung up and glared at Hayley. "I can't believe you didn't tell me that you kicked a slipper in Bruno's face. You said he didn't make you feel better but he didn't make you feel worse. You said *nothing* about bad behavior." She shook her head in disgust and muttered something about "*so* embarrassing."

"I did not kick the slipper in his face," Hayley said quickly. "I kicked it over his head. It's possible he could have interpreted it as just a reflex. You're probably okay."

"Wait a *minute.*" Suz looked from one girl to the next. She pointed her finger accusingly at Hayley. "You went to Bruno Maffri?"

Audra's expression morphed instantly from pissed to triumphant.

Suz whipped around and glared at her. "Aha! You were just waiting for the moment to strike!"

All due respect to Audra, Hayley didn't consider the results of the past few days a triumph, per se. Well, it may have been a triumph for Audra, but not exactly for Hayley. She leaned forward between the two girls to put it in perspective before things got ugly. But Suz wasn't finished. She moved her finger under Audra's nose. "You were just waiting for the right moment to stick it to me. That's why your hives went away. You think you've bested me."

Audra pulled back slightly and looked with masterful condescension at the finger hovering under her nose. With deliberate slowness, she opened her purse and removed a black-lacquered perfume applicator. "Would anyone like a dab? It's new. It's called Sheik Factor. The scent is supposed to conjure images of being fawned over by gorgeous men with oiled chests."

Nobody answered.

"Oh, please." Audra waved one languid hand in the air in her best bored manner. "I wasn't hiding anything. And did you hear me gloat? I think not."

"It was a silent gloat," Suz insisted.

Audra calmly dabbed a spot of perfume on both sides of her neck. "Whatever."

Suz didn't bite back this time. She just leaned forward slightly and sniffed the air around Audra. Hayley could see that she was already forgetting to be mad as her attention latched on to the mysterious perfume bottle and the notion of oiled body parts. Damn, Audra was good.

Unfortunately, Diane's already low supply of intuition hadn't kicked in. "To be honest, I was at the Bruno session and it wasn't pretty. And you'll notice that we haven't heard Hayley say anything that would attribute success to Bruno. In fact, from the memorial service to Bruno, the whole thing's more like a giant saga of failure than anything else."

"Jesus," Hayley muttered.

"Objectively speaking, of course," Diane added, as if that made it sound better.

"Not true," Audra said. "The Bruno teachings simply haven't kicked in yet. I can't speak for the other advice she's been getting, of course."

"Was that some sort of underhanded comment directed at me?" Suz asked.

"I can't say I know what you mean. I wasn't specifically referring to your role in Hayley's calamities," Audra said, looking down her nose. "I'm sorry your little two-step lesson plan didn't work out, but, *really,* Suz." The "really" part was drawn out as far as it could go.

"It's not as if your plans worked out right either, remember? Your brilliant advice lost Hayley her job in the first place."

"That's correct," Audra said, proudly. "I helped her lose the *old* job she didn't want. And thanks to my brilliant advice, as you so rightly call it, Hayley now has a *new* job."

Diane and Suz gasped loudly, in unison.

"Whoa. I do not have a new job. I have a job *interview.* If I'd taken a job, I would have told you. There is a very big difference. An interview in this job market is hardly significant enough to start making excited phone calls. Not to mention, getting the interview has more to do with Audra than it does with Bruno," Hayley said.

"Well, if you want to give me all the credit, I'm not going to argue with that. But if you think Bruno's magic hasn't kicked in yet, things can only get better." Audra carefully put her Sheik Factor bottle back in her tote.

Diane snorted. "Magic? I wouldn't go that far. The guy's good, but it's not magic."

Hayley agreed with Diane, but she didn't want to make Audra feel bad. The thing was, regardless of who was responsible, what her pal considered a wild success was a situation that made Hayley feel like she was well on her way back to square one.

An interview for a job at a company suspiciously similar to the last one, and no guy. Hardly the point of this rather exhausting exercise in self-improvement.

Diane must have been thinking along the same lines. "Well, it sounds like the job situation is a little more under control, but I've got to ask about this Grant guy. Suz told me you had a perfect opportunity to ask him out. He approached you. He gave you his business card. So what happened?"

"The same as always." Hayley looked down at her latte, mumbling, "Attractive people make me nervous. You all know there's, like, this whole sphere of aesthetically pleasing people that I simply cannot deal with. Which I'm sure is the major reason I messed up my chance with Grant."

Diane's forehead wrinkled. "I'm not sure I understand. . . ."

"*I* don't even understand it. I figure, you know, I'm above average. I'm not saying I'm some genius supermodel who's trying to save the world, but I'm not a completely repulsive human being." Too brightly Hayley added, "Now, give me an ugly guy any day and I'll just walk right up and introduce myself."

"That's the part I don't understand." Diane looked at her dubiously. "I think we've pretty much exhausted that 'he's so attractive he scares me' theory."

The three girls nodded and Diane continued. "To begin with, I understood Suz's exercise was designed to help you expand your horizons beyond the small circle of men who happened to approach you, to a wider circle of men, attractive or not, but hopefully attractive, whom you were mentally prepared to approach and proposition."

"I agree," Audra said, flashing Suz a conciliatory smile. "And I must say that I find it hard to believe that with such a small amount of time passing between lesson and practice, everything Suz taught you could go to hell in a handbasket just because the man has beautiful forearms and good teeth."

"They're extraordinary forearms, not just beautiful. Otherworldly," Hayley corrected. "And I've never seen teeth so gorgeous."

"Regardless, the fact remains that, as you so eloquently put it, just the other day you dry-humped a delicious Spaniard clothed in Armani trousers in a coat closet, with no problem. *Armani*, okay? Just try and convince me this Sergio wasn't aesthetically pleasing."

"I was completely wasted. I still can't verify his nationality *or* his pants. For all I really know, the handsome Armani-clad Spaniard might actually have been some creep from New Jersey wearing synthetic pants from Target."

Audra shuddered. "Really?"

"Why do you always dis New Jersey?" Diane asked.

"I don't know. Probably because it's a foreign place with a bad reputation that no one from San Francisco understands or has ever visited," Hayley teased.

Diane huffed. "I have relatives in New Jersey, remember?"

"Have you ever been to see them?"

"No," Diane confessed. "We make them come here."

"He wasn't from New Jersey, believe me. I was there. Although I can't speak to the pants." Suz turned to Hayley. "You're not going to get out of this so easily."

Audra used her pinkie to carefully tuck a few glossy strands of escaped hair back behind her ear. "Diane's right. Level of attractiveness can't possibly be the fundamental issue. When we watched that . . . that . . . *film,* you said you had a big problem. An overall problem with urban malaise. You have a problem getting yourself to make any kind of forward movement. In any scenario. Not just with men."

"And I really thought we'd handled the guy part of that whole issue at the Beer Garden." Suz shook her head. "It was like you regressed or something."

"Yeah," Diane said. "It's like that movie where they give the retarded man some pills and he gets really, really smart, but in a horrible, tragic twist, after he peaks at some genius level of intelligence, he becomes even more retarded than he was originally."

Hayley rolled her eyes. "Yeah, it's just like that. Great. Fabulous." She slumped back in her chair, sulking.

The three girls looked at each other over Hayley's head. After a pause Diane said, "You know, Suz is the only one who's actually seen Grant. What about this guy has you so crazy?"

Suz ran her tongue over her lips and wiggled her eyebrows.

Hayley giggled. "Well, there's that. But on the whole, it's still a bit unclear. I'll just say that up front. I mean, aside from the fact that he's good-looking, he's got an attitude thing going on. I think he knows he makes me a little off balance, and I'm not sure I want to like a guy who likes to do that."

"Sounds like shades of the Asshole Complex," Diane said.

Hayley sighed. "I don't know if that's quite it. He was really nice about the Fred thing that first time we met, and also he's a policeman. He's out there keeping the peace, defending our community, you know, doing those policeman things. It's kind of a mix. I don't know, whatever it is, I'm just really into it. Even the sexy pseudointimidation part."

"Thwack! 'Please, sir, may I have another?' Thwack!"

Hayley snorted with laughter. "Uh, right, Suz. Something like that."

"When good girls love bad, bad boys," Audra teased. "Really, a man in uniform. What honest woman doesn't like that? A man in uniform who obviously is attracted to you, who has just enough attitude to be interesting without being—we are hoping—excuse my French, an asshole. No contest. Seriously, though, I do wish you'd get on with asking him out, because he might have some good-looking friends for the rest of us."

"There's no such thing as a millionaire policeman, Audra," Diane said.

"I didn't say he couldn't be corrupt."

Hayley tossed back the last few drops of her latte and wiped her mouth with a napkin. Crumpling the napkin in her hand, she said, "You know the thing that's really bugging me? It's the wink. What do you think that was about? And is it normal for strange men to act so cavalier about personal space? Does that mean he likes me or he's trying to scare me? And why do you really think he came to the memorial service? Does it mean he has a conscience? Or does it mean he thinks I'm a slam-dunk? But if he thinks I'm a slam-dunk and is therefore interested, why would he leave without asking me out?"

"You were supposed to ask him out," Diane pointed out.

Hayley's patience was slipping. "That's not the point here. He didn't know that. I didn't ask him out and he didn't ask me out. We came away from the moment with nothing."

"Which proves you're equally ineffectual on that score and may be a match made in heaven."

"What I'm trying to get to the bottom of is why he would wink if he weren't interested."

"Why would a guy wink at all, though?" Shrugging, Diane added, "Maybe he had something in his eye. Guys don't really wink anymore."

Suz shook her head. " 'Scuse me, but guys do *so* wink. Didn't Sergio wink at you? Spaniards wink all the time."

"Spaniards?" Hayley repeated weakly. She could feel the conversation getting away from her again.

"No, it's true," Audra agreed. "Many a fine young Spaniard has winked at me. And they don't wink for no reason. It means he's interested. I confess I find it extremely arousing."

"Sergio didn't wink at me." Hayley wrinkled her forehead, trying to recall all the details. "At least I don't think so. I don't really remember."

"Well, I disagree with Audra. I think a Spanish wink is more like conversational punctuation than a sexual pass fraught with meaning." Diane looked around the table sagely. "Not everything means something."

"So you're saying there are rules for Spaniards and different rules for other men?" Audra asked.

It was time to put the kibosh on the Spaniards thread and get the conversation back on track.

Hayley put her palm out and said, "I have nothing against Spaniards, Aud, but what I'm really interested in is, 'Can I get a contact number?' What's that all about? It's the word 'contact' that I find unsettling. If he'd said 'phone' or 'home' or 'personal' or something like that, I'd have a sense that he was going to ask me out. But why didn't he ask me out right there, if he was planning to ask me out at all?"

"That was an interesting choice of words, wasn't it?" Diane assumed the "thinker" pose, chin on fist. "There's a certain formality to this guy I find really interesting. The way he said 'deceased' instead of 'dead,' 'vomit' instead of 'puke,' and now 'contact' instead of 'phone.' He must have done well on the SATs."

"Well, maybe not," Audra said. "I don't think they're all related. 'Deceased' and 'vomit' are very specific word choices. 'Contact' is almost deliberately vague in terms of its lack of clarity regarding whether his interest extends to business or pleasure. No connection, in my opinion."

"Yes, but maybe it's not the vagueness-specificity continuum we should be paying attention to. Maybe it's—"

"*Maybe,*" Suz said with a smirk, "*maybe* he simply wanted to provide Hayley and her friends with endless hours of analysis on this very subject."

"Oh, God, you're right. Listen to me," Diane wailed. " 'Vagueness-specificity continuum'? I'm a freak! What's going to become of me?"

"You always get like this near graduation." Suz squeezed

Diane's shoulder. "Everything always turns out okay, doesn't it?"

"It only turns out okay," Diane said, "because I immediately start studying something else. Maybe if I duff the Human Sexuality paper and get an F, I won't have to graduate this year."

"You can't duff the Human Sexuality paper," Hayley said, alarmed.

"Why not?"

"Because it's about me! That in and of itself is a concern to me. And now you're talking about writing a *bad* paper about me and sex. That's just . . . just . . . you can't. It's offensive. It might end up in the public domain. It could be misinterpreted. I'd never live it down. No guy would want anything to do with me—I'll be having imaginary sex for the rest of my life."

"Imaginary sex? Are you having a lot of this imaginary sex right now?" Hayley just glared at Suz, who added, "Like anyone who matters is going to be reading Diane's graduate school research paper." She snickered. "Oh. Sorry, Diane."

Diane lifted weary eyes to Hayley. "Don't worry; I was just saying that. I don't have it in me to underperform. And you're right. This is just par for the course. I think I'm just tired or something. It's been all work and no play. I've been skipping the MBA beer busts, and maybe I just need a drink. How about Monday martinis at the Zodiac?"

"Yeah, I'm in," Suz said.

"In," Audra said. "I need a stiff drink myself, what with all that's been going on."

"Likewise," Hayley added.

"Good." Diane smiled weakly. "And really, I'll be fine. This must just have something to do with closing in on thirty."

Audra gasped in horror. "You *had* to mention being thirty. Oh, dear God. Can I not bask in the glory of Hayley's progress for the length of even one conversation? I was just out of my bad mood." She pressed her fingers to her forehead.

"What's wrong?" Hayley asked.

"Nobody's turning thirty anytime soon," Suz said in an exasperated mutter and was duly ignored.

"You know how I told you we had the bonus meeting at work the other day?" Audra asked. "Well, it doesn't look like the amount is going to be what we were hoping for. In fact, you and the rest of your startup cronies are responsible for this."

"Whoa." Hayley sat back out of range of Audra's accusing finger.

"We did all the work. We provided all the capital. We made the money happen for you. But your business models all sucked, excuse the expression, and you couldn't figure out how to make a profit. I've never seen such bullshit financial management in my entire life. Your people are the stupidest people I've ever met."

Hayley swallowed, but Audra wasn't finished. "Now we're seeing the final results, and it's not pleasant. The money has vaporized! It's *your* fault I'm not going to be a millionaire by the time I'm thirty. It's *your* fault. You and your people."

"My people?" Hayley asked, trying to avoid laughing in Audra's face.

"Yes. You sloppy techie people and your lattes and your BMWs and your expensive clothes and your goddamn sense of entitlement. You people disgust me. Back when it counted, I should have stood out in the Mission District picketing with those creepy artists who thought they should be getting apartments for free just because they could make pretty pictures."

"But—"

"I'm not finished yet. I can't believe the ridiculous sums of money your people pulled in—are still pulling in—for jobs a person with half a brain cell could do . . . and it was *my money*." She inhaled a very deep breath and exhaled very slowly. "There. Now I'm finished. Well, what do you know? I feel better. That's been bothering me for a while." She picked up her latte and took a sip.

Hayley gestured to her friend's latte mug. "But you like lattes and Beemers and expensive clothes. The only differences between you and 'my people' is that you've got more of all those things—and you've actually got taste."

Audra appeared to be fairly well assuaged by that statement. She put her hand up to her neck and ran her fingers over her Gucci necklace, making sure it was still properly positioned.

Suz elbowed Diane. "I thought she *was* a millionaire."

"Maybe if she didn't spend so much."

"Is a millionaire just someone who's made a million dollars? Or is it someone who could spend a million dollars no problem and still have money left over? A million dollars isn't what it used to be."

Diane just shrugged. "Maybe she's just using the term 'millionaire' as shorthand. Maybe she really means 'multimillionaire.' "

To her credit, Audra declined to supply any details of her undoubtedly bountiful wealth. She just sat back in her chair with a self-satisfied smile and seemed content to leave it at that.

"Well, I'm really sorry about your bonus, Aud," Hayley said. She looked at Suz, a half smile on her face. "Looks like both Diane and Audra are experiencing some medium-grade distress. A little building tension, it seems. Do you have some anger you wish to express?"

Suz laughed. "Don't Bruno me. I'm fine. Although . . . Nah, I'm fine."

Audra nudged Hayley with her shoulder. "I didn't mean to take it out on you. Venture capital used to be fun. Now it's depressing. I'm just mad at your industry, that's all. Not you."

"Well, I guess you have a right to be mad at me about Bruno, anyway." Hayley still felt bad about that. It would be awful if Bruno blamed Hayley's behavior on Audra.

"Well, you owe me," Audra said. "So promise me just one thing. Sometime between now and drinks tomorrow night, I want you to just lie quietly and think about what Bruno asked you to do. Just imagine one small scenario." Audra raised her arms and made sweeping gestures in the air. "Visualize success. Okay? Promise me you'll give it a try."

"Okay, okay," Hayley said, rolling her eyes. "I promise."

Chapter Twelve

She was a genius supermodel trying to save the world. Her name was Emma de la Fressange, but the boys just called her M. She needed only one letter. She was that good, with enough charisma, MENSA-level intelligence, and devastating beauty to blow away even the most jaded of men.

She stood six feet tall, with long blond hair and a body that stopped officers dead in their tracks. Some had even been known to seek medical attention from the MASH-unit ophthalmologist after making eye contact.

On Saturday nights she danced and sang in a pitch-perfect voice tinged with a foreign accent of unknown origin—French, perhaps?—in the hottest nightclub in the city just outside base boundaries. But her real job was as an expert marksman in a covert military operation sanctioned by the United Nations that mobilized only for extremely righteous purposes.

She'd go out on jungle missions in her black fatigues and combat boots, concealing her shining tresses under a black helmet, just pining away for the love of the chief intelligence specialist as she shot the villains dead with her sniper gun.

He was a painfully handsome man, the chief intelligence specialist. A man with a tormented soul who was at this moment sitting shirtless in front of her by the campfire mixing up a pot of franks 'n' beans, his muscled chest gleaming in the light of the flames.

He was the American officer Lt. Grant Hutchinson. The one man she truly loved. The one man who didn't seem to know she existed.

Or did he?

Something was different about him tonight, she thought as he stopped stirring and walked around the campfire with his handcuffs in one hand and one eyebrow raised.

Would she like to practice special-intelligence search procedures? His voice was deep. Manly. She couldn't find the words to answer him, couldn't speak. She just raised her hands and let him carefully lock the handcuffs around her wrists, panting as his hands traveled down the planes of her perfect skin. He gently stripped her clothing off and slid his hand between her legs, his long fingers heading for the promised land.

It took him only sixteen seconds to take her where she needed to go; she came hard, just as the bells of a far-off native cathedral began to chime—

Brinnng!

Hayley sat straight up in bed, wide-eyed and breathing as if she'd just run a marathon . . . or something. She fanned her face with her hand to try to bring down the temperature.

Suddenly she stopped and looked at her hand. Did she actually orgasm? Or did she just dream an orgasm? Did that count?

The phone rang again. She leaned over to pick it up and looked at the clock, then shrugged. She'd napped practically the entire afternoon, but what the hell. The only thing on today's agenda was Martini Monday.

"'Lo?"

"Hello. I'm calling for Hayley Smith. This is Grant Hutchinson." There was a pause as he apparently waited for her to remember him, during which Hayley leaned back against the headboard in shock. After a moment of silence, he added, "We know each other through Fred Leary." And then he sort of chuckled.

There was another pause, during which he was probably wondering whether or not she had taken offense to the crack, but Hayley was now actually standing on the bed holding the phone out at arm's length in front of her with her right hand and doing the Tiger Woods victory fist pump with the other.

"Hello?"

She put the receiver back to her ear. "Oh, hi! This is Hayley."

"Hey. Hope I'm not calling too early."

"No, not at all. I'm just . . . I'm up. Up and about. I've been up for hours. That's right, um, getting an early start on the day, like I always do. What's up?"

"I've got two tickets to Friday's Giants game and I called to ask you if you'd like to go out to dinner first and then hit the stadium for the game."

Boom. No dicking around. No idle chatter to warm up to the point. This was a man who knew what he wanted . . . and he wanted her. Unless . . . that thing about Fred. Wait a minute. "This is a date, right? No corpse?"

"This is a date. Just the two of us. Fred's not invited."

Sense of humor confirmed! "In that case, I'd love to." Hayley gave the thumbs up sign to the stuffed giraffe perched on the bureau at the far end of the room.

"Great. Do you like Italian?"

"Love it. Uh, what time? Where? Where do you want to meet?" She slapped her forehead and winced. She sounded like she'd never done this before.

"Uglioto's? I could pick you up at six."

Within five minutes they'd very efficiently swapped addresses and Grant had hung up. The whole thing happened so fast, Hayley was left a little stunned, dangling the receiver by its cord. Very slowly she bent down and hung up the phone.

And then the enormity of the situation dawned on her. "Yeeeessss! Visualize success, baby."

Oh, my God, it works!

• • •

Hayley raced into the swanky downtown martini bar, roughly grabbed Audra's head, and planted a kiss on her friend's perfect hair. "It works, it works!"

"My God, what on earth are you wearing? It's . . . it's . . . ugh." Audra recoiled into the back of her chair. One hand attempted to smooth down her hair; the other moved to cover her mouth as she swallowed convulsively.

"It's a muscle T. Drove over and bought one from Bruno on my way here. They'd just closed up for the day. Had to pound on the door for a while before they'd let me in but what the hell, I'm just happy it comes in black."

"It's disgusting. The armholes are too large. I can see your bra."

Suz reached over and held the T-shirt taut. " 'Visualize success.' Oh, boy. Do tell."

"Ooh! Is that my drink?" Without waiting for an answer, Hayley took a big gulp of apple martini.

"Uh, go easy on that, Hayley," Diane said. She smoothed a hand over the front of a hooded maroon fleece, which was clearly a new addition to her sweatshirt wardrobe, and added, "Man, *I* wouldn't even wear that."

Hayley ignored her. "Wonderfully, fabulously delicious." She grinned, then pulled the cocktail glass toward her and took another giant swig, looking up in time to see the girls exchanging amused glances.

"How's it going with you all? As you can see, things are just dandy with me." She nudged Audra with her shoulder. "I owe you one. Bruno's a goddamn genius."

"I know." Audra smiled, but she was obviously conflicted. She seemed quite pleased that Bruno was responsible for Hayley's mystery success, but she hadn't recovered from the muscle T and was half shading her face away from Hayley with her hand. Her loyalty to the guru clearly did not extend to his wardrobe. "Well, don't keep us waiting. What happened?"

Hayley savored the moment. Very slowly and very deliberately she crossed her arms over her chest and leaned back in her chair. "Grant Hutchinson asked me out for Friday night."

Audra forgot about Hayley's shirt—and apparently her competition with Suz—and shrieked jubilantly.

Hayley nodded. "That's right. Grant is the guy. He's the One. This has multiple date potential, at the very least. I just know it." She paused, then added, "Okay, well, 'the One,' maybe that's a little strong. The point is, I have a date on Friday night. I am now a girl with a date on Friday night."

"Well, this is terrific news," Suz said. Hayley produced her most brilliant smile. But then Suz went on to say matter-of-factly, "Can't say I'm surprised. You played it just right. You already went to third base. That's like a guarantee."

Hayley deflated slightly. "What? That's not how this all came together. What happened between me and Grant in the office . . ." Her thoughts got garbled and she huffed. "Going to third base does not guarantee anything."

"It does when I'm involved."

"What exactly does third base consist of? Is there an actual definition?" Diane asked.

"If it were a guarantee, Suz, then why was I even concerned for one minute about whether or not he'd ask me out?"

Suz lackadaisically set down her drink and made a big show of checking out the bar crowd for fresh prey. "You were supposed to ask *him* out."

"You have no logic in your arguments." Hayley shook her head in disbelief. "They're just like crazy little sentences that come out of your mouth to confuse people." She looked at Audra and Diane for backup. They looked thoroughly amused, but no backup appeared to be forthcoming.

Hayley turned back to Suz. "You're suggesting that he asked me out because I gave him enough for him to know that I'll sleep with him?"

"Well, you do plan to sleep with him, don't you?"

"Well, yes, but that's hardly the point."

"Isn't it?"

"Maybe in your universe. Insult me if you must," Hayley said, looking pointedly at Suz. "But *I* am a girl with a *date* on Friday night. And *you* are merely a girl with a Friday night."

"She may not have a date, but she'll probably have a guy," Diane noted with a laugh.

Suz and Hayley ignored her.

"Don't get all testy, Hayley," Suz said. "We just don't want to see you disappointed with the long-term outcome."

Hayley gaped. "You'd think you could be happy for me. You're all just jealous."

"Absolutely," Suz said. "The guy is hot. I'm hugely jealous. I've always been partial to the police baton fantasy. I'm usually lying facedown in satin hot pants across some policeman's lap. He takes his baton and—"

"I know *I'm* jealous," Audra interrupted. "And I haven't even seen him." She lowered her gaze and whispered almost belligerently, "I've always wanted to make love to a man wearing a police uniform."

Suz choked on her martini.

Diane thumped Suz on the back, nodding. "I may not be on the prowl right now, but from what Suz told us, I wouldn't kick him out of my bed. Make no mistake: We're all completely jealous."

"Oh. Well, in that case. Fine." Placated, Hayley relaxed back into her chair, sipped at her drink more moderately, and let the high of Grant's call settle back in.

"I got-ta daaate, I got-ta daaate," she chanted. Then she paused, pointed across the table at Diane and Suz, did a little shoulder shimmy, and chanted a little more. "That's right. I got-ta daaate . . . I got-ta daaate . . . with someone I actually want to daaate . . ."

The girls winced at Hayley's cadence-challenged ode to the joys of dating, but Diane said, "Let her enjoy it while it lasts. She's interviewing for that new job tomorrow, and who knows what's going to happen with that."

Hayley stopped chanting. "I heard that. I'm not going to take it if it's just the same old thing."

"Do you want to practice for the interview?" Audra asked hopefully.

Hayley looked at her as if she were crazy. "Are you kidding? I can't think about *that.* I need to start preparing for my date. Maybe later."

Suz opened her bag, fished around, and pulled out a fistful of condom strips, which she dumped next to Hayley's cocktail glass. "Here. Now you're prepared."

Audra whipped out the bar menu and opened it up to shield Suz from the other patrons. "For God's sake."

"That's not what I meant." Hayley turned red and hastily pushed the condoms back at Suz. "I was thinking more along the lines of a haircut." She frowned, now mentally reviewing the contents of her closet. "I've already got those great shoes I need to amortize some more. Just not sure what I'm going to wear with them."

Diane picked up one of the condom strips. "Aren't you on the pill?"

"Why would I be on the pill?" Hayley asked. "And don't make me state the obvious."

"I'm on the pill to regularize my cycle."

"What a waste!" Suz giggled.

Diane looked at her pityingly. "You are woefully oversexed to the point where I think it's depleting your brain cells. You just sit there giggling like a loony. I'm almost positive it's from being manhandled so often."

Suz turned away from Diane back to Hayley. "So how far are you planning to go?" she asked.

"Well, as far as he can." Hayley snorted, quite pleased with her own joke.

"No, I mean do you think he's a one-position guy or a two-positioner?"

Audra made an exasperated sound.

"Uh." Hayley looked at Diane for translation, but she just shrugged. "Is this something I need to plan ahead for? Usually I find that the less I'm actually thinking about what I'm doing when I'm having sex the more successful I am at having it."

"Well, let us know. If he turns out to be a two-plus-position guy at the first go, he might be a keeper. You want someone without too many inhibitions for the long haul," Suz explained.

"What do you know about the long haul?" Hayley asked, now amused.

"I don't know. I'm just saying." She paused. "On the other hand, that's something I haven't considered before. If you go through too many positions up front, maybe he figures he's done it all and he won't see you again."

"You never *want* to see them again."

"So for me, I might as well go for the variety pack. You, being more the girlfriend type, might want to stick to the basics."

"You know, I think this is both more than I need to know and more than I *should* know. I'm going to be trying to get into the mood and all this talk is going to have me analyzing the whole thing."

"Nah. Just forget I brought it up."

"Uh, okay."

Before Hayley could wallow in sexual insecurity, Diane changed the subject. "Where're you guys going on the date?" she asked.

"Uglioto's, then a Giants game. Isn't that neat? It's so classic American romance." Hayley hugged herself, happy just thinking about it.

Audra looked dubious. "'Classic American romance?' Baseball?"

"Yeah. A romantic Italian meal followed by America's favorite pastime. Baseball."

"Your first date is a baseball game," Diane repeated.

"Yeah, so? Why are you looking at me like that?"

"Do you like baseball?"

"I'm fine with baseball. I mean, I don't know enough about baseball to dislike it. What are you trying to say?"

Diane sat back and folded her arms, a smile on her face. "He's testing you." She nodded, impressed. "Nice."

Chapter Thirteen

Strategy. It all came down to strategy.

The way Hayley figured it, all she had to do was score a job offer. If she could just do that, it would take some of the pressure off. It would help her confidence, and even more important, it would lock down the promise of an income again.

She didn't want to say anything to her friends, but the money situation was starting to get a little tight. So all Hayley wanted to do at this point was get one job offer in the pocket. Just to get the ball rolling.

It wasn't hard to find the office of Mouth-to-Mouth Recitation, because it was literally blocks from her old job. The biggest apparent difference between the two offices was that the elevator was out of service in this one.

So Hayley trudged up three flights of stairs in her stilettos until she reached the landing. Trying not to sound totally winded, she approached the company receptionist and smiled. The girl looked about sixteen years old and answered the smile with that familiar sort of world-weary startup-worker expression that belied her youthful appearance.

She was sitting there with a fancy phone headset squeezed over her fuchsia-dyed crew cut, eyeing Hayley with a sullen expression, emphasized all the more by her black lipstick.

It was unclear what the girl had to be so snotty about. Hayley looked dubiously at the receptionist desk. It was fashioned out of spare plywood, had obvious splinters hanging off it, and looked for all the world like one of San Francisco's more inexperienced carpenters had put it together.

Whatever. One more time, with feeling. Lean. Extend. "Hi. I'm Hayley. Jane. Smith." Smile. "I have an interview with George Bassum."

The receptionist immediately perked up. "You're Audra Banks's friend!"

"Yeah, do you know Audra?"

"Her firm helped us get funding. We looove Audra. George Bassum—the guy you'd work most closely with—he's in triage right now, so I'm going to take you on the company tour first."

She punched a button. "Crystal, it's Amy. I'm going off-line for about fifteen, twenty minutes. Interview. Right. Can I transfer calls to you? Great." She took off the headset and laid it on the desk. "Why don't we start with the employee kitchen? It's really spectacular."

She stood up and strode off down the hallway, with Hayley trying to keep pace as she stumbled behind her in her long black pencil skirt. The skirt really flattered the lower body, but it didn't allow full leg extension. Of course, Hayley hadn't expected to be doing much running.

They stepped into the employee kitchen. "This is our espresso machine," Amy said reverently, as she waved her hands over the machine like a game-show hostess.

"You grind your own beans over here," she said, "And then transfer them to here . . . it can make two cups at one time, has a frother over here, on the right, but you gotta be careful because it has a tendency to spritz out at you . . . and in this cupboard we have the vanilla and chocolate powder sprinkles."

Her voice grew stern. "We *only* use dark French roast from Peet's Coffee ground on five for a gold filter. Milk is brought in weekly and you can choose from nonfat, one percent, low-fat, or half-and-half, and we can special order acidophilus if you have a problem. Here, let me make you one."

"No, it's not—"

But Amy was already in high gear, protesting that it was a Mouth-to-Mouth tradition to greet people with her signature coffee-making skills. "I'll give you milk if you want it, but you really oughta drink it straight."

She made it sound like it wasn't really a choice. Hayley studied Amy's face as she carefully prepared twin espressos.

This had to be some sort of test. Interesting. Most tech companies used mind games. Like when those pompous Microsoft interviewers asked you to figure out how to land a plane when the surface area you were given was a perfect square, then sat back and watched you try to come up with an answer that was sufficiently creative and unique.

Now *this* was the kind of test Hayley could appreciate. And Amy was clearly an accomplished barista. After a couple minutes of processing, Amy handed her a paper cup filled with about three inches of espresso.

"Thanks."

Amy downed hers like a kamikaze shot.

Hayley eagerly lifted the cup to her lips. Her eyes teared up before she'd even taken a sip.

The brew was so strong it smelled like kerosene vapors. This was no "welcome" espresso. That much was obvious. But with Amy watching, Hayley had only a few seconds to figure out the score.

Well, if she failed to drink it, she might not get an offer. *Bottoms up.* She downed the drink in two gulps.

Hayley smiled at Amy in spite of her blurry vision and tossed her cup in the trash.

Amy didn't miss a beat. "And here's the soda refrigerator. The regular canned soda is free, as is the bottled water. But we ask employees to make a fifty-cent donation for the Odwalla smoothies. You put the money here. Any questions? Well, you've worked in startups before, haven't you? You know the drill."

I certainly do. Hayley smiled. "We didn't get bottled water at my last startup."

"Well, a lot of the employees work at least part of the week out of the Silicon Valley office, which is located on a nuclear waste Superfund site. So never drink the tap water. Even here. You don't know who from Sillyville's been around touching what."

"Oh. Okay." Hayley looked fearfully over her shoulder at the empty espresso cup lying in the trash.

"Anyway, we have a company beer bust every Friday. Free pizza and beer and a big bowl of candy. You know, Snickers and stuff." Amy reached up into a bowl sitting on top of the refrigerator and pulled down a candy bar, which she held out to Hayley. "Have a chocolate bar."

Hayley looked at the chocolate bar. It was a little early for candy, but she wasn't about to show weakness. She smiled at Amy and took the chocolate bar. Amy stood there and watched Hayley unwrap it and start eating.

When Hayley was about halfway through the candy, Amy opened the soda refrigerator and pulled out a Mountain Dew. "You must be thirsty. Here." She opened the can and pressed it into Hayley's free hand.

"Uh, thanks." Mountain Dew had just about the highest caffeine content on the market. Add her morning coffee to the extra-strength espresso plus a Mountain Dew and a chocolate bar and what you got was something akin to mainlining caffeine straight into the bloodstream.

Hayley recognized a fit test when she saw one. It wasn't even the strangest test she'd heard of in the industry. And she could handle it, all right, although she probably wouldn't sleep for a couple nights.

Amy popped the lid on her own Mountain Dew and left the kitchen. Hayley followed behind, tossing the candy bar wrapper in the trash behind her.

"The bathroom's here on the left," Amy was saying, "Unisex. I have to be honest with you and tell you that it's not nearly as exciting as it looked on *Ally McBeal*. Have you ever noticed that on TV, you never actually hear anyone . . . Oh, sorry. I should probably just get on with it."

Amy paused briefly in the hall and took a swig of soda, gesturing to a row of offices with her elbow. "Executives get real offices. They're lined up by that wall over there. That dark-haired woman?" She pointed through the glass wall of one of the offices. "That's Lucy Tedescho, the editor-in-chief."

She started walking down the hall again and said, "So. We're looking for someone with creativity to work on the editorial staff writing headlines and maybe a little blurb copy. We're looking for someone . . . how should I put this . . . we're looking for someone who can do 'snarky.' "

"Snarky?" Hayley stopped in her tracks.

Amy turned around in surprise when she realized she wasn't being followed.

"Yeah, you know. Hip, urban, fashionable, a voice that says 'we're insiders, we know, and we're willing to tell you so you can be cool, too . . .' you know, 'snarky.' "

"Well, that's great, because I specialize in snarky." *In fact, I got fired from my last job for excessive snarkiness. How about that? Heh. Well, that and for creating "a hostile work environment." Okay, don't say that out loud, Hayley.*

"Fantastic. Well, if you don't have any questions about the job, I guess our interview is over."

Hayley looked at Amy in surprise, and the girl smacked her forehead with the ball of her hand and said, "I'm such a dunce. Did I forget to introduce myself? I'm Amy Mathers. I do the same thing you'll be doing, but in a different editorial department."

You'll be doing? You'll? Maybe it was just a slip. From her own experience interviewing, Hayley knew it was sometimes hard to remember that the person being interviewed was just a potential candidate. But it could very well mean that she was heading toward an offer. It was a very good sign.

"There's one thing I want to make sure you understand," Amy was saying. "You know how hard it is to get venture capital funds these days. Well, it's very important that we try to conserve cash right now. It's part of our new company mission statement."

She broke off suddenly and said, "Which reminds me, please

remember to tell Audra how *psyched* and *thankful* we are that she's keeping us on the funding list."

Huh? Okay. Whatever.

Amy was back on track. "So anyway, that's why we all take a shift as receptionist. It's either that or give up the free drinks, and nobody wants that, of course." She laughed. "You've pretty much seen the best part of the office. We'll just go see if George is ready. On the way we can drop in on some of the people on the team so you can get a better sense of what it would be like to work here."

Hayley almost wanted to say that she already had a pretty good idea of what it would be like to work there, since it appeared the loft plan was the same one as at her old job.

And the floor layout looked pretty much the same as at her old job.

And she already knew what it was like to work in sweltering heat.

Amy led the way through the maze of cubes, introducing Hayley as "the editorial candidate." Finally she stopped in front of a cube with a large swath of fabric draped over the doorway. It was embroidered with a Chinese symbol.

She knocked on the cube wall, and a man pushed aside the fabric and beckoned them inside.

"This is our copy chief, George Bassum," Amy said. "George, this is Hayley Smith. You two will be working closely together. George, Hayley liked my espresso; isn't that nice?"

Hayley could see Amy's thumbs-up reflected in George's monitor screen. *Will be working. Will be.* Hayley's hopes soared.

And then she took a closer look at George Bassum.

George stood in his cube with Post-its stuck on each finger of his left hand and a copy of *Feng Shui for the New Economy Workplace* in his right hand. He raised the Post-it-blanketed hand in an open-palm greeting. Prior to this, Hayley would have thought that a man with a plaid short-sleeved shirt and pants featuring an elastic waistband couldn't get geekier, but apparently she'd been wrong.

"Thanks, Amy." In a stilted voice he added, "And I'm sure she liked the soda and chocolate as well."

"Yes, she did, George." Amy and George exchanged some very transparent nonverbal communication and then Amy left.

"Hayley, come on in."

Hayley stepped into the tiny cube. There were Post-its completely blanketing the inside of his workspace.

"This is my fortune corner," he said, gesturing with his head. A yellow Post-it was pinned to the wall. He'd written "fortune" on it. "I'm really hoping we'll still go IPO. Hey, while you're here, go have a peek at the cube next door. It's a good one. The loft temperature-control box is built into that cube. The new editorial person will be sitting there."

Hayley walked out and around into the adjoining cube. Her heart sank. It looked pretty much the same as the cube from her old job, but there were two significant differences.

The first difference was the fact that the temperature-control box was mounted to a giant column that seemed designed to support the loft ceiling. It stood right in the middle of the cube, and it wasn't clear whether she'd be able to move her chair back far enough to stretch out her legs under the desk.

And that was the other thing. There was no desk. On the floor lay a phone, a hammer, a pile of nails, and a stack of wood.

George came up next to her, and he must have seen the disturbed look on her face, because he rushed out the words, "Don't worry; we'll have the ergonomics expert help out after you build your desk. And you'll probably want to borrow my feng shui book when I'm done." He pointed into the cube. "You'll want the computer positioned right over here, so that when you're working on it, stress can flow straight through the door and out of your life forever."

Hayley noticed that he was speaking as if her getting the job were inevitable. Staring first at the support post and then at the pile of wood, she couldn't quite pin down exactly what she was supposed to be feeling.

She clasped her hands together in front of her because they'd started to shake, and took a deep, steadying breath. "Does this job involve a lot of stress?" She made it sound joking, but she wasn't really joking.

"Oh. No, of course not. You've been in the on-line magazine biz. You know we've got deadlines, but between you and me, working on this content isn't exactly rocket science."

He elbowed Hayley in that way that made it seem like they were buddies or something, members of the same non–rocket scientist club. "Well, do you have any questions?"

Hayley knew she was supposed to have questions. Any self-respecting interviewee came prepared with questions—questions thought out carefully to make one look intelligent, interested but not overeager, perfectly oriented for the job. She should ask questions if she wanted an offer.

For a moment Hayley couldn't breathe. She'd been so busy preparing for her date with Grant, she'd never gotten around to preparing any questions. Her heartbeat accelerated, and the idea of finishing up the interview as quickly as possible took on even greater appeal.

Hayley pulled her references sheet out from her portfolio and said, "No, I think I understand exactly what the job is all about. I have my references here if you'd like them."

George waved the document away. "Oh, that's not necessary. Audra Banks recommended you personally. When would you like to start?"

A pain ripped through Hayley's stomach, a pain so sharp that she actually made an audible distressed sound. The toxic combination of Mountain Dew and espresso was absolutely churning inside her.

"I'm sorry, I didn't catch that," George said. "*When* would you like to start?"

Audra. It all made sense now. Audra had actually gone and sealed the deal before Hayley'd ever stepped foot in the door. *Damn her.*

There was just supposed to be an offer. Just an offer. And it was supposed to come over the phone while Hayley was at home so she could listen as the answering machine picked it up. And then she was supposed to decide if she really wanted the job.

You need to make a decision, Hayley. Just make a decision. Yes or no? She clutched her portfolio up against her unsettled stomach and stared at George.

"Yes." Everyone was making it so damn easy, and she needed cash flow. "The answer is yes."

George gave her a curious look, and Hayley remembered that she hadn't actually answered his question.

She had the sweats now, and was feeling totally suffocated by the time she heard herself say, "Next Monday?" Her voice sounded tinny and very far away.

"Perfect. It's as good as done. Let me just ping your new manager. She'll come negotiate salary with you."

Hayley forced a smile and leaned her full weight against the doorway of George's cube while he typed out an instant message.

And as she stood there, feeling as if she were within an inch of death, a tiny fluffy white poodle marched down the hall and trotted past the cube door, its red, rhinestone-studded leash trailing behind it on the floor.

Hayley closed her eyes. Maybe it was a mirage. She felt like shit—maybe she was having caffeine-induced hallucinations and the poodle was just a nightmarish vision.

"Aww," George said. Hayley quickly opened her eyes. George was looking over his shoulder and making a purring sound, of all things. "Did our little doggy just go by? That's Killer. Get it?" He laughed. "You'll love him. We all do. You do love dogs, don't you?"

He asked in that way that dog lovers did, like if she said no it meant she must be an ax-murdering, sexual deviant, antienvironmental unacceptable excuse for a human being. Like she should be taken to the supply closet and shot dead with a staple gun.

This was a no-win situation. If she said, "Sure, I love dogs," she'd have to fake it for her entire term of employment, which was too exhausting to contemplate. If she said, "I hate dogs," she might not get the job.

The thought did occur to her that choosing the second option would essentially provide her with her last chance for escape off a train that was picking up some serious steam as it left the station.

The trouble was, she didn't care for the image of her lying in a cloud of dust on the railroad tracks, while a white poodle stood on its hind legs barking at her from the caboose.

"Hayley, is that you? What a pretty name!"

Hayley's head snapped up. Her eyes narrowed as she watched a woman who put the "perk" in "perky" practically skip down the hall toward her.

Just this one look and Hayley could see that the woman practically screamed "this manager installed by venture capital firm to assure financial integrity." She looked totally out of place in a conservative navy suit and white pumps. White pumps! Audra had some nerve dissing *Hayley's* people.

"I'm Eileen Stone. I'll be your new manager. This is very exciting. Let's go get you all official, why don't we?"

Hayley almost dry-heaved right there.

She stumbled out of the cube without even a good-bye to George, and followed Eileen, who was apparently following Killer.

"Killer, baaabbbby." Eileen made little kissing noises, too, as she and Hayley trailed behind the dog all the way to a conference room.

Once inside, Eileen picked Killer up, set him in the middle of the table, opened her file, and gave Hayley a brilliant smile. "We're just pleased as punch to have you join our little team, aren't we, Killer?"

Hayley's lip curled with disgust, but it did occur to her that if Killer was a purebred maybe he wouldn't be as stupid as Ponzi. This was some consolation.

After all, Hayley liked to think she wasn't an unreasonable person. With all the strength she could muster in her weakened state, she made eye contact with the poodle . . . and did her very best to produce a friendly smile.

While Hayley and Killer eyed each other, Eileen had been discussing salary and benefits for the last twenty minutes. Hayley could barely listen to what she was saying. Her stomach was like a boiling cauldron, and somewhere between the employee kitchen and George's cube, she'd acquired the attention span of a toddler.

"Well, I guess we're in complete agreement, then." Eileen pushed forward the employment contract and held out a pen.

Huh? Oh. Whatever.

Hayley reached across the table for the pen, and suddenly Killer leaped forward, poodle fangs bared, and went for Hayley's hand.

"Goddammit!" Hayley snatched her hand back. "For fuck's sake, just toss me the goddamn pen, will ya?"

For a moment she thought she'd blown it, and she reeled back in a bizarre wave of relief and self-loathing. But then she remembered that Audra apparently held this company in the palm of her hand. She knew it and Eileen knew it.

Clutching Killer to her chest with a look of abject fear trained on Hayley's face, Eileen very slowly surrendered the pen and rolled it across the table.

Hayley's heart must have been beating at twice the normal speed when she picked up the pen in her fist and gave Killer a withering glare.

An unstable mental patient with hostages, indeed. *Ha!* Then, holding her churning stomach with one hand, she signed the contract with the other.

Thirty minutes later Hayley stepped outside the building with a new employee folder crammed with information about the benefits of working for Mouth-to-Mouth Recitation. She took off her shoes and leaned against the side of the building in the shade for a little while.

When people started to leave the building for lunch, Hayley finally peeled herself off the wall and walked toward the bus stop, shoes in hand. She was shaking and practically hyperventilating by the time she got there, and babbling to herself to boot. "It's okay, Hayley, baby steps."

Bottom line was that it was always better to look for a different job while you still had one. That's what everybody always said.

So, this was actually a good thing. Yeah, a good thing. Even if it did feel really, really wrong. Which it did.

Chapter Fourteen

It was a calculated move, having Grant pick her up at her house. Not that Hayley'd had a whole slew of these incidents to compare as of late, but normally when she was going out on a date with a virtual stranger, she'd take the precaution of meeting him at a safe place and driving herself there.

But Grant was different.

First of all, he was a public servant, a man working for the good of the community. A law enforcement officer, for God's sake. If you were going to trust a stranger to be a good guy, you might as well trust a police detective.

Second of all, there wasn't much a reasonable guy would try to do on a first date that Hayley didn't want to do with Grant, so it wasn't like there was going to be a problem in that department. Sure, she had mad money, but she wasn't too concerned about not having a getaway car, all things considered.

What Hayley *was* concerned about was the fact that she was so freaking nervous. Now that career progress was once more derailed by landing a job exactly like the one she'd had before, the significance of the date had taken on distorted proportions.

She'd spent the balance of the week working herself into such a frenzy that she'd gotten to Friday evening thinking that if she and Grant didn't end up having sex when all was said and done, she'd have to up and move to Spain and have a go at things there.

With all that in mind, Hayley took special care with her looks, making sure that she felt secure in that department, at least.

She picked out a black skirt and top, and made it special by adding a black beaded sweater that hit right at the waist. She considered wearing the stilettos; she really wanted to, just to get that extra boost in confidence, but she was afraid of stepping in nacho cheese spread at the game and settled on a pair of slides instead.

Last but not least, Hayley dug her black CK baseball cap out of the closet and stuck it in her purse, just in case. And with forty-five minutes left to go, she sat on the bed and waited for the doorbell to ring, obsessing as to whether or not she was overdressed.

When Grant arrived, he was wearing a lightweight barn jacket, khaki pants, a cream-colored button-down shirt, and a pair of those cute, rugged shoes with the lug soles. He just looked adorable—so J.Crew catalog delicious that Hayley wanted to drag him into her kitchen and brand him on the ass with a giant smoking "HJS."

Really the only hitch was that he picked her up in an SUV. The problem wasn't just that Hayley recognized SUVs for what they were: evil, gas-guzzling, vision-obstructing vehicles created in the deepest bowels of hell.

No, it was more that she couldn't actually get in the vehicle without his help. The car was too high; her skirt was too tight. Not that she couldn't appreciate the physical contact it required to get the job done, but Hayley decided that if Grant ended up being her boyfriend, the SUV was the first thing about him she was planning to change.

But then again, he wasn't going to end up being anything of the sort if the date completely sucked. And with that disturbing thought, Hayley surreptitiously smooshed her lips together to make sure her lipstick was evenly distributed. She wasn't going to leave anything to chance.

Uglioto's was about fifteen minutes away, and, to his credit, after circling the nearby streets once for parking, Grant drove straight to the valet. No nonsense. So far, so good. He obviously wasn't a cheapskate.

As the valet wrote out the ticket, Grant turned to her and said, "So it's family-style. Hope that's okay." Hayley gulped, and his hand froze in midair as he reached to turn the car off. "*Is* that okay?"

She'd forgotten about that—that Uglioto's was family-style. Hayley smiled brightly. "Yeah, that's just fine. That's great." She looked around curiously as they walked into the restaurant and waited for the hostess to escort them to their table. Family-style. It *was* cozy in here, with the white or red linen tablecloths and tiny votives throwing off an intimate glow. *Hmm.* Maybe he was indicating his interest in developing a committed, long-term relationship.

Hayley glanced up at Grant. With her luck? Nah. More likely it was just his way of flushing out any strange eating habits on her part early on in the mating dance. Oh, God, the pressure. Something like that could be the difference between "go" and "no go."

Grant seated Hayley, then took his own chair. "You seem a little unsure about the family-style concept. I'm really not a picky eater, so you can go ahead and decide on something for both of us." He seemed taken aback by Hayley's startled reaction at that comment and added, "Or we can just order separately."

"No, it's great. It's just that it, you know, it, uh, makes you think." Hayley smiled and spread her napkin out on her lap.

"What does it make you think about?" He looked suspicious.

"Oh. Oh! Whoa, whoa. No, it doesn't make me think about having a *family*." Hayley snorted a laugh, then flushed. "No, it's just that there are implications. In terms of the process of us ordering something to share."

He seemed to find that quite amusing. "Like what? This sounds interesting."

Hayley looked at him carefully. Did he really want to know or was he just making conversation? Oh, well. They had to talk about something. "Well, let's say, for example, that you ask me to choose"—Hayley picked up her menu and glanced at the choices—"and I insist on . . . here, I insist on eggplant parmigiana because it's the only vegetarian dish on the menu." She looked up at him. "Well, that right there could be a double turnoff."

"For who? Me?" He picked up his menu and had a look.

"Right. Well, you or any other guy. Because everybody knows men think eggplant is just about the vilest substance there is, and because unless you're vegetarian, you'll realize immediately that the filet mignon you're so fond of will become a lightning-rod issue throughout our entire relationship."

He glanced at her over the menu. "Our entire relationship?"

"Right, well, of course, that only matters for the long term,"

Hayley quickly assured him. "Obviously, we aren't worried about having a *relationship* just yet, and besides, I'm not vegetarian anyway. There's more, of course, but I think you get the picture."

"Yeah, I get the picture." He looked the tiniest bit deer-in-headlights, like he thought it was funny but he wasn't sure how serious *she* was.

Hayley was mortified. Her smile faded and she buried her face in a glass of water.

"Everything okay?" Grant asked.

Everything was not okay. The fact was, she wanted him to like her. If she was going to make progress, him liking her was basically a requirement. He *needed* to like her. As simple as that.

Okay, not quite so simple. She also wanted hot sex, a notion that seemed increasingly foreign, in spite of how often she'd been bandying the term about in conversation with her friends.

Of course, there was no way she was going to say any of these things to Grant. Especially not the part about how this simple date was inextricably tied to her quest for self-improvement and personal momentum. He'd think she was a Hare Krishna or something and leave the table. People just didn't say things like that.

And now she'd gone and scared him by talking about relationships! He must think she was crazy. Quickly, she went for damage control. "You know what, I just think it's really best to be honest. I mean, this dating stuff is bad enough, with all the built-in awkwardness and people not being themselves. So I'm just going to come right out and say it."

Grant leaned forward with a pained expression on his face. "You're not going to ask me if I'm your boyfriend now, are you?"

"No!" Hayley was horrified. How embarrassing. Although . . . was the idea *that* offensive to him? "I just wanted to say that I think we should keep it simple and eat something like lasagna, and not read anything into it."

"Lasagna sounds great." He smiled casually, but Hayley still felt uneasy.

After they'd ordered, with salad to start and a bottle of red wine, there was a silence that Hayley didn't know what to do with, so she tried to fill it with conversation he could relate to better. "My friend Suz, the one I was with at Fred's memorial service? She's been trying to get me to do the Citizen's Police Academy with her."

Grant nodded. "She's the one who went into the confessional at Fred Leary's memorial service and was praising Jesus at the top of her lungs?"

"Oh. Well, I was outside and didn't hear that part. Sounds like her, though."

"She's interested in policework?"

"She's interested in policemen."

He laughed. "Got it."

"You know, speaking of Fred Leary, I still don't know how he died."

"No foul play, if that's what you're asking. Natural causes. The heart, I think."

"God, that's more depressing than suicide or murder."

Grant's eyebrows arched.

"Well, at least somebody's making a conscious choice in those scenarios." Hayley laughed and then stopped suddenly. Okay, he must think she was a real sicko now. She cleared her throat. "Er, I guess what I mean is that there's something particularly sad to me about Fred working himself to death."

Grant just nodded.

Nice going, Hayley. You're such a downer. You just totally turned him off. "Sorry, that was kind of maudlin. There's such a thing as being too honest, I guess." She laughed a little too loudly, then turned to her food and just started chowing down like there was a time limit or something.

This is turning into a disaster. I suck at this. Finally she put her hands in her lap and just stared at her plate as she chewed on a bite of lasagna. She'd been so fixated on the idea of getting a date with Grant, it hadn't really occurred to her to worry about what would happen once she was on it.

"What's going on under there?" Grant asked.

"Excuse me?"

Grant pointed to her lap, and Hayley held up her napkin and looked at it in surprise. She'd twisted it into a knot. "Oh, this? Oh. Nothing."

"Mmm." He nodded. "We've gotten off to a bit of an odd start, don't you think?"

Hayley smiled weakly.

"I wonder why that is." He contemplated a wad of cheese at the end of his fork.

Was he going to analyze how bad the date was right in front of her? Hayley shuddered and he looked up at her.

"Are you cold?" he asked.

"No, I'm disgusted."

He put the fork down on the plate without taking the bite. "You're disgusted?"

"This isn't working. I'm saying stupid, sick things. I'm talking about dead people."

Grant looked at her curiously. "You know, I don't offend as easily as I think you think I do."

"Oh. Okay." Hayley nodded. What else were you supposed to say to a statement like that?

He studied her for another long moment. "I've noticed that you have kind of a twisted sense of humor, but the minute you realize you might be laughing at something inappropriate, you make yourself stop laughing."

"You think I have a twisted sense of humor?" How disconcerting. Would that be a compliment or an insult?

"Yeah, I do. You can take that as a compliment," he said, gesturing casually with his fork. "I don't like boring women."

Hayley's eyes widened in surprise. *Well, that answers that question.* She chewed on her lower lip, then cocked her head and said with a smile, "I don't recall that I've given you that many examples of my twisted sense of humor."

"Oh, there've been a couple of good ones. Like the first one about Fred's corpse. Before things got out of hand."

"Oh, right. About smelling Fred versus the engineer." Hayley giggled into her hand. "I wasn't exactly joking. You thought that was funny, did you?"

"Yeah. But I was busy being concerned about you. Those wide swings in emotion . . . I didn't want you to go into shock."

Hayley pulled back. Was he trying to say that he thought she was moody? Didn't he know a man was never supposed to call a woman moody?

"I was unusually put-upon that day, I think you should know," she explained defensively. "And I also think you should know that I'm really not that squeamish. It was merely the fact that I actually *knew* Fred that made me so emotional. I think I'd be really good around an anonymous dead body. I could be quite capable, take charge, all that."

She didn't want to belabor the point or seem overanxious to show him that she could relate to his job. But she wanted him to understand that she could handle these things.

"You know, maybe we should talk a little more about what happened. Clear the air," he said suddenly. "Maybe that's what's"—he waved his fork in the air, trying to find the right words—"between us."

She looked up at him in surprise and blushed. "Oh. Sure. Which part?"

His eyebrow went up. "Well, the part where you and I almost had sex within spitting distance of your colleagues."

"There's a visual for you," Hayley said, and laughed again.

"Is there anything about that day you want to talk about?"

"Not especially," she admitted. "It was, um, not an incident I've come to regret, actually."

"Me neither," he replied with a grin.

Hayley smiled back. Things were taking a turn for the better. Much better. "Well, then I guess that's all there is to say about it. But if we're clearing the air, do you want to tell me what you were doing at Fred's memorial service?"

He shrugged. "I'd kind of written you off because of the unique circumstances of our first meeting, but I was . . . intrigued, say, by what happened. I actually called you at work but you'd already quit, and they weren't keen on giving me your home phone."

"You went to the memorial service to find me." Hayley grinned. "Cool."

Nodding, Grant said, "Even then I wasn't sure how you felt about the whole thing. You seemed mostly interested in persuading me you weren't a murderer, but I figured, what the hell, I'll give you a call."

"And here we are," Hayley said. "By the way, in the interest of full disclosure, since we *are* being extremely frank here, I didn't quit. I got fired."

"I know. They told me. I was trying to be nice."

She shook her head and laughed, then excused herself and went to the bathroom to freshen up for the baseball game.

Actually, not too much damage had been done over the course of the meal. Hayley scrunched her hair a little more, then pulled a travel toothbrush and mini-toothpaste out of her purse. When she bent over the sink to brush her teeth and opened her mouth, the first thing she saw was a wad of lettuce stuck between the two teeth just left of center.

In shock, she just stared at the lettuce for a moment, then quickly gargled and washed it out. Gone. *Now,* it was gone.

Salad was the first course. It was the *first* course! *Oh, God.* Hayley swung her head down and stared into the sink. Just when she was feeling *good* about things.

Why did dating have to be so complicated? If the salad had been lodged in her teeth since the first course, it had been there for something like an hour. She'd talked, smiled, laughed . . . had the lettuce been there the whole time and he hadn't said anything?

What kind of a guy would put a girl through that on a first date? No, Grant wouldn't do that, would he? In spite of the embarrassment factor, he'd told her about her skirt in the employee kitchen, hadn't he? Maybe guys didn't take the food-in-the-teeth thing as seriously as women did. But obviously he *had* to know she would see it at some point.

Was it some kind of a power trip? Was he trying to keep her off balance again? What a jerk! Of course, it wasn't impossible that the lettuce had spent the majority of the hour in a back molar somewhere and had jostled to the front only recently. But really, how likely was that?

All those stupid things she'd said over dinner . . . since she'd met him, in fact. But then why was he being so nice about it all? "I don't like boring women." *Yeah, right. Talk about a line.*

Hayley glared at herself in the mirror. Maybe he was just pretending to like her, pretending to be having fun because he knew there was a baseball game still to get through. It wasn't like Hayley had never pretended to have a good time before, just to be polite, and then made it clear much later that she wasn't interested.

Her confidence shaken, Hayley finished brushing her teeth, reapplied her lipstick, and went back to the table.

Grant looked at his watch. "We have time for some dessert, if you're interested."

Hayley was on the fence about that one. Frankly, escape was the more appealing option. But he'd bought tickets to a baseball game and it would just be too rude to bail out.

Besides, if things were that irredeemable, she might as well pork out on dessert. No point in worrying about appearances. She had an excellent metabolism, anyway. "Dessert would be great," she said glumly. She pointed to the dessert card propped up in the center of the table. "I'll have Death by Chocolate."

• • •

For some reason that Hayley was unable to explain, Grant seemed totally unfazed by anything that had transpired at the restaurant. He gave no sign of enjoying any power-tripping that may have resulted from the implementation of a Lettuce Humiliation Scheme. In fact, in the car on the way to the baseball stadium, he didn't act in the least like he wished he could simply open the passenger door and push the seat release.

Even stranger, after they'd parked and entered the stadium, Grant took her hand and held it as they wove through the crowd, all the way to the beer vendor. Since he was also holding a baseball mitt, Hayley couldn't read anything into it when he had to let go of her to pay for and carry the beer.

She surreptitiously glanced up at him as they circled the inside of the stadium toward their section. He appeared completely at ease. Hayley, on the other hand, was totally confused and filling up with an embarrassing amount of what she could only think of as "stupid joy."

Why had she wasted so much of the dinner obsessing and worrying? The chemistry was still there. It was definitely still there. The hand he'd held was tingling so much, it was practically numb.

"The seats are low on the first-base side," he said, holding up his mitt as they walked out into the stands and down the aisle toward their seats.

Hayley wasn't too sure about the significance of that statement, so she just smiled and sat down where he indicated. "I've got a question for you."

"Shoot."

"Is this a test?" she asked.

"Is what a test?"

"This baseball game."

He froze for only a second, then put the beers in the cup holders and tossed the tray under his seat. Then he looked at Hayley, giving her his full attention, a huge grin on his face. "What gave it away?"

"You manipulative bastard," Hayley said, laughing, feeling truly relaxed for the first time all evening. "My friends guessed. What kind of test are we talking about here?"

He took a sip of beer. "It's an old classic. I'm testing for the 'Baseball Trick.' "

"The Baseball Trick? Do go on."

Grant shook his head in mock-disbelief that she'd busted him on it. "The Baseball Trick. When a woman wants to get a guy to fall for her, she pretends to love baseball in order to trick the guy into spending nine innings a pop in her company every game he has tickets for, until his defenses are so low and he's so lulled into the familiarity of her company that he begins to think of her as his girlfriend and suddenly she is. That's the Baseball Trick."

"That's the Baseball Trick," Hayley echoed in a teasing tone.

He shrugged. "Yep. I was curious to see what your reaction would be to the game."

"That's incredibly pathetic, mildly disgusting, and downright insulting. I can't believe you would suggest such a thing," she said sternly.

She was just joking, but he actually looked a little worried for a moment, so Hayley took pity on him and smiled. "But I'll take it as a compliment. The fact is, I don't know enough about baseball to pretend I like it. But I'm enjoying myself now, anyway."

"I'm glad," he said, and put his arm around her shoulders.

Hayley sucked in a quick breath, and settled in.

For the next couple hours they watched the game. He kept his arm around her shoulders, all the while pointing out the players on the field and explaining the intricacies of baseball strategy.

Diane had guessed the game was a test of some sort. Hayley wished she'd asked some questions back then, because if anybody knew about strategies like the Baseball Trick it was Diane.

Suz and Audra were better at suggesting strategies for women to implement, but Diane was better at analyzing strategies put forth by men. Among the three of them, they would undoubtedly have a couple of suggestions to make regarding the Baseball Trick and how to properly implement said manipulation.

Too late now, though. Grant already knew she didn't know a thing about baseball . . . and he knew what to look for. Not to mention, Hayley wasn't in the mood for manipulation. Not with this guy, anyway. The problem was, she liked him more than she thought she would. She wanted much more from him than just hot sex, though that was still imperative.

Grant pointed to her empty beer cup. "Would you like another beer? I know I could use one."

"Sure."

"I'll be right back." He tossed her his mitt. "Watch out for those foul balls."

Hayley watched him climb up the aisle, and then when he disappeared into the concession area, she turned back around and put the mitt on her hand. It was enormous. And it was warm from his hand, which made her stomach flip-flop.

It was kind of fun, this baseball thing. Nothing wrong with baseball, nothing at all. She could *totally* imagine herself as the girlfriend of a baseball fan, no problem.

Spending warm nights drinking beer and watching the game in the temperate San Francisco breeze, spending cold nights drinking coffee while huddled with her loved one beneath a stadium blanket.

Hayley stuck out her gloved hand experimentally, pretending to catch a ball on her right side, then on her left. She was so caught up in the fantasy of being a baseball wife that she was hardly cognizant of the guy next to her saying something about a line drive.

"Sorry, what did you say?" she asked pleasantly, looking up from the mitt.

"Look out!" he yelled, and lunged toward her.

Hayley recoiled in horror as three hundred pounds of large, orange-garbed male came at her. Grant's mitt fell off her hand. A hot dog catapulted into the air from somewhere in front. Arms reached out on all sides. Baseball caps tumbled from heads, and beers, jostled from their cup holders, spilled down the steps.

When she turned to look at whatever it was that had everyone in such a state, a large white blob appeared before her very eyes. It seemed to hover and bob in space a few rows ahead, growing larger and larger . . . flying closer and closer . . .

Hayley blinked. "Holy shit!"

She threw her arms up across her face as protection and tried to duck down when the guy in the seat in front of her lost his nerve and retracted his mitt.

Through the crook of her elbow she saw the round white missile homing in on them all. She squeezed her eyes shut. The seconds before impact seemed like minutes.

No! No! No! Not when everything was starting to go so well! This was so ill-timed, Hayley couldn't believe it. How many times over the last few weeks had she prayed to be delivered into a vegetative state by having her head bashed in by a solid object moving at high speed? But *not now!*

A terrible pain shot through her left hand, and before she could react, the giant orange man toppled over, slamming her to the cement between the rows in front of her seat.

"Is it halftime?" Hayley asked him before passing out.

Chapter Fifteen

"Hayley? Talk to me. Say something. It's me, Grant."

Hayley could feel him stroking her hair. He was holding her right hand; her left hand hurt.

"Hayley, you're worrying me." Grant put the back of his hand against her cheek and Hayley swallowed, enjoying the sensation of his skin against hers. There didn't seem to be much to be gained by waking up, that was for sure.

"There you go, you're waking up now. You just swallowed. That's a girl."

Damn. Hayley opened her eyes a crack. " 'Lo." God, he was cute. And he was looking at her with wide-eyed concern as he stroked her hair and her cheek.

He murmured her name, and then ran his hands down both of her arms, then both of her legs. *Oh. Foreplay! Excellent.* Hayley sighed ecstatically. He said something about "everything else seems okay," which she didn't quite understand, but since he kept moving his hands all over her body and didn't seem to be looking for an answer, she figured it didn't matter.

Whatever had happened, it was worth it. As long as she was physically capable of taking full advantage of him. Hayley wanted him. Badly. And here she was horizontal. All the prerequisites fulfilled. She licked her lips and sighed again, a deep, throaty sigh. Grant's touch was so . . . erotic. And she hadn't been qualified to use the word "erotic" in a long, long time.

She could hear the sound of her own breathing coming in little shallow pants as he took her head in his hands and ran his fingers through her hair again, gently pressing along her temples and then smoothing a hand over the crown of her head.

"Hey, hey!" Grant called over his shoulder. "I think she's having trouble breathing."

Oh, shit. They weren't alone.

Some woman put her head next to Grant's, the two looking down at her from the bird's-eye view. Grant looked at the woman, which made Hayley immediately jealous. She narrowed her eyes at both of them.

"I checked her for any other thumps on the head and bone breaks. She seems fine, but then it seemed like she was having trouble breathing," Grant said.

"Hmm, let me do a quick check for internal injuries," the woman said. "I understand a large man fell on her spleen."

Just my luck. Look, sister, the only internal injury I'm dealing with here is an irregular heartbeat caused by your interruption.

The woman manhandled Hayley without a word and finally cleared her and left.

Hayley struggled to sit up. "See, I'm fine. I can breathe."

Grant wouldn't let her sit up. "Just stay down for a little longer, okay?"

Hayley looked around at the unfamiliar surroundings and then yielded to the pressure of his hand pushing her back down on the cot. "Where am I?"

"We're still at the game. In First Aid. How do you feel?"

Hayley thought about it for a moment while she stared up at him. "My left wrist aches a little and so does my head. But it's not really terrible or anything." She looked at her left hand. It was bandaged.

"I'm pretty sure it's just bruised, but I had her wrap it up just as a precaution," Grant said. "Wanted to keep the wrist immobile for a little longer."

Hayley wrinkled her forehead. "What happened?"

"Apparently a pretty serious line drive went foul and glanced off your hand. The only reason you went unconscious was because the spectator to your right fell on you. If you hadn't put your hands up, it would have been your face, though." He swiped his thumb slowly across her lower lip.

"Jesus," Hayley whispered. *Do that again.*

"Yeah, I know." He frowned and added, "Maybe I shouldn't have left you. I should have just waited for the beer vendor."

"Don't be ridiculous. Most people don't get personal protection in the stands. I don't know why I should get special treatment just because you happen to be in law enforcement."

He laughed and said, "True. But people *have* been killed by getting hit in the head by a baseball. Sad, but true."

"The ball wouldn't have killed me. It was that guy. Death by giant orange male. The foreign tourists would probably think it was part of the ballpark entertainment. The last thing I'd hear would be the mournful ringing of that cable-car bell up above center field, and the last thing I'd see would be the replay of the incident and an image of my broken body projected up on the Jumbotron for all to see. Tragic."

"You're starting to sound like yourself again. What is it with you and this death obsession? It's morbid . . . but oddly appealing," Grant murmured.

He slowly moved his thumb back and forth over her lower lip again. "I think death turns you on. You only wear black. You ordered Death by Chocolate for dessert. You have . . . how should I say this . . . interesting and not altogether undesirable reactions around corpses."

"I could ask you the same question. You always seem to show up when there's a corpse around." Her voice shook a little, but she didn't care. As long as he kept looking at her that way.

"Well, I'm a police detective. The corpses come with the job." And then just like that, he leaned down and kissed her.

Hayley had no time to prepare or analyze, because there it was. It started out sort of tender, probably because she'd been injured and he didn't want to hurt her. But Hayley put her good arm around his neck and pulled him closer, made him kiss her harder. *Oh, wow, oh, wow. Whatever you do, don't stop now.*

Someone in the room coughed politely, and Grant pulled away and looked over his shoulder. The First Aid woman. Hayley rolled her eyes.

"Just kissing it and making it better," Grant said, then looked back down at Hayley and winked.

Oh, the wink! Divine.

"Well, if it's better now, perhaps you should be getting her home." The woman stepped forward and handed Grant a baseball, pointing to a scrawled signature on the white leather. "He said he was sorry and he'd try to hit 'em straight next time."

She disappeared again and Grant looked back at Hayley. "You sure you're okay?"

"I'm really fine," she protested, starting to feel a little panicky that he'd decide for her own good that he should end the evening early and just take her home.

"You're fine?" he repeated.

"I'm really fine. My wrist aches just a teeny tiny bit. I don't even have a headache anymore. I'm really, really fine."

"How fine is fine?" He paused for a moment, then grabbed her by the collar of her sweater and kissed her hard.

For a minute Hayley thought she might not be fine after all. Her head started to swim. Just his fingers on the back of her neck made her feel warm all over.

And then he pulled away, and the two of them stared at each other, wild-eyed. "You know, I think you said earlier you had a thing for honesty," he said. "Well, here's something for you to chew on."

It was Hayley's turn to be nervous. Jesus, what if he had some sort of transmittable disease? She hadn't really prepared for something along those lines. "Yeah?"

"My intentions aren't honorable. I have things in mind."

Hayley clutched at a fistful of his shirt. "Things?" she said hoarsely.

"That's right. After-dinner things. Post–baseball game things." Grant played with a wayward lock of her hair. "So. That being said, should I take you home, or would you like to see the Renoir in my bedroom?"

"Only if it's from his pre-Impressionist period," Hayley answered happily.

"Good. Because you've gotten a little tense again." He pulled her hand off his shirt. "We'll have to do something about that." He helped her up and put his jacket around her shoulders.

Hayley leaned into him, smiling like a lunatic. Thank God something was working the way it was supposed to.

• • •

Grant parked the car in his apartment parking lot, then jumped out and was at Hayley's door in a second. He seemed to be in a big hurry for a guy who normally acted so casual, so calm. Hayley smiled to herself. That's right, he *wanted* her.

A guy with his own parking spot wanted her. *Nice.*

Grant slammed the car door shut, grabbed Hayley's purse and put it over her shoulder, then lifted her up, face-to-face, so that she had to wrap her legs around his waist to hang on. He leaned her back against the SUV and started to kiss her neck, his hands snaking under her skirt.

Hayley's body had a good memory, at least, and it remembered everything about the first time they'd gotten together in her cube at work. She was ready to go in no time and only mildly concerned about the fact that they were taking care of the foreplay in a public parking lot.

He must have had the same thought at some point. Hayley had no idea how they got into his apartment with him still carrying her like that, since she didn't think he could actually see where he was going. But there they were; he was kicking the door shut with his foot and carrying her over to what she assumed was his living room sofa.

He must have been inspired by the almost delirious "game over" look on her face, because with a complete lack of finesse, Grant just went nuts.

It was a gung-ho, no-holds-barred, totally aggressive play. Exactly what Hayley needed. And she was pretty confident that he wasn't just blindly lusting every which way but loose, because he seemed to have her name on his mind, grunting and moaning it until it turned into a rhythm. Quite flattering, actually.

And this next part was so cool. Hayley would have been more than willing to conduct the entire event right there on the sofa, seeing as how it would meet the requirement of being a horizontal situation, but Grant obviously viewed it as a mere halfway point.

He picked her up again and carried her into his bedroom, pulled down the sheets with one hand, and tossed her roughly on the bed. And now the clothes were coming off in that random pulling-and-tugging-and-landing-inside-out sort of way.

All of a sudden he pulled back and said, "I don't mean to kill the mood, but do you have a condom?"

Hayley sat up and used a pillow to cover her top. Unfair question! If she said yes, it was equivalent to wearing sexy underwear—the expectation would be obvious. If she said no, there might very well be no sex, and that was unacceptable at this point.

Why the hell didn't *he* have one? Of course, it was sort of sweet, because it meant he didn't think she was a slam-dunk. But what if it was more like he hadn't really gotten around to deciding if he wanted to sleep with her or not, but now that she'd made it clear she was ready to go, he figured he might as well? That was not a flattering concept.

Well, she was pretty sure she had one. Hopefully it wasn't expired. *Ha-ha.* But better not to commit right this second. Keep it unclear. "I don't know." Hayley tried her best to keep the irritation out of her voice. "Don't you have any?"

"I hope one of us does." He opened up the little drawer of his side table and rummaged around. "Damn. I must have used them up."

Used them up? You sex maniac. You dirty dog. You stud muffin. You egomaniac. Ha-ha. Jesus Christ.

This, right here, was the trouble with condoms. Hayley was all ready to bail, but then he looked at her and said, "I'm so sorry about this," and he seemed to be extremely disconcerted. Hayley's poor, underexercised little heart just went pitter-patter. "No problem. If you wouldn't mind getting it for me, there might be one in my purse."

He pulled on a robe that was hanging off his closet doorknob and retrieved Hayley's purse from the living room.

She stuck her hand in her purse and fished around in the bottom. *What's this? Oh, my God.* "Um, I think we're . . . covered. That friend of mine, Suz . . ." She pulled out a fistful of condoms of every imaginable variety. "Never mind."

Grant cocked his head and shook it, smiling. "All right, then, where were we?" He stripped the robe off and got back under the covers.

The pace picked up again and Hayley managed to find that nice, blurry place in her head where she didn't have to concentrate. That was, until he asked her a question.

"What's this?"

It was more of a rhetorical question, actually. Hayley blushed as he moved down her body and licked the tiny black daisy tattoo just above her pelvic bone.

"I like this," he said. "What do *you* like?"

What do I like? The question threw her. "I don't know," she answered breathlessly. "Just do whatever . . . you do." *Don't ask me that. Just take charge of this.*

And he did. It didn't take Hayley long to figure out that this was no college fuck. This was a serious fuck, and that realization seemed to change everything. Grant knew what he was doing... and he was doing it extremely well.

Which was why Hayley started to overthink the situation. He was taking his time. He was making it as much about her as it was about him. She wasn't used to accomplished sex.

The problem with this being a serious fuck was that it drove home the concept that this entire scenario could be different. This could have potential. There might actually be a real adult relationship somewhere in the midst of all this, if she didn't blow it.

"You still with me?" Grant asked.

She moved her gaze down from the ceiling and looked in his eyes. He hovered above her with a quirky smile and his hair all over the place. She didn't want this to be just a one-night stand. Not that she didn't want to have sex with him... She absolutely did. But at the end of it, she wanted there to be the possibility of something more.

It was one thing to have a goal. And have that goal be to get a guy. And to analyze the getting of that guy with your friends in a sort of academic, joking way. But there came a point where you realize it wasn't just "get a guy." It was "get a particular guy," because there was something you really liked about him.

And the "get" concept seemed much sillier and more insignificant than the reality of the wanting felt. And she wanted Grant. But putting out every time she saw him probably wasn't going a long way toward showing him she was about more than just sex. And he, being a guy and all, couldn't be expected to necessarily interpret anything else.

"So, uh, tell me what it's like being a police officer," Hayley asked.

He pulled back slightly, one eyebrow cocked. "Right now?"

"Maybe we should get to know each other a little better before we do this."

"Do you want to stop?" He rested his hand on her thigh.

She swallowed and opened her mouth to say something. Nothing came out but a shaky breath of air and an uncontrollable grin.

He slowly skimmed his fingers up her thigh and then . . . hello! "I don't think you necessarily want to find out about a typical workday at the San Francisco Police Department right now." He leaned down and whispered in her ear, "But let me know if I'm reading this wrong." Then he chuckled.

Hayley laughed nervously in response, but was promptly cut off by a wave of pleasure that blindsided her nervous system and made her literally arch off the mattress. What on earth was he doing down there? And could she take it home with her?

And for once in her life, instead of analyzing everything, Hayley just stopped thinking and let it happen.

Which was really the best thing she could have done.

"How you doing?" he asked sometime afterward, when Hayley lay sprawled across the bed, numb or paralyzed or something similar that was causing her to go into a trancelike state.

She looked over and then did a double take. He was ready to go again. "Oh, my God," she said before she could stop herself. Then she just laughed. Turned out, every last bit of creativity *hadn't* been completely sapped out of her.

When all was said and done, he was as trancelike as she had been. It was all he could do to roll over and wrap himself around her.

She was thinking up something incredibly witty to say when his breathing suddenly became suspiciously even. She glanced over her shoulder and found Grant already asleep.

Men. So predictable. But she had to give him bonus points for falling asleep in the spoon position. It wasn't like he'd rolled over and fallen asleep as far away as possible.

In fact, if one were to analyze it just a bit further, one could say that not only was he spooning, but he was in "boyfriend" position, with his face in her hair and one arm flung over her waist. That was definitely a good sign. . . . Wait a minute. Hayley's eyes flew open. A good sign unless it was reverse psychology.

An hour and a half later, after the entire evening was mentally calibrated, analyzed, compartmentalized, and fully assessed, Hayley finally fell asleep.

Chapter Sixteen

The minute Grant closed the bathroom door and turned the shower on, Hayley reached over the side of the bed and grabbed her purse.

She pulled out her cell phone, stared at it, then stuck it back in her bag. Then she pulled it out again . . . stared . . . stuck it back in her bag.

Last night was incredible. Grant was incredible. Maybe she should trust her instincts with whatever was going to come next. Maybe she didn't need advice.

Hayley pulled the phone out of the bag and stared at it some more. Who was she kidding? She couldn't take the chance of doing something stupid. It was her first night with the One, and she didn't want it to end up having been a one-night stand. Suz had so much more experience with this stuff.

Hayley leaned back against the headboard with the phone in her lap. She could hear Grant singing something in the shower; he had a pretty good voice, actually. And from her vantage point in the bedroom, he didn't appear to have any hobbies or habits Hayley objected to.

The walls displayed some police academy and baseball memorabilia, and from what she remembered of the other rooms, the rest of the apartment was pretty classic.

The bottom line was that he seemed like a keeper, and Hayley didn't want to take any chances. This was too important to go solo on. She quickly dialed Suz's cell number and put the phone to her ear.

"What's up?"

"Hi, Suz, it's me."

"Hey, hey! How was your date last night?"

"It hasn't actually ended yet, if you get what I'm saying," Hayley whispered.

"What? Oh! Excellent! Mine either."

"Figured. That's why I called your cell. I'll make this quick. Here's the thing. I'm not exactly sure about the proper protocol here. You know, with the morning after and all. I don't want to mess this up."

"Protocol?" Suz chuckled. "Okay, first things first. Whose place are you at?"

"His. Pretty nice apartment. He must have rent control."

"That's nice, but we need to focus. Can I assume he's out of range?"

Hayley glanced at the bathroom door. "Yeah, he's in the shower. He offered to let me use it first, but I wanted to call you right away."

"You have some options. Your decision should be partially based on how good he was in bed, whether or not you want to see him again, and whether or not you are *likely* to see him again."

"I'm with you. Keep going."

"Well, you can bolt. It's traditionally a male technique, but I've used it quite successfully, many times. But if you choose this one, you'd better hurry, because it's best done in the middle of the night, while they're in the shower, or while they're cooking breakfast, depending on where the kitchen is located."

At this point, Hayley started to question the wisdom of involving Suz, but what was done, was done.

"I suggest using the bolt if, a) you really don't want to see him again, or, b) you want to see him again but you want to play hard to get, which is risky, because now that you've slept with him, if he thinks you weren't up to snuff, it's pretty much all over. But in that case, now that I think about it, that's an argument for bolting right there."

Grant started to hum the *M*A*S*H* theme song and Hayley smiled into the phone. "I want to see him again. Definitely. And I don't want to play hard to get. That sounds way too complicated for me. The advanced class. The big thing is that I don't want to seem like a lot of trouble. You know what I mean?"

"Mmm. Did he ask you to leave or offer you a ride home last night?" Suz asked.

"No . . . well . . . last night he offered to drive me home in the *morning,* but he wasn't suggesting that he drive me home right after the deed."

"Good, good. Was there snuggling of any kind after the deed was done? And if so, how would you describe the nature of the snuggling?"

"There was snuggling." Hayley smiled at the memory. "It was highly satisfactory, although I don't have much to compare it to. I'd describe it as more than token snuggling but not excessive. Not the kind of overblown snuggling that would make you feel stupid the morning after. He, uh, he actually kissed my forehead before falling asleep. Heh."

"Impressive."

"Oh! The water just stopped." Hayley looked toward the bathroom in panic. "He's done showering. I gotta go, I gotta go."

"Okay, pay attention. If he really doesn't look like a bad mistake right now, and there's a low embarrassment quotient, let him drive you home. But consider that you're going to be together in the car for fifteen to twenty minutes of morning-after weirdness. Are you with me?"

Morning-after weirdness? That did not sound appealing. Grant started whistling in the bathroom, and Hayley quickly said, "I don't know about that, Suz. What else you got?"

"Okay, if you want some middle ground, call a cab but wait for him to get out of the bathroom first so you can tell him you just didn't want him to go to the trouble of driving you home."

"Jesus, this is a little complicated."

"Just use the Rule of Three. It's very simple. Do this. He's going to ask you if you want a ride home. Protest. Twice. 'No, no, I couldn't let you go out of your way like that . . . it's too far . . . yadda yadda.' Protest twice, and if he asks a third time, you're gold. It means he really wants to. And take the ride so *he* knows you really want to. Rule of Three, got it?"

"Suz, I gotta go."

"No prob. But now you owe me details."

"Sure, sure. I'll tell you everything on Sunday." Hayley hung up just as Grant emerged from the bathroom wearing only a towel around his waist.

Oh, wow. I think I'm in love. Ha-ha. Not really, but I could see it happening.

He looked curiously at her cell phone and then back at her. "Your turn."

"Great." *Uh-oh.* She hadn't quite done the logistics right. Now she'd have to get out of bed naked in front of him, unless he went into the kitchen. "You know, I think my, um, my, um, my keys are in the kitchen. Would you mind . . ."

"No problem." He went into the closet and pulled on some sweats, then left the room. As soon as he was out the door, Hayley scrambled out of bed, pushed her clothes into a giant pile on the floor, picked up the pile, and ran into the bathroom.

She locked the door behind her and took a deep breath, then got into the shower. When she was finished, she dressed herself in last night's clothes and went into the kitchen.

Grant was sitting at the table with the newspaper and a box of Raisin Bran. "Can I offer you some breakfast before I drive you home?"

Protest once: "Oh! I don't want you to have to drive across the city just to get me home."

He looked at her in surprise. "Okay. But it's really no trouble. I'm more than happy to do it."

Protest twice: "No, seriously. It's too far. Have a nice breakfast and I'll take a cab. No big deal. I've got the number for a cab right here."

He was silent, looking at her curiously for a moment. Then he just smiled and shrugged. "Sure, whatever you prefer." He took the cab card from her hand and picked up the phone.

• • •

At Girlie Brunch, Diane shrugged, impressed. "Wow. That was quite a date. It started off miserably, took a turn for the better after you got whopped by the ball, escalated into something pretty incredible, and then kind of ended with a whimper."

"It did not end with a whimper," Hayley insisted. "I admit I could have implemented the Rule of Three with a little more finesse, but for a first try, I think it went down okay. It was *not* a whimper."

She was only insisting so much because she really *was* worried that it had ended with a whimper. But Grant had to know better than that. After all, they'd lived through that ridiculous dinner.

Audra bit her lower lip and rested her chin in her hand. "You're making me want to go out on a date."

"So how long until he calls me, you think?" Hayley asked.

Suz shrugged. "My guess would be Tuesday. He probably wants more of what you gave him, yet he'll give you a couple of days to keep up appearances."

"What do *you* guys think?"

"I think Suz is right," Audra said. "Tuesday makes sense. It's early enough in the week to make a second Friday or Saturday date without suggesting that either party had nothing better to do. But it's not so early he looks desperate or disrespectful that he's calling you soon because he wants more sex."

"I'm a little concerned about this Rule of Three, I have to be honest," Diane said, frowning.

"I've used the Rule of Three a million times and I don't ever recall wishing the outcome had been different," Suz said.

"But the thing is, you're so different from Hayley. If the outcome wasn't quite what you wanted, I don't think you'd really care. But Hayley would care. I think you approach the Rule of Three differently, and I also think you've had more experience using it."

Hayley's stomach sank a little. She'd been pushing that last little exchange with Grant out of her mind, but it kept popping back up and bugging her. When she thought about it in hindsight, it felt like a bad memory. Like the one blot on an otherwise perfect date. Much better to think about the good parts. "It was the best sex of my life. In a way it's kind of horrifying, because it points out what I've been suspecting all along."

"Which is?" Suz asked.

"That my sex life up until now has consisted almost entirely of bad sex. Bad college sex. I'm not saying I didn't enjoy messing around or getting riled up. But when it comes down to the serious action, we're talking about a career filled with unexceptional and sometimes totally unsuccessful sex with guys I don't think I was really all that thrilled to be having sex with. Yuck. It all seems so depressing . . . and sordid."

Diane nodded. "Now you see where I'm coming from. I swear to God, I have enough credits to apply for a minor in bad college sex."

Hayley giggled. "I hope he calls me soon. In any case, it's taking my mind off the job."

"Are you all set for your first big week?" Audra asked.

"I almost don't even care," Hayley said. "How bad could the job be, if things are going this well with Grant?"

Audra leveled her with a steely gaze. "You are glad you took the job, aren't you?"

Hayley snickered. "I'm not one hundred percent sure, actually. Some of it's a bit of a blur given that for at least part of the interview I was completely out of my head. What? It's true. I can't be held entirely responsible. They drugged me. At some point, I think I started to drool. By the time my new boss put the forms in front of me, I'd ingested something like ten thousand times the recommended daily allowance of caffeine. Not to mention all the sugar, plus a vicious dog incident that I'm hoping was a drug-induced hallucination."

"I don't think there *is* a recommendation for ingesting caffeine," Diane said.

"My point exactly. *Not* recommended. The whole thing was, like, outside the realm of my control. I practically stumbled out of the building. I was *hyperventilating*." Hayley started laughing at the memory.

The three other girls looked at each other in confusion. It made Hayley want to laugh even more.

Diane lifted an eyebrow and waited for Hayley's giggles to die down. "Are you suggesting that accepting the job was an accident? That you did so under the influence or under duress? That you won't take responsibility for your actions? And that you find this disaster humorous somehow?" She ticked the questions off her fingers and shook her head in disbelief.

"Of course not! I'm beyond all that." Hayley was pretty sure, anyway. "I just think it's a funny story, and I'm saying that several factors combined, and I ended up getting rushed into making a choice that I might not have made under different circumstances. Sure, it was like this really terrible moment when it happened. But once I was away from the office, and my head—and my system—started to clear, it just seemed . . . hilarious."

"Hilarious?" Audra asked, tightly.

"Correct me if I'm wrong." Diane looked first at Audra and Suz, then turned to Hayley. "But I think I speak for all of us when I say that normally you'd be much more upset about this. What transpired—and with all due respect to Audra and her assistance setting up the interview—I'd have to say that what transpired is a kind of a setback for you. You do see that?"

Audra huffed. "*I* wouldn't call it a setback." She paused and looked down at the table. "Well, not exactly."

"No, no," Hayley protested. "Let me finish. Because then I got on the bus, and I thought to myself, "you know, it really is okay, because not everything has to happen at once." And then after my date with Grant it became even more obvious. Because even if I hadn't made particularly impressive strides via proactive decision making in the job department, there was still him to be optimistic about."

"And now we get to the crux of the issue," Suz said. "Like I said, if it weren't for Grant, you'd be freaking out about the job."

"I don't think that's true." Hayley crossed her arms over her chest.

"I think Hayley has the right positive attitude," Diane said. "Aside from what you *don't* have in terms of satisfying employment, what you *do* have is a physically appealing man who is, at a minimum, interested in sex for some reasonable time span which, when you look at it objectively, is nothing to scoff at if one is coming off an unwanted eighteen-month dry spell, which you are."

"Exactly," Hayley said, although at this point she was hoping that more than sex was involved.

Diane gestured to Audra and Suz. "And two out of three agree that the guy is harder to come by than the job in this town. So if you can really get the guy part nailed, I think the hard part's over."

"My thoughts exactly." Hayley smiled at Diane and uncrossed her arms.

"That statement had double entendre written all over it. Anyone want it?" Suz asked.

Audra shot a warning glance at Suz. "Leave it alone, Suzy." She turned to Hayley.

"You're absolutely right. It doesn't all have to happen at once, and you don't have to stay there forever. I'm not a proponent of job hopping, but it's not going to affect me in the slightest if you don't stay long. I just thought it would give you some level of comfort, you know, so that you could relax a little more and get your bearings."

"I think she's plenty relaxed," Suz said, and snorted.

She tried to whisper something in Diane's ear but Diane pushed her away and said, "Yeah, Hayley, you take the job, and then start looking for what you really want to do—while employed."

"And that's exactly my plan." Hayley sighed. "There is the fact that I haven't addressed what it is I really want to do. But frankly, I'm just not even equipped to deal with that at the moment. I've got other things on my mind." She paused. "Grant *will* call... right?"

Chapter Seventeen

The first day of work wasn't so bad. Nobody actually expected you to get anything done, and there was a certain novelty to everything.

It helped that Hayley was still basking in the delicious glow of His Royal Grantness, and spent most of Monday in the supply closet pretending to get stocked up. In reality, she just stood there practicing the lighthearted tone she planned to use when Grant called her on Tuesday.

By rotating between the supply closet and the employee kitchen, Hayley figured people would just assume she was in training. The only downside to that strategy was that by Tuesday morning, people really did seem to think she knew what she was doing.

Not that anything had actually been explained to her by anyone, but Hayley figured that was pretty much par for the course. In fact, no one had even come by to deal with the desk situation, and she hadn't been issued a computer yet, so she put two chairs together and stuck her personal laptop on the one and sat in the other.

On Tuesday afternoon Eileen finally called Hayley with her first assignment. It was hard to concentrate, because every time the phone rang Hayley would jump, thinking it was Grant.

It wasn't until Tuesday night that it occurred to Hayley that something was wrong. She was eating a frozen pizza at her kitchen table with the telephone sitting in the spot she would otherwise have put Grant's table setting when the question popped into her head: Had they all miscalculated?

Was it possible? It couldn't be. All three girls agreed that if he were interested, Tuesday would be the most likely day he'd call in this particular situation. The weekend plus one working day.

Hayley didn't fall asleep for a while that night, the terrible sinking inside stronger with each passing hour that the phone failed to ring.

Wednesday was brutal.

Ring!

" 'Lo, this is Hayley speaking."

"It's me."

Suz. Hayley's heart dropped. "Hey, Suz. No, he hasn't called yet."

"Bummer. Well, I'm sure there's a reasonable explanation. Maybe you gave him such a workout he can't lift the phone." She laughed but stopped abruptly when Hayley didn't join in. "I'm sure he's on an out-of-state case or something."

"Well, that's entirely possible. I appreciate the call, Suz."

Ring!

" 'Lo, this is Hayley speaking."

"Hello, it's Audra."

Hayley's heart dropped. "Hey, Audra. No, he hasn't called yet."

"Oh, dear. You know, I'm quite sure there's a plausible explanation. Have you heard about the Fisherman's Wharf Strangler? I'd be willing to bet he's been assigned to that case. They're on victim number three now. Must be keeping him very busy."

"You've got a point there. I'd actually not heard of the Fisherman's Wharf Strangler. That's good to know. Thanks for calling."

Ring!

" 'Lo, this is Hayley speaking."

"Hey, it's Diane."

Hayley's heart dropped. "Hey, Diane. No, he hasn't called yet."

"Oh. Well, there's got to be some kind of explanation. I'm thinking it has something to do with sexual politics. He may be expressing some kind of need for power by waiting one day longer than normal before calling you. But he'll call real soon, I'm sure."

"That's an excellent theory. You're probably right. Gotta run, though. Thanks for checking in."

Hayley hung up and went to the employee kitchen for a candy bar. She didn't want to take the chance of missing Grant's call while she was out at lunch.

Turned out she should have gone to lunch.

By late afternoon, the animosity toward the job itself that had been building up in Hayley's soul since the interview was at peak level.

This general animosity, on top of the residual disgust from her last job, combined with a very specific animosity toward men resulting from what she was beginning to think of as the Grant Debacle, had begun to manifest itself in disturbing ways. Most notable was her all-consuming desire to bash in George Bassum's head repeatedly with his miniature Japanese rock water fountain.

The fountain may have been providing George with minute-to-minute Zen, but the trickling sound made Hayley have to pee constantly. And as Amy had insinuated, the unisex bathroom experience was not at all as seen on TV.

And that wasn't the end of it. At this point all of Hayley's five senses had become hyperaware of her surroundings. The mere sound of George Bassum's three-times-daily Cheerios snack scraping against the side of a Dixie cup, and the accompanying sounds of his very thorough mastication, served as a kind of never-ending reminder of the hell she'd gotten herself into. This was no laughing matter.

Chew, crunch, swallow . . . smack, chomp, chomp, chomp. Slurrrp.

Hayley snarled at the wall separating her cube from George's cube. *Feng shui,* this, *asshole!* She turned back to the computer screen and stared loathingly at the cursor that had been twitching on line fifteen for the last twenty minutes.

Yep, there was George Bassum, and then there was this assignment.

The last thing Hayley wanted was to be thinking about sex. Because thinking about sex made her think about Grant. And thinking about Grant made her very upset, as the likelihood of his calling became less and less probable.

But as fate would have it, her first assignment was to catch up on a bunch of articles sorely neglected from the Food & Sexuality special feature.

She'd already spent the greater part of her morning trying to boil down "Ten Ways to Get Sexual Satisfaction from Ordinary Kitchen Tools" into a snarky two- or three-word headline.

Hayley took a deep breath and tried to clear her thoughts. *Okay. "Tantric Tooltime"? No, too specific and too esoteric for the mainstream readers.*

"Come in the Kitchen"? Probably can't use "come."

How about a play on words invoking the turkey baster? "Cock-a-doodle-doo"? Hayley couldn't help giggling, even though she didn't want to.

Or perhaps the more direct call to action, "Lick My Spoon"?

George popped his head up over the cube wall. "Uh, Hayley, I need that headline for the kitchen tools article now."

Crap. "Right. Okay. Uh, I'm going to go with, 'G-spot, Gee whiz!' With an exclamation point at the end. It's extremely general, but it has the right playful attitude. Kind of a playful . . . fifties-housewife sensibility. I think it will go nicely with the retro illustration of the egg beater."

" 'G-spot, Gee whiz!' I like it," he said cheerily, and disappeared into his cube again.

Fuck cheerful people. Hayley rolled her eyes and looked down at her notes for the next assignment. Eileen had described it as a series on recipes from history's most famous prostitutes.

The first installment featured English muffins baked by Sally Salisbury, a popular nineteenth-century whore from a tiny village in northern England.

"I cannot believe what I'm doing for a living," Hayley muttered.

Is this what I've come to? This is pathetic. I'm sitting here in a job I never wanted, waiting for a guy to call. The fact that this jerk hasn't called me is literally consuming me to the point where I can't concentrate on the job I never wanted.

Is this all something I should be getting upset about? Is this what my life is supposed to be about?

What is the meaning of life? What's to become of me? Hmm . . . How about "Guilty Pleasures" . . . ? No, not snarky enough.

You're born, you live, you die. And that's it. And somehow, while we're here on earth, we're supposed to do what we can to pass the time in the best way we know how. Be the best, the happiest person we can be.

"Strumpet Crumpets!" That works. . . .

I just need some traction. I just want . . . I want. . . .

"Hayley. How's it going?"

Hayley slowly turned to face the cube doorway. It was Amy. She still wasn't too sure about Amy. "Uh, hi. It's, uh, well, it's coming along. You know how it is, first few days and all. Heh."

She should just say everything was great. That was what people wanted to hear. "How's it going?" was really not a question. It was a statement. A statement that could be loosely translated to mean, "I don't actually want to know how you're doing, but I don't want you to think that I'm an uncaring bastard, because you'll probably end up doing my peer review when it's time for promotions."

"I certainly do." Amy paused and looked around the inside of Hayley's cube. "I was wondering if you'd like to take a coffee break with me. Maybe I could help you out with any questions you have."

"Sure." Hayley saved her document and walked back with Amy to the employee kitchen. "So what are you working on?"

Amy grimaced. "It's pretty bad. I just got a new assignment, and I'll be on it for, like, twelve weeks. It's some sort of endless online miniseries featuring the autopsy reports of dead Hollywood celebrities."

Hayley perked up. It sounded a hell of a lot better than what *she* was doing. "Really? Tell me more."

Amy shrugged. "Well, it gets to the heart of those important questions. Was there really a gallon of cum found in Summer Sazinki's stomach? Did Mama Cass really choke on a ham sandwich?" She sighed. "It's real hard to come up with creative, snarky blurb copy about dead bodies. You don't want to swap, do you?"

Amy was joking about a trade, obviously under the assumption that nothing could be worse than corpse subject matter, but Hayley knew a good opportunity when she had one staring her in the face.

"Absolutely," she said quickly, "I will absolutely switch with you. You take Food and Sexuality. I'll take Celebrity Autopsies."

"Thanks! I owe you one." Amy's eyes got all round, like all this really mattered or something. It made Hayley feel old and jaded.

"No problem at all. Say, Amy, how long does it take before someone comes around and builds my desk? I've been sitting on one chair and operating my laptop on the seat of the other." Hayley laughed. "I was kind of hoping it would be sooner rather than later. But I don't want to complain or anything, since I just started. Know what I mean?"

Amy looked at her strangely. "When I saw your desk wasn't up yet, I was wondering. You're supposed to build your own desk. Didn't you know that? It's kind of a team-bonding thing."

Excuse me? "I'm supposed to build my own desk? As a team-bonding 'thing'?"

"Well, yeah. Like I said, the money's an issue right now, so we've all got to pitch in." Amy's voice became incrementally tight. "You *are* a team player, aren't you?"

"Absolutely. I'm absolutely a team player. So, uh, heh, where's the team that's going to help me build my desk?" Then in a chirpy voice she hoped did not sound as fake as it really was, she added, "This will be fun. I can't wait to get started."

Amy's eyes narrowed, and Hayley instantly knew she'd made a terrible mistake. There were always two groups of people at these companies: the ones who bought in and spent their lunch hours kissing up to the managers, and the ones who spent their lunch hours talking trash about the ones who bought in. Amy bought in.

"I thought you'd been in Silicon Valley for a while, Hayley," Amy said snidely. "There is no 'team' that builds desks."

She might as well have added, "you raving imbecile," because that was what her tone implied.

"The team part of it is that everyone's done it. It's like an initiation, if you will." Amy's voice softened and she added almost reverently, "This might sound crazy, but you can't imagine just how creatively satisfying it is to get down on your hands and knees in your cube and really become one with nature. You know, handling wood. Really, you can't imagine."

You're right. I can't imagine.

Amy came up close to Hayley and spoke softly in her ear. "I don't mean to scare you or anything, but just remember that the first two weeks are like probation. You're here on spec. And the CEO doesn't look kindly upon employees who haven't built their desks within a week of starting."

Hayley swallowed and resisted the urge to back up. "It's already been three days."

"Yeah, I'd get on that if I were you. Oh, and by the way, you did check the list, didn't you?" Amy pointed to a piece of notebook paper tacked up on the bulletin board by the refrigerator.

Hayley squinted at the paper. "No, I didn't, actually. What's the list for?"

"It's the reception floater chart. You're on today. Don't worry, you can take the calls in your cube and transfer them. Just grab a headset from the supply closet and you can multitask!"

"Just grab a headset and you can multitask! How fabulous! It's so easy! You just add water!" Hayley mimicked in a baby voice after Amy left the kitchen.

Ten minutes later, Hayley was crawling around on the carpet in her cube, hammer in hand, her skirt hiked up to her thighs.

If she moved too far away from the phone, the headset yanked out of its socket and disconnected the call. But without full extension, it was hard to align the wood properly and still handle the receptionist duties.

Hayley had nothing against the great outdoors, but there was a reason she never had the urge to date a mountain man. As it stood, she was developing severe rug burn, two nails on her right hand were broken, and her arm ached from holding the hammer for so long.

At ten o'clock that evening, she declared the construction work finished. All of the supplied pieces of wood were connected in some way, which was good. Of course, the result more closely resembled sculpture than office furniture, which wasn't so good.

In fact, it was only after Hayley had taken her computer equipment off the chair and arranged it on her new desk that she realized there was a problem. She'd built the desk with a pretty severe southward lean that caused her laptop to slide toward the edge.

Finally she realized she'd have to place a couple extra nails sticking up halfway at the front edge of her computer to keep the equipment from falling off.

Driving in the last nail, Hayley missed and banged her thumb.

It seemed like things couldn't get any worse. But then again, it was only Wednesday.

Chapter Eighteen

"This is the nadir of my life." Hayley stared at her giant bandaged thumb. She didn't really need a bandage by now, but she was so low she'd do just about anything at this point to get a little sympathy.

"Isn't 'nadir' a little extreme?" Audra asked.

"It's meant to be extreme. It means the lowest point," Suz snapped. "Right, Diane?"

Diane didn't answer. She was desperately trying to flag down a waiter with her empty water glass.

Audra turned to Suz. "I know what 'nadir' means! Don't patronize me."

Diane scored her water and chugged it.

Hayley looked at Diane. "I guess you're wondering what happened."

Suz interrupted. "I'm not in the mood for this. My life is starting to suck, too."

"We're working on Hayley." Audra sniffed disdainfully.

"We're always working on Hayley!"

Diane slammed her fist down on the table. "Will someone please give me their glass of water?" She looked a little surprised by her own outburst.

Hayley handed hers over and looked around the table pointedly. "I took the job."

"Yeah, we know that," Suz said in a throwaway voice.

"It's a nightmare," Hayley insisted.

The four of them just sat there blinking at each other.

Hayley started to panic a little. "You don't understand. I had to make my own desk! Do you understand that? Look at my hands. And look at this." She lifted her skirt and stuck her leg out. "Look!"

"Why are you wearing stilettos at ten o'clock on Sunday morning?" Suz asked.

"She needs the extra confidence," Audra said. "I just wear them because they make my legs look incredible."

"No, my *knees*! Look at my knees. It's what they call teamwork. How fucked-up is that? I'm by myself getting rug burns and splinters and they call that teamwork. Audra, you're right. My people suck. And that's not all." Hayley paused dramatically. "There's Grant. Or should I say, there *isn't* Grant."

"Uh-oh," Suz said.

"Oh, no," Diane said grimly.

"Oh, yes. It's all gone to hell. The Grant thing imploded. I'm in the abyss. He never called."

They probably had all figured it out by the time she'd actually said it, but a shock wave went through them nonetheless.

"He never called," Diane said to Audra.

Suz leaned forward.

"He never called," Diane and Audra chorused to Suz. Hayley winced.

"He never called," Suz repeated incredulously, staring at her fork. "What a dick."

Audra shook her head and looked up at Hayley in disbelief. "He *never* called?"

Hayley scrubbed at her head with her hands until her hair stood on end. Scowling, she admitted, "No, he never called. Um, I think we've established that fact now. Maybe we could move on to the solution phase." To no one in particular, she repeated, "This is a nightmare."

Audra looked at Suz. "I thought you were giving her relationship advice. What happened?"

"Her advice sucks," Hayley muttered, thinking she'd done so under her breath.

"Hey, what the *hell*? My advice would work just fine for ninety-nine-point-nine percent of America's women." Suz turned back to Audra. "Hayley is just an oddity, okay? It's not my fault. She's an exception to the American norm."

"Maybe I should move to Sweden," Hayley said. "Maybe they'll accept me there. Maybe Swedish men aren't complete jerks."

"I slept with a Swede, once. He had the oddest—"

"Stop right there." Diane put her hand over Suz's mouth. "We don't want to hear about *you* or *penises* or you *and* penises right now. You got that?"

Suz fought back and pushed Diane right off her chair when she couldn't dislodge her friend's hand.

Diane grabbed Suz behind the neck with her other hand and took her with her to the floor. The two started to grapple, half under the table, half in the aisle.

Hayley gawked at them and put her head in her hands. "Please, God, stop the pain."

"Stop it!" Audra screamed, poking at Diane and Suz with her shoes. "This is gross embarrassment . . . and you have no idea where that floor has been!"

Both Suz and Diane stopped fighting immediately and said, "What?" in unison.

"Get off the floor. Right. Now." Audra lifted her heel and poised her stiletto right up near Suz's eye. "Get up now, or one of you is going to lose an eye."

Suz pressed her palm over the edge of Diane's sweatshirt cuff, so all Diane could do was lean back out of range.

"Yeah, Suz, let go of me," Diane warned. "It's all fun and games until someone loses an eye."

"Ha-ha. Then it's just fun you can't see," Suz retorted, her eyes narrowed.

It appeared to be a standoff until Diane played her trump card. "I think I'm going to throw up," she said weakly.

Suz got up immediately. She and Diane took their seats and Diane, who actually looked substantially green, grabbed Suz's water and proceeded to down it in one continuous swallow.

Hayley looked at her friends through her splayed fingers. "This is Armageddon."

"Oh, stop being so dramatic, Hay. We'll get you out of this," Audra said.

"You got me into this," she mumbled, but was duly ignored. Then louder, "I refuse to take responsibility for my own actions!"

"What is she ranting about now?" Suz asked.

"I have no idea," Audra said.

"Would you all please stop yelling!" Diane yelled. "I've got a serious hangover. You're all making me sick."

Hayley shook her head. "It's like I prop up the one side and the other side flops over."

"What the hell are you talking about? What's propping and what's flopping?" Suz was clearly at the end of her patience.

"I'm a Mr. Bean video. A bad slapstick comedy." Hayley picked up her coffee mug and continued. "I might as well just dump my latte on my head, pull a fake string of snot out my ear, and learn to live with it! This is catastrophe."

"Did she just say the S-word?" Audra asked. "Uch, that's so icky."

"The S-word? Snot? I'm describing the end of the universe and you're objecting to the use of the word 'snot'? Where are your priorities?"

"My God," Audra said, now apparently quite alarmed. "Diane, don't you have any sedatives in your backpack?"

"Why does everyone assume I have drugs? You're the one with the therapist. It's vaguely insulting!"

"*You're* vaguely insulting!" Audra grabbed Diane's purse and rifled through it, pouncing on a bottle of pills that she ripped from a brown paper bag and held up with a triumphant shriek. "Ha! Uppers or downers? Which is it, Diane?"

"You don't even know the difference!" Furious, Diane grabbed Audra's wrist and slammed her arm to the table. "It's folic acid, you idiot."

"Oh, my God, you're taking acid? Well, I guess that explains your belligerent behavior this morning. I don't think we should give Hayley any."

"Folic! Folic!"

"Stop swearing at me!"

"Oh, my God, this is not happening." Suz stared at Audra and Diane in disbelief. "Audra, *folic acid.* Women of childbearing age are supposed to take it. How can you not know this?"

"Maybe because I have no interest in childbearing at the moment." Audra rubbed her wrist, most likely exaggerating the amount of pain she was actually feeling. Then she pointed at Diane. "And she's not even having sex. What are you expecting, Di, some sort of immaculate conception?"

Diane snarled. "If you weren't one of my best friends I'd tell you to go to hell."

Audra gaped at Diane in disbelief.

"What are you all getting so upset about?" Hayley looked wildly among her friends. "I'm the one with the problem here! It's my problem! I need help! Somebody help me! Help!"

A silence fell over the diner.

"She's fallen and she can't get up," Audra said snidely.

Hayley considered that. *My God, what an apt metaphor.* She was the proverbial old lady with the walker lying on the carpet. She heard an odd, high-pitched, panicky sound come out of her mouth.

"Mind your own business," Suz snapped over her shoulder. The other diner customers instantly swiveled their heads back around to their own tables.

Suz turned back to Hayley. "Pull yourself together! You broke the dry spell. You had sex. You apparently had great sex. Isn't that something to be happy about?"

"I'm doomed."

"Nobody said personal change was easy," Suz noted. "I don't know. Maybe we should write to Oprah and get Hayley one of those Life Makeovers. Let's face it. We're mere amateurs. I think it's clear to all of us Hayley needs a professional. A *really good* professional."

"Oprah depresses me," Diane said. "The only books she ever likes are about downtrodden people with horrible childhoods. And the fact that their current lives are incrementally less horrible than they were before is supposed to be uplifting in some way."

"You're in an unusually foul mood this morning," Suz said.

Diane ignored the comment. She must have been keeping her feelings about Oprah inside for a long time. "She's an angst peddler. We have plenty of angst of our own. Do we need to supplement it with other people's angst? Between the three of us plus this month's Doomsday Hayley special, there's more than enough angst to go around. . . ."

"Doomsday Hayley?" Hayley didn't like the sound of that.

Diane's voice was getting hoarse, so she started talking louder to compensate. "But the American public just follows Oprah's lead anyway, becoming collectively more and more depressed as a society while spending significant portions of their paychecks purchasing what Oprah tells them is good for them to read so that when they talk about the books to each other in their book clubs, they can pretend they're deep and literary individuals. . . ."

Hayley started to get alarmed. Diane was flushed bright red now and looked a little glazed. Still talking, she started to stand up, but Audra reached over and pushed her back down.

Suz started to hum the national anthem in the background.

"Secretly they hate these stories, but they read them anyway and bring them to their book club meetings, sitting on living room floors across the nation, getting fatter and fatter eating homemade cookies while they disappear to the bathroom in pairs to swap prescriptions for antidepressants when they think the rest of the group members—whom they mistake for deep, literary individuals—aren't looking."

Diane was breathing heavily now, the air whistling audibly through her raspy throat. "Oprah does not understand my problems. She doesn't understand Hayley's problems or Suz's problems or Audra's problems."

There was a long, long pause; then Suz snorted. "Somebody woke up on the wrong side of bed this morning."

"I woke up on the floor of the bathroom wearing just a bath mat, actually." Diane swallowed, then winced and grabbed Audra's water.

Hayley watched her drink it down and said, "I don't think Oprah's even doing the book club anymore. She's doing classics now, so you're safe."

"That doesn't make her safe. I thought all the classics were depressing. Or at least angry. Isn't that a requirement, or something?" Suz asked.

Audra waggled her index finger at Diane and said, "You're missing the point. You just don't understand Oprah's gestalt. The more depressing someone else's life is, the better you feel about your own."

"That's pathetic," Hayley said. Of course, pathetic was relative. She should know.

Audra sniffed disdainfully. "Just because you don't understand something or personally enjoy it doesn't mean it's stupid. I love Oprah books. And Oprah would love Hayley. I bet she'd devote two entire episodes to her."

"Oprah would hate me," Hayley said.

"She'd love you," Suz said. "There's so much to work with."

"I gave her a session with one of my therapists," Audra grumbled.

"Great idea," Suz said. "They've been so successful with you."

"You're being such a bitch," Audra snapped. "Sometimes you make me hate you."

"I don't make you do anything."

Audra and Suz were clearly busy, so Hayley turned to Diane. "What am I going to do?"

Diane lifted bleary eyes. "You need to look at the bright side," she said in monotone.

"I'm supposed to look at the bright side. I think the bright side is a sham. I think it's a complete fabrication. Something people say to get unhappy people to shut up . . . oh. Right." Hayley shrank back in her chair.

Suz poked her head in. "Why don't you just think of it this way: You can cross 'policeman' off your list of things you must do once before you die."

"Um, Suz? 'Policeman' really wasn't on my list of must-do-once-in-life. I was really going to be okay without checking off that accomplishment."

Suz just shrugged.

"Here's the point. There was this epiphany, remember? I made a plan and I thought things were going to change, if I just gave it a shot. But I'm right back where I started." No emotion was registering on anybody's face. Hayley tried to be more specific. "No guy and a new job that, for all intents and purposes, is exactly the same as the one I managed to get out of, except my paycheck says I'm making less money. I mean, do you see how severe this is? I'm off the charts. I don't know what I'm going to do. This *is* the *worst* time of my life."

"The worst? The *worst* of the worst?" Suz looked around the table. "The worst moment in Hayley's life? It's not like anybody died."

"Fred Leary died," Hayley pointed out. "He died in the cube right next to me, remember? He was dead for days before—"

Audra interrupted. "Okay, it's not like being stood up on your wedding day."

Hayley sat there, stunned. "There *is* no wedding day; don't you *get* it?" she wailed. "We had sex and he never called back! And then I had to go to this crappy new job and think about sex. For three days, sex, sex, sex. But now that it's finally worth thinking about, there's no one to have it with."

Audra leaned forward. "Okay, I find this interesting. I really do. It's riveting. But for everyone else in this restaurant? For them it was quite possibly a major overshare. Can we all just keep it down?"

Suz waved a languid hand in front of Audra's face. "Who gives a damn who hears? It's probably the most interesting stuff they've heard in a long time."

"Well, *I* give a damn," Audra yelled, pushing Suz's hand away from her face. "Not that anybody cares what I think. You're all too busy yelling and insulting me. Let me tell you something. I. Give. A. Damn!" She looked around the table, her eyes narrowed, the most scathing expression she had in her repertoire embedded in her features.

She stood up, turned her back on the table to face the rest of the diner, straightened her spine, tossed her hair, and said to the attentive crowd, "I *heartily* apologize." Then she jammed the strap of her purse onto her shoulder and walked out of the restaurant without looking back.

"Peachy. Just peachy." Suz sighed impatiently. "Now you've really done it, Hayley."

"What did I—"

"We've tried everything. I swear to God. For now, I guess you're just going to have to pull your ass out of bed tomorrow morning and go to work like the rest of us. I just cannot deal with this anymore. I've got developing issues of my own. Not that anyone's interested." Suz packed an entire pancake in her mouth and got up, chewing all the way out the door.

"I'm outta here," Diane mumbled.

"Diane?" Hayley blurted out. "You're leaving me, too?"

Diane turned to Hayley, her face tinged an unhealthy green. "Jesus, look at me. I think I'm gonna puke. I'm not gonna make it through the rest of the day, much less make it to any of my classes tomorrow."

Diane started to walk away from the table and Hayley just spontaneously snaked her arm out and grabbed her by the cuff of her sweatshirt, which was already looking substantially stretched out from the altercation with Suz.

Diane snatched her arm away. She shook her head, wiped her sweating face with her sleeve, and shuffled toward the door holding her stomach.

A few minutes later Hayley took her head out of her hands and looked up. Diane's handheld lay on the table. She jumped up and raced to the door with it, but Diane was nowhere in sight. Hayley sighed and returned to the table to wait for her friends to come back.

Fifteen minutes later the waiter apologetically reclaimed the table for some waiting customers. Hayley walked out of the diner into the stifling Sunday midmorning. She took a long look up and down the block to make sure she wouldn't miss them if her friends turned around and came back, but she didn't see any of them.

In a bit of a daze, Hayley started off down the street toward her apartment. Waiting on the corner for the red light to change, she considered her situation. Was the abyss worse than the nadir? It was probably just the difference between having to climb out and having to climb up. Either way, she was in it and down it.

The light flipped to green, and Hayley started across the street. Without warning, her heel caught in the rough cement, and with a lurch the stiletto on her right shoe snapped off and sent Hayley sprawling. Her purse spilled and Diane's handheld went skidding across the pavement.

Hayley immediately started bawling. It was to the point where crying wasn't going to make things any more embarrassing than they already were. As she hiccuped and swiped at her eyes while scooping her belongings off the dirty street, the question came to her again; abyss or nadir? It was the kind of question Diane could answer. Except Diane apparently wasn't speaking to her right now. And neither was Audra. Or Suz, for that matter. None of them were.

What the hell just happened in there? It *wasn't* always all about her. Was it? Maybe they were right. Maybe she was expecting too much. Did anybody ever really get what they wanted? Like Suz'd said, she'd just have to pull her ass out of bed like everybody else and go to work.

As she knelt on her hands and knees in the middle of the street, the thought occurred to her that maybe she really *didn't* have to. Technically, she didn't *have* to do anything. A little chink in the armor, the hazy suggestion of something that Hayley couldn't put her finger on, faded in and then back out again.

The light changed again and a couple cars started honking. With her head down so the people she passed couldn't see the tears streaming down her cheeks, Hayley picked herself off the ground, snagged her broken heel off the white crosswalk line, and limped toward her apartment.

Well, her friends had been right about one thing. *That* wasn't the worst of the worst. *This* was.

Chapter Nineteen

Hayley sighed deeply, dramatically, as she shuffled over to the coffeemaker and flipped the switch. She watched the coffee drain in an endless, murky stream into her travel mug. Endless and murky. How appropriate. She sat down at the kitchen table, staring at Diane's Palm, which lay in Grant's theoretical breakfast spot between the phone and her right shoe with its superglued stiletto.

Suz would have been so proud. On this grim Monday morning at seven o'clock, Hayley had, indeed, managed to pull her ass out of bed. It was not pleasant. And frankly, Hayley wasn't sure she could stand the thought of repeating said ass pulling for the next, oh, forty years of her life. There had to be something worth getting out of bed for, but this just wasn't it.

Maybe she needed something different. If she wanted something different, and if she wanted to avoid this soul-sucking experience otherwise known as unsatisfying employment, maybe she should just go back to school, like Diane always did. That way she could check out of real life for a while and stop fixating on her problems. Perhaps in time they would just go away. Or at least become irrelevant.

Hmm. There might be something to that. Hayley reached across the table and snagged Diane's organizer. Poor Diane had looked like death warmed over yesterday, and nobody had been particularly sympathetic. She'd said she wasn't going to class today, so maybe Hayley could make nice by taking notes for her while she checked things out for herself. She turned the machine on and poked the stylus at the calendar icon.

Diane's ten o'clock Monday class was scheduled in Warren Hall. It didn't say which class, though. Hayley figured it didn't matter, since she just wanted to get a sense of whether going back to school was really a viable option.

She tapped the stylus thoughtfully against the table. She'd have to call in sick. Eileen might not take that too well, seeing as how today marked only her second week of employment. Maybe she could just say she needed thumb surgery and ask if she should call a lawyer. That would probably shut her up.

A couple hours later, Hayley entered the lecture hall and found a seat in something like row 103, skewed nicely toward the left side of the room. She felt pretty safe, but it was strange to be back in college.

School had seemed like such a pain at the time. Now it felt sort of comforting. Like a giant cocoon. A place where expectations were low, yet hopes were high. A nice, peanut-butter-and-jelly place to be.

She looked to her left and accidentally made eye contact with the guy occupying the seat next to hers.

"Hi," he said, scoping her out.

Hayley scoped him out and then surveyed the other occupants

of the lecture hall. No wonder Diane wasn't interested in dating. It was like a bunch of twelve-year-olds masquerading as underclassmen. *Yuck.*

"Hi," Hayley said in her most uninterested voice, hoping that would be the end of it.

The kid looked confused. "It's, like, the end of the semester. You been here before?"

"Uh, no." What was he, the lecture police?

"You an exchange student?"

Bit of a dim bulb, this one. "Yes, I am. I'm from Sweden," she said sarcastically.

"Sweden?" He looked excited.

Hayley shuddered and looked away. Maybe things *could* get worse.

He tapped her shoulder. "Welcome to America. I'd be more than happy to, uh, ya know, help out. Culture shock can be, like, a real bitch. I'm Carson. Car. Son."

He stuck out his hand and Hayley stared at it. "Uh, Inga, here."

Was there no peace to be found? Hayley looked at her watch. Ten minutes to go. Ten minutes before she could sink into mindless oblivion, serenaded by the delicious droning sound of a tenured professor. Somehow she hadn't appreciated the anonymous quality of college when she'd actually been there. But she appreciated it now.

"Hey, Inga, do—"

"Do you mind if I read your newspaper?" Hayley asked quickly, pointing to the stack in the empty chair on Carson's opposite side.

He smiled nervously and handed it over. Probably figured he was getting somewhere. Hayley opened the front section full span, providing a shield between her and Carson. On the facing page was a picture of a happy couple holding hands at the zoo. It was faintly nauseating.

Carson peered around the side. "I could take you there. It's, like, a real American thing." Hayley looked at him in horror, and he quickly added, "Not like a date or anything. Like culture exchange."

"We have zoos in Sweden." She folded up the newspaper and handed it back to Carson, muttering, "Shiny, happy people. Must be models."

Carson tossed the newspaper back on the seat next to him, then pulled a binder out of his backpack. He turned to a blank sheet of paper and scrawled, *Lecture 12—Professor Atkins—Human Sexuality.*

Hayley stared at the title. Of course. It would be.

"Can I please have everyone's attention?" The professor down on the stage clapped his hands. He appeared to be what people generally described as an eccentric, looking more like a mad scientist than an expert on sexuality. His white hair stuck out on all sides of his head and his crowning glory appeared to be a tie in the shape of a trout.

"Today we're going to do things a little differently," he said. "I need a couple of volunteers."

The seconds ticked by. The lecture hall remained silent. At first the silence felt good. And then it started to seem really strange. Hayley looked around, but no one said a word. No one raised their hand. No one stood up.

And all of a sudden, the idea formed. Was this her chance?

She was all prepared just to go and sit there, absorbing the anonymous bliss of public-university academia, sheltered from the real world and all its annoying dilemmas. But in the three minutes that ticked on endlessly while the professor waited, waited for someone, anyone, to step out of the crowd, Hayley watched her fellow students and wondered if she should change her mind.

They just sat there like students tend to do, staring anywhere at all, at their mechanical pencils, their handhelds, the ceiling, each other, anything to avoid notice. To avoid being called to participate. To avoid asserting themselves.

The world was full of people thinking too much about what other people thought of them. Afraid to make a decision for whatever reason.

"Just remain as still as possible," Carson whispered. "Don't do anything and he'll pass right over you."

"I wasn't planning to do anything. I was planning just to sit here and absorb. Just fade right . . . into . . . the crowd . . ." Hayley cocked her head and considered that. "Just be a passive observer," she murmured.

Fade into the crowd. That would be less than zero. That would put her back to where she started, but worse.

At the start of this whole thing she'd complained about an inability to move forward, but at least she'd been standing on solid ground. Now she was just begging to disappear, check out, fall into the crowd as it moved in circles like mindless cows.

"Hey, you okay?" Carson peeled one of Hayley's hands off the armrest and looked at her palm.

She snatched her hand away.

"I think you're cramping up or something. Don't worry, he won't call on you if you scrunch down in your chair like this."

"Look, Carson, I'm not a mindless cow."

"Huh? I think that's, like, the wrong idiom or something."

Hayley stood up. She looked down the rows of students all the way to the bottom, where the professor stood onstage, waiting. She waved her arms in the air. "Over here! I'll do it. Hey, Professor. Pick me!"

"Inga, what are you doing? Nobody in America volunteers . . . nobody does that. Sit down!" Carson started to panic, pulling on Hayley's sleeve until the fabric ripped under the arm and he had to let go.

Hayley smiled at Carson. He looked desperate, powerless, as if he'd realized he was unable to pull a poor, hapless exchange student away from certain death. Hayley knew she was grinning like an idiot and she didn't care.

"Well, come on down, then," the professor shouted up happily. "What's your name?"

Hayley continued walking down the mountain of stairs toward the front of the cavernous lecture hall. If this were a movie, she'd be moving in slow motion, the doors to the lecture hall would open of their own accord, and white light would be streaming into the room as Hayley moved toward the podium, her hair rippling slightly in a light breeze. "I'm Ing . . . no, I'm Hayley Jane Smith, that's who I am," she called out.

She reached the bottom and turned around to face the lecture hall. She could see Carson with that horrified expression still frozen on his face.

Hayley waved and watched all the student heads swivel to look at Carson. It was kind of amusing, so she waved to some random person on the other side of the room and watched them swivel again. She turned to the professor. "They're so malleable, aren't they?"

He was looking at her oddly. In a good way. Like he'd found a kindred spirit or something. "Now we're going to need a male."

"Here, I'll pick." Hayley stepped to the edge of the lecture stage and surveyed the faces. Her spontaneous volunteerism seemed to have caught their attention, because, instead of staring mindlessly at the foam-tile ceiling, they were staring at her.

Hayley honed in on a beefy fellow who quickly looked down and started flipping the pages of his notebook in some effort to look as inconspicuous as possible. She needed someone manly. Er, as manly as she could possibly get under the circumstances. "You. I want you," Hayley said, pointing right at him.

From the corner of her eye she saw Carson put his head down in his hands. Hayley grinned. This felt terrific. "Don't worry, Carson," she called up to the 103rd row. "Everything's under control."

Carson answered by slouching down in his chair until Hayley could see only the very top of his head.

"Well, let's go, young man. Pick up the pace," the professor said. The beefy fellow slowly stood up, looking around at the rest of his class. They stared back at him, whispering and giggling. He was obviously getting no support from them, so he gingerly made his way toward the stage.

He walked onstage and stood next to Hayley, smiling uneasily, trying to look cockier than he undoubtedly felt, given that he kept shifting his weight from one foot to the other.

Hell, she'd picked him out of the crowd. He ought to feel pretty good about himself.

The professor came up between Hayley and her prey and put one hand on each of their shoulders. "We're going to do a role-play here called 'He Said/She Said.' But first we need a subject matter over which men and women tend to disagree. May I have suggestions from the audience? Just call it right out."

"A one-night stand," Hayley said immediately, leaning over to speak into the professor's lapel microphone. The audience laughed. Beefy Guy blushed and dropped his pen.

The professor shrugged. "A one-night stand it is. Fine. Hayley Jane and . . . I'm sorry, what's your name?"

"Steve." It came out hoarse, and a snicker went through the crowd.

Hayley began to feel sorry for the poor guy. After all, whatever was about to happen, just because he was male she shouldn't make him pay for Grant's lack of good manners.

On the other hand, wasn't that how things worked? The next girl paid for the trespasses of past women who had undoubtedly done something bad enough to make Grant Hutchinson sleep with them and not call them back. It was simply payback time.

"Okay, Hayley Jane, you seem to have a real grip on this assignment, so I'll just let you launch right into it, and if the two of you get stuck, I'll ask a question to get you back on track. Go right ahead." The professor set his stopwatch and waved his arm to start the show.

Hayley turned to Steve and smiled. "Hi, Steve. We had sex on Friday night and you never called."

You could have heard a pin drop. Steve's Adam's apple bobbled convulsively. His eyes grew big and round. His legs started to spasm. No longer just redistributing his weight, he literally picked up one foot and put it down again, then picked up the other foot and set it down again. It was almost as if he were trying to run away but couldn't move.

Well, he wasn't going anywhere. Hayley wanted some answers. She put her hands on her hips. "We had a one-night stand and you didn't call me."

"I—I'm sorry?" He swiped at his nose with his sleeve and looked helplessly at the professor.

The professor just waved his lecture notes in a "keep-going" motion.

"That's it? You're sorry?" Hayley asked.

"Wait a minute." The guy stopped bobbling around. "Wait a minute." He was thinking pretty hard. It seemed as though he wasn't used to it or something. But he was definitely thinking. Finally he said, "I'm *not* sorry."

A few hoots, hollers, and some laughter floated down from the bleacher seats. More confident now, Steve added, "You have a one-night stand with a girl and you don't call, it's 'cause you don't want to call her, not 'cause you're sorry."

The professor nodded sagely. "Mmm . . ."

"Why don't you want to call her?" Hayley asked.

He shrugged. "Because there's nothing to talk about."

"But there was lots to talk about on Friday."

"That was before we had sex."

"Well, yeah. How about if I called you? Would you be impressed by that?"

"Don't call me." He held both palms up in warning.

"Why not?"

"Because it's lame."

Hayley gaped at him. "It's 'lame'? It's not 'lame.' It's . . . courageous."

"It's embarrassing." He looked at her as if she were crazy. "It's major humiliation waiting to happen. You some kind of, like, sadist?"

"Masochist." *Idiot.*

"Yeah. One of those."

Hayley wasn't ready to give up. "So I shouldn't call you?"

"No way . . . well, maybe if you called me again I'd take you out, but only to have sex with you again."

"That's disgusting."

"Men are disgusting." He said this as if it were a point of pride.

Hayley shook her head. "You're all a bunch of idiots."

"Not really. If I keep calling to have you keep coming over to have sex and you do, that's pretty fucking smart of me. Heh-heh, heh-heh."

"Language," the professor warned.

Steve and Hayley both ignored him. Hayley was horrified. "Are there any clues as to whether you intend for the next date after the one-night stand to be an actual date or an excuse for sex?"

"Nope."

"No?"

"Nope. You wouldn't be able to tell right away. You'd just have to take your chances."

"*What?*"

"You're gonna have to take your chances."

"My *chances*? I'm supposed to just take my *chances*?"

"Uh-huh."

"Steve?"

"Yeah?"

"Were those pot brownies you ate for breakfast? Did you slip a little hallucinogen into your coffee before class this morning?"

"Uh—" He looked extremely puzzled.

"Yeah, buddy, you heard me right. Or maybe it's just that you're *completely insane*."

Steve looked over at the professor who seemed equally nonplussed by the situation as he clutched nervously at his trout necktie.

But Hayley wasn't finished. She grabbed the professor's sleeve. "He's got it all wrong. You don't just walk away and leave things to chance. That's not going to work. Not to mention, these things are all relative. You have to take into account the particular circumstances of the encounter. I mean, we have a history of sorts. We have a corpse together. I don't *want* to walk away. And that's what you have to ask yourself—what do you *really want*?"

She turned to the audience. "Specifically, what do you want? Figure it out and then don't just sit there, avoiding. Do something about it. Don't just accept. Step out in the world."

And as she stared out at that sea of faces, suddenly Hayley realized she wasn't worried. The economy might be tanking and the dating landscape might be looking pretty bad, but for the first time in a long while, she wasn't worried.

She took a deep breath, raised her fist triumphantly in the air a la Bruno, and yelled, "Ask yourself what you want . . . and *go for it!*" Then Hayley raced up the aisle like some sort of possessed television evangelist and blasted through the exit doors as the class burst into explosive applause behind her.

When she finally got back home, Hayley dumped her purse on the bed and took off her stilettos. She studied the shoes, noting the worn patches on the toes and heels, the areas where the black leather had scraped off the sides, and how the stiletto tips were dull and uneven. She smiled to herself. It looked like she'd managed to fully amortize them, after all.

She put the shoes in her closet and dragged out her storage box into the bedroom. Rummaging through it for a while, she finally found what she'd been looking for. It was the crane mobile Fred Leary had given her as a holiday present last December.

Some of the cranes were smashed up, so she smoothed them out as best she could, then retrieved a hammer and nail from her kitchen utility drawer. She returned to her bedroom, stood on the bed, and hammered the crane mobile into the ceiling above where she slept.

Immensely satisfied, she brushed the chips of plaster off the bedcovers and lay down on the bed with her arms behind her head, staring upward as the cranes swayed in an invisible breeze.

What did you try to tell those kids, Hayley? You have to ask yourself, what do you really want? Specifically, what do you want? Don't just sit there, avoiding. Do something about it. And don't pretend you're doing something; really do it. Step out in the world. No gimmicks. Don't waste any more time.

Okay, then. Here goes.

Chapter Twenty

Hayley's heart was pounding. This was a recipe for disaster. A reasonable woman did not just go confront a guy over a one-night stand. It made a person look like a psycho. Or a stalker.

And it wasn't as if Hayley could blame Grant, exactly. Who had sex with a guy on the first date and expected to ever see him again? What was she thinking? Why had that seemed like a good idea?

On the other hand, it wasn't really a first date, was it? And it wasn't like she'd picked him up in a bar. After all, they'd had quite a bit of conversation prior to the sex. One could even consider the corpse incident "datelike," since it had included conversation, a little Q-and-A, and some lead-up groping.

So the sex they'd had last Friday maybe wasn't really sex on the first date; it was more like sex on the second date, which sounded much, much better. . . .

But the bottom line was that she'd slept with him early on in the relationship, and he did not call afterward. That did not bode well for this impending confrontation.

The poor guy might have no choice but to embarrass both parties by explaining that he was really sorry but not interested—and he thought he'd managed to communicate that point by not calling.

Hayley figured that since seventy-five percent of the scenarios she'd played out in her head on the way over had some form of humiliation involved, the best thing to do would be to make the whole exchange as private as possible . . . and get it all over with as fast as possible.

Walking into the police station was a little strange. Hayley felt inexplicably guilty, like her past transgressions, however small, would load on the check-in computer screen the minute she said her name. She leaned over the desk and craned her neck to see.

"Hi."

Hayley whirled around.

Grant leaned his hip against the desk, arms crossed.

"Hi," Hayley echoed. At least her voice didn't crack. That was something. She studied his face. He didn't look annoyed. He didn't look much of anything . . . he was essentially unreadable. Not very helpful.

No pain, no gain. She swallowed and cleared her throat. "Okay, Grant, here's the thing." She prodded his chest with her index finger. "I've got something to say to you."

He looked down at her finger, which Hayley had to admit seemed a little pathetic, poking somewhat ineffectually at the broad expanse of his chest.

Then he looked around the busy room and said, "Why don't we go in back?" She thought she saw the flicker of a smile, but it could have been a flicker of something else entirely.

As she followed him back into the depths of the building, Hayley quickly said, "I'm not going psycho on you, I promise. I just want to understand the logic here. This is a growth opportunity for me."

"What logic?" he asked as he opened the door and ushered her into the holding cell area.

Hayley grabbed on to the cell bars with one hand and pretended to study the metal with great interest while she prepared for the big moment.

Hanging casually off one of the bars in an effort to look nonchalant, she took a deep breath and looked right in his eyes. "Why didn't you call me? It's obviously not because you were hit by a bus."

He looked genuinely surprised. Or else it was a well-honed, well-practiced reaction. Hayley chose to remain suspicious. She put up her palm and said, "Hold on; before you answer, let me first say that I'm going to put myself in your shoes. I'm not an unreasonable person, so I'm going to try and—"

"Can I talk now? That was a simple question and I have a simple answer."

"Uh, sure."

"I go into the bathroom, you get on the phone with somebody. I offer you a ride home, you take a cab instead." He shrugged, suggesting it was all quite obvious, self-explanatory even.

She tilted her head. "A simple answer. Okay. I'm in your shoes. I'm in your shoes and girl and guy have one-night stand. Well, it's not obvious that it's a one-night stand at that point . . . in any case, girl makes phone call on the morning after and takes cab home in the morning *to save guy trouble* and not make it look like she's going to be expecting too much from him."

His lips pursed in an encouraging way, sort of like her interpretation hadn't occurred to him. A beat of silence passed between them, with the two of them just looking at each other.

"Sorry, it's not coming to me. And you figured what?" Hayley finally asked, embarrassed all over again that she had to press him for an answer. She didn't like the idea of seeming needy or pushy. She was definitely losing hope . . . and her nerve.

"I figured that was it. You weren't interested. You didn't want a next time." He stood there, so matter-of-fact about it.

Hayley studied his face. It just wasn't true what women said about the male brain. About it somehow being illogical and dysfunctional. It wasn't that at all. Well, maybe it was dysfunctional, but it was more like it was hyperlogical to a fault.

If A equaled B and B equaled C, in the male world A equaled C, simple as that.

But every intelligent woman knew it wasn't that simple at all. A might very well equal B, and B equal C, but if A is, say, depressed, B can't find the car keys, and C just gained five pounds, well, obviously there are some variables in the equation that men apparently aren't equipped to deal with.

Hayley slapped her forehead with the palm of her hand. "I was following instructions." She sighed heavily. "If there is one thing I've learned it's that other people's protocol *cannot* be guaranteed to apply to anyone else. I really need to stop seeking so much outside advice. I should follow my instincts. I wasn't going to make that call to Suz at first, but then I kind of chickened out."

He looked at her like she was crazy. "I'm not sure I'm getting all this. What advice were you following?"

"Suz's advice about the Rule of Three," Hayley answered sadly. "I protested that you didn't have to take me home three times and you only insisted on taking me home twice. If you'd insisted one more time, we wouldn't be having this conversation." Boy, it really *did* sound stupid when you took a step back and thought about it.

"Maybe you *should* stop taking so much advice," he said.

Ouch. At least he looked like he thought it was funny instead of looking like he wished she'd hurry up and go. But maybe it was just because he was so polite.

Okay, I'm going to say it. Be bold, Hayley. Expand your horizons. "I never meant to give you the impression that I wasn't interested. In fact, I thought I was doing the right thing to try and show you that I did want a next time. Frankly, I don't have a tremendous amount of experience with these, er, one-night-stand situations."

"You seemed experienced enough to me," he said. "I had no complaints."

Was he flirting with her now? *Go for the kill! Go for the kill!* Hayley's mind reeled, trying to analyze all the possible meanings and implications of his statement. Wildly self-conscious, she finally just cleared her throat and, fighting the urge to close the door first, said, "Well, then, just so you know, I'm interested."

He smiled but he didn't say anything. Hayley got the impression he was making her pay a little bit for dashing out on him in the morning. It was actually quite flattering, if she was reading him right. If.

Well, the only thing worse than putting it out there that you were interested was being forced to ask about reciprocation with the possibility of getting it thrown back in your face. But she'd come this far, and so far he'd been receptive. He wasn't making it easy or anything, but he was teasing in a nice way.

Hayley looked down at her shoes for support. They looked like crap by now. They'd lost all of their designer glory, frankly, and failed to supply any of the kick-ass confidence for which they'd originally been purchased.

If they weren't so damned symbolic she'd have thrown them away by now. But, shoes or no shoes, Hayley was feeling surprisingly kick-ass all of a sudden.

She cracked a sly smile. "Suppose I were to ask if *you* were still interested?"

He grinned and crossed his arms. "Suppose I said yes?"

Hayley's stomach fluttered. "Suppose I did something about it right now?"

"Suppose you did?"

She tugged nervously at the collar of her shirt and said, "I'm going to kiss you, you know. I hope you don't have a problem with that, seeing as how this is your place of work."

"We didn't seem to have a problem in your place of work. But whatever you decide, you'd better get on with it. I think we've got a suspect to incarcerate." He pointed over her shoulder to the open door.

It was a little disconcerting, what with a burly, uniformed policeman complete with giant beer gut and a seedy-looking guy in handcuffs staring at her. Hayley gave them a hand signal to get a couple of extra minutes. She took Grant's elbow and set him against the bars of one of the holding cells a little farther into the room, out of the sight line of the open door.

He let his arms rest at his sides, watching, waiting, a little more amused than Hayley would have liked.

"Okay. Here goes." She grabbed the bars on either side of him and walked up to him, real close. Then she kissed him. He seemed to like it. A lot. So she moved closer, put her hands in his hair, and kissed him harder.

When it became clear that she was requiring more oxygen than seemed to be available, Hayley broke off the kiss. Somewhere along the line, Grant's arms and hands had gotten more involved in the situation, and Hayley was also happy to note that he seemed a little breathless himself.

"Uh, Hutchinson. Can we cage this guy, or what?" The burly policeman stood in the doorway, leaning against the doorjamb looking bored.

Hayley blushed to her roots and cleared her throat.

Grant grinned. "Just one sec." He looked down at Hayley. "I've got to get back to work."

"Okay, I think it's safe to say you're definitely interested. In that case, I'm going to ask you out on a second date."

Grant nodded, waiting.

"Just give me a moment. Okay, here I go. Right now. Right here. Here goes: I was wondering if you'd like to go out with me again sometime."

"Yes, I would," he said. "I think you're just crazy enough to be appealing."

Hayley grinned and released the breath of air she'd been holding.

"That wasn't so bad, was it?" he asked.

"No. But we have to acknowledge that, by this point, it was kind of a shoo-in."

"The kiss could have been a tease," Grant said. "I could have said anything. I could have said no."

"Nah."

"Why not?"

"Because we've already been past third base. I'm a slam-dunk, a guarantee, the gold."

He gave her a once-over. "Can't say I wouldn't enjoy a repeat."

"I hope that's not the only reason you're interested."

"Bit of a risk, isn't it?"

Hayley gaped in mock-disbelief. "So it's like that, is it? Well, don't get your hopes up, because I'm calling the shots this time, and we are going to do things a little differently."

"Is that so?" he challenged.

"That is so. And for our next big destination date, we are going to, uh . . . we are going to . . . we're going to the San Francisco Zoo. That's right, we're going to the zoo."

Grant blinked, looking substantially less than enthusiastic. "The zoo?"

"It will be the perfect opportunity to get to know each other a little better."

"True." He didn't look all that convinced.

"Besides, they've just upgraded the petting zoo and we can pet the goats and stuff. You know, buy food pellets out of the vending machine and feed them. It'll be fun."

He pretended to have to give it some thought. "You did sit through a substantial portion of a baseball game," he said.

"It was fun. I would've sat through the whole thing if I'd remained conscious. And believe me, it has nothing to do with the Baseball Trick."

"I know," Grant admitted, then laughed in disbelief. "Fine. The zoo it is. Sounds terrific. Clearly feeding goats is something no man should pass up." Then he shook his head. "If this doesn't demonstrate my 'interest,' I don't know what will."

Precisely.

Chapter Twenty-one

Asserting oneself could be deliciously contagious. Once Hayley got used to it, it was difficult to stop. Or maybe it was that she didn't want to stop.

Hayley had no idea what the final outcome of the Grant Thing would be. Maybe he was full of shit and seeing this thing through just long enough to get her back in bed for one more round.

Or maybe it would actually turn into something, become a boyfriend/girlfriend scenario and blow up three months down the line.

Or maybe he was the One.

Hayley put her hands behind her head and leaned back in her office chair. She had no idea, but as it stood, she didn't particularly care. For now she had what she wanted, and she'd gone out and done it herself.

The sound of George slurping and smacking in a prolonged effort to reduce his Cheerios to a digestible pulp brought home the fact that not *everything* was quite what she'd like it to be.

The fact was, she didn't want to be here. The trouble was, she had rent to pay. She could be mercenary and suck it up until she'd squirreled away some money and brought her savings back up to a safer level. Or she could chuck it all and take another path.

She knew what she *should* do and she knew what she *wanted* to do. Glancing over her shoulder out of habit, Hayley confirmed that no one was watching. She went on-line and started surfing the techie job sites.

"Hayley Jane, how *are* you?"

Goddammit, Eileen! Hayley twitched in her chair with a start and immediately killed her browser window. How embarrassing. The second week of work and she got caught looking for another job.

"Hayley, we've got a problem." Eileen let the word "problem" hang out there all cheerful and long-voweled in that perky voice.

Hayley still hadn't put her finger on what exactly it reminded her of, but it rivaled George's Cheerios-smacking on the fingernails-against-blackboard scale of annoying noises.

Ever since the incident with Killer in the conference room, things had been a little uneasy between her and Eileen. They both faked a smile whenever they met in the employee kitchen, but this was the first time Eileen had ever stopped by Hayley's cube. Of course, that may have had something to do with fearing for her personal safety.

"That's right, we've got a problem," Eileen repeated. Apparently she was waiting for Hayley to react. Inside, Hayley was reacting . . . to Eileen's beige polyester pantsuit. *Heh. No, seriously, Hayley. Concentrate. Okay. So.* She and Eileen had one thing in common: Together they had a problem. Well, whatever it was, it couldn't be good.

And under these circumstances, how bad could something that couldn't be good, be?

"Why don't you have a seat, Eileen, and we can discuss it." Hayley picked a stack of papers off her guest chair and made a welcoming hand gesture.

Eileen sat down, primly folding her hands in her lap. She smiled hard enough to pop a couple of lightweight dimples.

Hayley stared at her. Was she going to fire her? Could they have decided already that she wasn't up to snuff? Perhaps it was the way she'd put her desk together.

Was this a mercy killing?

A wave of delightful anticipation swept through her, and Hayley realized just how much she'd like to cut bait. Hell, a mercy killing—getting fired with a chunk of "mistake money" when you really wanted to leave all along—was as good a method as any.

Trying her best not to look inappropriately hopeful, she said, "We're both professionals. I'm sure we can come to an understanding, whatever the problem is."

Eileen rubbed her lips together. "It concerns your writing."

"Oh." Hayley wrinkled her forehead, then added helpfully, "Too snarky? Or not snarky enough?"

Eileen produced a toothy smile, then leaned over and patted Hayley's knee. "I'd like to take you to lunch."

Hayley cringed reflexively, because Eileen's expression reminded her of Killer's look just before he'd lunged for her hands. "Uh, okay."

"It's not too snarky. And it's not that it isn't snarky enough. The problem is . . ." Eileen paused, letting the moment string out. Suddenly she looked like she was going to give Hayley a tasty treat or a present or something.

Alarm bells went off in Hayley's head. She swallowed fearfully, just as Eileen finished up with, "... the problem is that we love it! We absolutely love it. I'm taking you to lunch because we think your writing is: Fan. Tastic!"

Hayley froze. "Oh." She cycled through a variety of expressions and settled on "crazed." "Oh!"

But Eileen didn't notice the expression. She just kept going, gushing and flapping about, using her hands excessively as she spoke. "I want to be honest," she was saying, "so I'll tell you that when we first met and there was that situation with poor Killer, I wasn't sure how you'd fit in."

Hayley just nodded.

"And then when I took a look at the sample URLs listed on that résumé Audra forwarded, I was concerned that we might have to help you make a little bit of an adjustment with your writing. Just a liiittle bit."

Her face was all screwed up and she was pinching her fingers together at the tips to bring home the point that the adjustment was extremely small. "But you've really come into your own in the last several days."

The corner of Hayley's mouth twitched as she struggled to hold back a laugh. "Really? And what was your favorite?"

Eileen leaned forward ecstatically. "For example, the piece on kitchen tools and sexual gratification?"

Oh, God. The woman managed to say that with a straight face. The fact that she said it in her high-pitched, squeaky animal voice made it even better.

"You're referring to, 'G-Spot, Gee whiz!'?"

"That's the one. It was just so clever!"

To her credit, Eileen was working real hard to make Hayley feel good, and frankly, under normal circumstances, she'd be doing a reasonable job. But these weren't normal circumstances... and Hayley wasn't normal.

And actually, she felt a little bit bad about stringing Eileen along, but it *was* kind of funny. "I'm so glad you liked it. I drew on the influence of the accompanying retro-fifties illustration... you know, the housewife and the eggbeater?"

Eileen sat back up, her hands flapping excitedly. "It's just... can I say we just love what you're doing. We love it. The click-through on your titles is incredible. And in just one week we've seen an unusually large increase in page views for the pages you've been working on."

Hayley wanted to tell her to calm down, or slap her or something, or maybe just come out and tell her not to be such an idiot, because that was what happened when you used sex in headlines to catch people's attention. Somehow she managed to control herself, which she thought was pretty impressive, given that she didn't have a whole lot to lose.

"I'm really looking forward to being your mentor, Hayley," Eileen said as she stood up and brushed off her pants.

Hayley's eyebrows flew up. "My mentor? You're planning to be my mentor?"

"Not everyone gets to have one. It means we'll be spending our lunches together discussing your progress and professional development."

Hayley flinched. "I really don't deserve this, Eileen."

"Oh, but yes, you do."

"Oh, but no. I don't," Hayley replied firmly. It suddenly dawned on her. The woman's voice was the equivalent of cheerful yellow baby chicks and furry little white bunnies. She'd rather be held under alien surveillance than deal with this.

Well, maybe not. Six of the one, half dozen of the other.

Suddenly Eileen sat back down again and pulled her chair right up close to Hayley's. "You know what? I just can't hold it in. I was going to tell you this over lunch, but I'll tell you now." She drew her upper body up as straight as it could go and said, "We're taking you off probation early. You can go ahead and order your business cards!"

There obviously wasn't going to be a mercy killing. Hayley stared at the woman in disbelief, surprised at how disappointed she felt. If she wanted out, she would have to euthanize herself.

Suddenly Hayley didn't feel like waiting to find a new techie job on-line. She didn't feel like waiting around for anything.

She felt a strange calm come over her.

There was no need to make a big scene. She'd allow herself one last indulgence, just a small speech, and then it was Quitsville.

"Actually, Eileen, I'm terribly sorry, but I simply don't think I'm capable of stooping to that level of degradation for the honor of holding such a glamorous, prestigious job in a smelly loft with no air-conditioning while bringing in the wages of an illiterate mango."

Eileen pulled back, confused. "Mang—I beg your pardon?"

" 'Illiterate mango.' I'm trying to drive the point across that only an exotic piece of uneducated fruit would want to work in these conditions." Hayley wheeled her chair around so that her back was to Eileen, and started to stack up the papers on her desk. "That's a fairly small audience. It appears I've made a mistake."

"Hayley Jane," Eileen said.

Hayley's eyes widened. *Wow.* The woman's voice went from hot to icy cold in less than ten seconds. Fluffy baby chick was now a frozen chicken entrée.

She slowly turned around to find Eileen looking at her with an expression of sheer disbelief, opening and closing her mouth several times, but totally unsure how to proceed.

Hayley wasn't sure whether it was the nonsensical tropical-fruit reference that had thrown her off the scent, or something else. She didn't actually care.

She smiled as pleasantly as she could and said, "It's okay. I was eventually going to quit anyway. At some point in the next few days it would have dawned on me that I should just quit as soon as possible. This is not where I need to be. Consider it no harm, no foul. I'll pack up and be out of here in an hour."

"You can't quit," Eileen choked out. "Nobody *quits* in a job market like this. Getting fired or laid off is one thing, but no sane individual quits."

"I don't recall putting 'one sane individual' on my résumé. I don't even have a 'hobbies' section on my résumé." *Hmm. Maybe I should get out more.*

Eileen slowly stood up, then wordlessly backed out of the cube.

Hayley sat back in her chair and watched her leave. When Eileen was gone, she put her head back and stared up at the ceiling. Same industrial-light-fixture ceiling laid in next to the building's pipe system.

And she just sat there. Blinking. Just sat there, quietly flapping her eyelids and taking in oxygen. It felt peaceful. There was none of the disquiet and worry she'd felt after getting fired, even though the bottom line was the same. She was unemployed. But for some bizarre reason, she just felt free this time.

Free.

Hayley giggled, then clamped her hand over her mouth. She regained her composure, then got up from the chair, got on her hands and knees, and pulled the empty box from her last job out from under the desk.

With a crazed grin, Hayley walked to the supply closet and tore a strip of stickers off the roll of orange circles. She went back to her cube and plastered *Basura* all over her box and packed up her personal belongings.

Chapter Twenty-two

"You skipped last Sunday," Diane said accusingly.

"Yeah, I know," Hayley said. "I was going to call, but I didn't think any of you were speaking to me."

"None of us have missed a Sunday for as long as I can remember," Suz noted. "No matter how late I've been up Saturday night, or whose house I'm at, I never miss a Sunday."

"I guess I just figured a cooling-off period would be good."

"We ordered your latte," Audra said, shocked. "It just sat there, a disgusting film forming on the top. We expected you to be here."

"Not to mention, your absence has already put us behind. We've been working hard on a new strategy," Diane said. "Audra's found a couple of exciting job alternatives, and Suz apparently met a gaggle of sailors you're supposed to choose from, and—"

Hayley burst out laughing.

"I don't know what's so funny. There's more, even. I've talked to Bruno about becoming his protégé, and even though he refuses to see you again, he suggested a couple of new techniques *I* can try out on you."

"You guys are so good to me." Hayley shook her head, truly overwhelmed. She'd been totally impossible over the last few weeks. And they'd hung in with her every step of the way. "The thing is, I'm totally under control. See, I've got some good news—"

She stopped abruptly. The three girls were smiling knowingly amongst themselves. "What?"

"Look, we understand that this is a difficult time for you," Audra said. "And there's no need to pretend in front of us."

Diane nodded. "And we also understand that you really want to be the one making the changes. So we're going to have you choose which one of us to work with first."

"See, that's a decision," Audra said encouragingly.

"But that's what I'm trying to tell you. The good news is that you don't need to worry about me so much. This time I mean it."

Audra put a hand on her hip. "Well, we *are* worried," she said. "As a matter of fact, we've been worried since last Sunday."

Suz nodded. "At first each of us assumed that you'd called one of the others, but when we met on Sunday and found out that wasn't the case, we were *really* worried. You never returned our phone messages."

"And you FedExed my Palm back to me," Diane said. "How exactly was I supposed to interpret that?"

"Sorry, I got really busy and I knew I'd see you today," Hayley explained. "And you just won't believe what I've accomplished since I last saw you." In a teasing tone, she added, "You are going to be shocked and amazed."

"We already *were* shocked and amazed." Suz propped her chin up with her hand. "I was going to go to the police station and get Grant to come with me to your apartment and break the door down."

"You were going to go to the police station and get Grant to introduce you to the other policemen," Audra clarified with a smile. "Suz showed us her new hot pants last Sunday." She waved her hand in front of her face, pretending to be overheated. "Silver lamé. Breaking down your door was just an excuse."

"And what was your excuse for volunteering to come with me? I'm thinking you were hoping to find someone in Internal Affairs so you could ask about those corrupt policemen."

Audra just shrugged. "I only said I was interested in going if you needed some moral support."

"I know what you said," Suz said, elbowing Audra.

"Suz needs more 'moral support' than you could possibly supply, anyway," Diane said.

Suz snickered, obviously quite pleased with the comment.

"Well, you'll be happy to know you're off the hook," Hayley said. "I don't need your help anymore."

The three girls studied her in silence.

"You heard me right. I'm looking into a whole new career. Nobody says you have to keep doing the job you thought you wanted when you were in college. There is absolutely no rule that says that even if you've spent years studying toward one thing in particular, you have to do it one minute longer than absolutely necessary."

"Who are you trying to convince? Me or you?" Audra asked.

"I'm already convinced. I went to Diane's lecture and now I'm convinced."

"You went to *my* class?" Diane asked.

"Well, I knew you weren't going, so I figured there would be a free seat," Hayley said. She put a hand on her heart and added, "I went to your Human Sexuality lecture and stood there on that stage looking out at a sea of malaise."

"What were you doing on the stage?" Diane asked fearfully.

"I'd volunteered for a role-play game."

"Oh, my God." Diane put her head in her hands and mumbled, "*Nobody* volunteers. My A."

"Don't be ridiculous. Nobody even knows I know you." Hayley laughed and added, "I told the guy next to me I was from Sweden."

"And he believed you?" Suz asked.

"Yeah, I know, pretty bad, huh . . . ? So, anyway, I stood there on that stage, looking at these people about four or five years behind me, about to make all the same mistakes. And I went home and basically asked myself, why do we do things we really don't want to do? And why don't we do more of the things we want to do? And why—*why*—don't we do something about it before it's too late?"

Diane looked a little stunned. "If you'd wanted to go to class with me, you could have just asked. I would have guided you. I could have explained what is and isn't appropriate in the collegiate environment. I know it's been a few years for you."

"I'm glad I didn't know." Hayley took a sip of coffee. "Fred Leary dies in the cube next to me and nobody notices. I'm willing to bet that all he really wanted to do was fold origami, not sit in some stuffy cube haranguing people over improper use of the subjunctive form. This is a good thing, Diane. I'm really looking forward to this."

She looked around the table. "I see you're all looking a bit skeptical. Let me put it this way. I tried all these things. Tried to force myself to go in different directions. Be more like you, Diane. More like Audra. More like Suz. What I really needed to do was just . . . let go and follow my heart and use my head." She shrugged as if it were the most simple and obvious explanation in the world.

"Follow your heart?" Diane put a hand on Hayley's forehead, ostensibly to check for fever. "You don't feel warm or clammy or anything. But that's the most clichéd thing I've ever heard."

"And there must be a reason for that." Hayley flashed her shit-eating grin around the table.

"Wait a minute. Look at her. She's suspiciously Zen. What happened?" Diane asked. "Something's happened to you." She drew in a sharp breath. "Oh, God. Were you approached by a cult?"

"Hayley's part of a cult now? Does this mean we can start using the collective 'we'?" Suz was laughing as she said it.

Audra looked horrified. "Don't laugh! Di may be right. We left Hayley alone, vulnerable and in the middle of a personal crisis. That's when those people strike. Is that where you were last Sunday, Hay? Some sort of strange New Age-cult Bible study? You didn't eat anything while you were there, did you?"

"No, believe me, that's not what happened."

"You see? They teach them to deny everything. This may require an intervention of some sort." She patted Hayley's hand across the table. "Don't you worry, Hay; we'll get you the very best." Audra pulled her hand back, took the cell phone from her bag, and started scrolling through the address book.

Suz subjected Hayley to some close scrutiny, then shook her head at Audra. "I really don't think that's it."

Audra put her palm up to Suz's face. "One sec. Intervention . . . intervention . . . drug rehab. No, wrong kind of intervention. Maybe D for 'deprogramming.' Ah, here we go. Let's see. 'Deprogramming, cult.' Now, which one should we call . . . ?"

Suz and Diane looked at each other. Diane nodded and said,

"Audra, you're not listening to her. Look at her." Audra looked up in surprise, then put the phone down and looked at Hayley.

"I did *not* get approached by a cult and I will *not* be requiring deprogramming," Hayley said. "Nobody told me to deny anything. Honestly. I just figured out what I needed to do for myself, and then I did it."

Audra looked at her, then at Diane and Suz, then back to Hayley. "Oh. Fine." Sheepishly, she tossed the phone back in her bag. "I guess I just wasn't quite ready to give you up as my project."

"Why don't you tell us what happened?" Suz asked.

And so she did. She told them about storming the police station and kissing Grant against the holding cell, and about prematurely *basura*-ing herself from her latest job.

Needless to say, they were speechless.

Hayley blithely sipped her latte while the girls picked at their food without really seeing it, stared off into space, or scratched their faces in wonder.

"Mother of God," Suz finally said.

The other girls nodded slowly.

"You quit your job," Diane said.

"That's right."

"And you confronted Grant on his own turf and came out of it with a second date," Audra said.

"That's pretty much what happened," Hayley said.

"Holy Mother of God."

The girls looked at each other and then scooted their chairs closer to the table.

Diane smiled her best psychiatric smile and put her clasped hands out in front of her on the tabletop. "Hayley, we all want to be supportive here. We certainly don't want to burst your bubble, do we?" She looked at Audra and Suz for support. They nodded obligingly. "But—"

"But what?" Hayley asked.

"But we don't want to see you get in trouble."

Hayley grinned a loopy sort of grin. "What trouble? I'm not in trouble. I'm distinctly out of trouble. Troubleless. Sans trouble."

"Be serious," Audra said.

"Okay, I'm serious." Hayley lifted her hands up questioningly. "Where's the trouble?"

"You seem to be unemployed. Again. With no more prospects than you had the first time around. Not that this is a problem for me," Suz said, "but last time I checked, you seemed to think this was a problem for you."

"I'm looking into other things. I may just leave tech behind for good."

"Leave tech behind?" Audra gasped. "You've been in tech your whole career. What on earth would you *do*?"

"Something else." Just saying it felt terrific. "I'm exploring my options."

"Okay, that's great. That's great," Suz agreed, not looking as though she thought it was really all that great.

An uncomfortable silence settled in among them.

"Let's just switch gears for a moment," Diane said. "About Grant. I think what you did was admirable. I really do, and it sounds like maybe there might be something to this relationship. . . ."

"But?" Hayley prompted, totally unconcerned.

"But what if he's just using you for sex? Are you mentally prepared for that possibility?" Audra and Suz looked at Diane and nodded their agreement.

Hayley considered this. "Well, I have to admit that I'm thinking that would . . . suck. And it's not entirely out of the realm of possibility. . . ."

The three of them looked at her, concern etched all over their faces.

"Let's just say that the guy is very accomplished at what he does." Hayley smiled and wiggled her eyebrows suggestively. "And I'm having a good time with him. So I'm going to try not to overanalyze every little thing." She shrugged. "Bottom line is, I'm not going to worry right now about where it is or isn't going to go."

"Okay, that seems reasonable," Suz said. "Very reasonable." There was another long pause and she added, "Is this something you'll want to worry about later?"

Hayley just laughed. "I hope not."

"What's next?" Audra asked.

"The zoo."

Diane choked on a sip of water.

"It was my idea to go, so don't try to tell me there's something called the Zoo Trick I should be aware of."

"There's no Zoo Trick *I* know of," Diane said. "Anybody else?"

They all shook their heads.

"The zoo?" Audra asked, trying to suppress her laughter. "How . . . cute."

"I think so," Hayley said. "I think this next date will be rather tame, and that's fine by me. Like I said to Grant, it's an opportunity for us to get to know each other in a no-stress environment. I figure, what could possibly happen at the zoo?"

Chapter Twenty-three

It just didn't get better than this.

Sure, things started to really heat up behind the popcorn stand after only fifteen minutes, but that was partly due to the fact that they'd had to postpone the date once because of an unexpected twist in one of Grant's cases . . . and they were *really* happy to see each other. Hayley simply reminded Grant about the purpose of the date and explained that she didn't want him to think she only wanted him for the sex and vice versa. He seemed to take it pretty well, although Hayley had to swat him with her empty popcorn container to wipe the smirk off his face.

So far they'd seen the lions and tigers and bears . . . in that order, because Hayley thought it would be funny.

While Grant watched indulgently, she'd oohed and ahhed at the animals in a manner she would have found repulsive and annoying in anybody else. But not today. Today Hayley and her man held hands. They shared food. They laughed at the tourists.

It was divine.

Hayley felt as if she were living one of those cheesy montage sequences, sort of *When Harry Met Sally,* but with giraffes and stuff.

Now that they'd spent the morning looking primarily at animals with fur, Grant requested that they stop in at the insect zoo, since it was on the way to the petting zoo.

Hayley wasn't all that thrilled to be checking out a bunch of insects, but she figured he'd been pretty patient so far, and if he wanted to look at bugs, then by God she would go with him to look at bugs.

Grant peered happily through the Plexiglas windows at the various specimens of yuck while Hayley walked behind him scratching and rubbing at phantom creepy crawlies on her neck.

"You need to see this." Grant waved Hayley over to his side and pointed through the Plexiglas.

Hayley stared at a spider with rust-colored tufts of hair on its spindly legs. She lifted one eyebrow and looked dubiously at Grant. "It's . . . er, nice."

"No, no. *This* one. You're looking at the Mexican Red Knee tarantula, which is a perfectly respectable spider, but I'm more interested in the black widow spider. . . ." He directed her gaze to an adjoining display. "Now, *that's* a spider."

He nodded in satisfaction at the display, while Hayley backed away in horror.

"I hadn't really thought about the fact that spiders might or might not have knees," she said in a slightly quavering voice. "But I'm not really a 'spider person.' Heh."

She looked down at the insect zoo brochure. *Ugh.* Nor, for that matter, was she a "hissing cockroach" person. *Oh, God.* Was Grant one of those men who refused to flush bugs down the toilet? Probably. After all, he was in the business of saving lives.

Hayley chewed on her lower lip, watching him. It was something to consider if they were ever going to move in together. No, wait a minute. She'd sworn she wasn't going to overanalyze or jump ahead of herself.

Grant looked at her and laughed at the expression on her face. "I think you might be shortchanging yourself. There is much to appreciate about the black widow spider."

In a teasing tone, he added, "Let it not be said that I was unable to appreciate the Mexican Red Knee tarantula, but the fact remains that it's the black widow I find particularly . . . appealing."

Hayley watched him stroll around the display, checking out the spiders from all possible angles.

She knew full well he expected her to ask. With a little laugh, she said, "By all means, don't keep it to yourself. What *is* so appealing about the black widow spider?"

"The black widow spider," he said with a *National Geographic*–special inflection, from the opposite side of the display, "has *many* appealing attributes. . . ."

He was circling around the exhibit toward her now, a predatory look on his face. Hayley shrieked happily and started to walk in the opposite direction. In response, he walked faster and faster after her, and she had to stop trying to outrun him or else go completely dizzy.

He caught up with her and stood behind her with his hands on her shoulders. "The black widow spider has a nice, curvy figure. . . ."

Okay, so he was using a little creative license right there, but Hayley figured she'd take it as a compliment, because he gently brushed his hands from her shoulders down what existed of her curves down the sides of her body and then away.

He put his mouth up close to her ear and whispered, "And a tattoo that only those up close and personal get to see . . ."

His hands moved up to her waist, and he pressed his palm over the spot where her teeny-tiny flower tattoo sat. Hayley thought she might pass out.

"According to the documentation," he growled softly, "the black widow spider has a bit of a temper. We've come to find that she's not always in a good mood, but we like her anyway. . . ."

Hayley just grinned like a fool.

"The black widow spider enjoys warmth. . . ." Hayley could feel Grant's hot breath on her neck and started having a little trouble with her own breathing.

Dammit! This date was supposed to be charming and romantic and cute. Who got turned on at the zoo? In the insect zoo?!

"The black widow spider likes to handle her man in her own special way," he said. "I hope you don't take this the wrong way when I tell you that she likes to suck the body of her man into her mouth and do with him what she will. . . ."

Hayley gasped and burst out laughing, then turned in to his chest to keep from making a scene.

Grant bent down slightly so he could whisper in her ear some more. "There are many, many things, you see, to like about the black widow spider. The Mexican Red Knee tarantula doesn't. Even. Come. Close."

"You're completely insane," Hayley whispered breathlessly into his shirt.

"Maybe so." He shrugged.

The separation in his shirt between the two buttons she'd accidentally dislodged distracted Hayley. Her proximity to the patch of bare chest seemed to be affecting her short-term memory. The notion of refusing to let the date end up with sex was just that: A fleeting notion. *Oops.* There it went. A fled notion. "What do you say we get out of here?" she asked.

She could hear the laughter in his voice when he asked, "But what about the petting zoo?"

"We can pretend I'm the goat." Hayley took him by the hand and made a run for the exit.

The Last Sunday

"That's not a latte, is it?" Audra's voice sounded shocked as she peered into Hayley's mug. "It's darker than usual."

"Why, Audra, you're extremely observant this morning," Hayley said. "This is not a latte; you are correct. This is a café au lait. I've decided to break with tradition and go for less milk, lower octane."

"She's breaking with tradition," Audra said to Diane.

Diane shrugged. "She's had an epiphany," she explained in a blasé voice. "And now she's acting out."

"Acting out? What's that supposed to mean?"

"You want others to believe that you really are making serious changes in your life, so you're doing things to make other people notice that something's different about you."

Hayley just smiled. She took a sip from her noticeably different café au lait and then went digging in her purse.

"What's that?" Audra asked.

"What?" Hayley asked, looking up innocently.

"The thing you just tried to conceal in your purse."

"What, this pamphlet?" She held up a pamphlet.

"What is it?" Diane asked.

"It's just a little something. I figured I'd wait for Suz before getting into it." She put the pamphlet back in the purse. "Where *is* Suz?".

"Maybe she's not coming. She might have overexerted herself last night," Audra said, glancing at the corner of the pamphlet sticking out of Hayley's purse.

"Just last week she lambasted me for missing a meeting," Hayley said.

"Suz isn't usually quite this late. I don't think she's coming. So you might as well hand it over." Diane tugged on Hayley's purse straps.

Hayley pulled the pamphlet back out of her purse and pushed it across the table to Diane.

"You're kidding, right?" Diane passed the pamphlet to Audra. Audra's jaw dropped.

"I'm not kidding. I can't help it if I find it interesting," Hayley said. "Seems like a person should pursue their interests, don't you think?"

Diane took the pamphlet back and read aloud, " 'The Fifteen Best Jobs for People Who Are Scientifically Interested in Dead Bodies.' " She gazed at Hayley. "*Scientifically* interested?"

Hayley shrugged. "It's put out by a science organization. They don't want to attract any weirdos."

"No weirdos. Right."

Audra stared at her. "No weirdos," she echoed. "So what are you thinking of doing?"

"Dunno. Paramedic. Autopsies. Something along those lines.

Haven't had a chance to really explore what's available. Hence the pamphlet."

Audra dabbed at her mouth with her napkin, looking fairly repulsed. "You screamed your head off when you discovered Fred Leary's dead body. You told us so. I'm not trying to put a damper on your newfound aspirations, but I think you need to be a little less squeamish if you're planning to work with the dead."

Hayley huffed. "I *knew* Fred. It makes a huge difference. I'd have no trouble dealing with dead people I'm not personally acquainted with."

Diane stared into her latte as though it had suddenly become distasteful. She shook her head. "Hayley, I want to ask you a question, but I don't want you to get mad at me."

"I'm not going to get mad at you. Ask me anything you want."

"Do you think all this will last?" Diane asked. "If in two weeks you still don't have an income and Grant won't take your calls, has something so profound happened to you that you won't be flipping out again?"

Hayley frowned, tracing the drawing of the chalk corpse outline on the cover of the pamphlet with her index finger. "Well, I don't know about 'profound.' Let's just say that I can see a little more clearly than before. The reasons I was flipping out before . . . well, they don't seem as valid to me anymore. What's the point of getting all worked up over a job? You know? I could get hit by a bus on the way home today, and then what would it all be for?"

"You don't have to convince me about that," Diane said. "I've been trying to avoid all sorts of jobs for years."

"What about the relationship side of all this?" Audra asked.

"Ah, the Grant Thing. In all honesty? I have to admit I hope that lasts awhile. And I won't pretend not to be upset if it all blows up. I really like him." Hayley swirled her drink. "I don't know; I hope it works. What else is there to say about it?"

"You must have *something* else to say about it. You haven't even mentioned your date. How did it go?"

Hayley giggled. "We played petting zoo. He has an excellent imagination. But I'm not saying anything more until Suz gets here. She'd make me retell the whole story, and I'm not giving out the details twice."

"Petting zoo. I see. So much for a nice, idyllic, get-to-know-you stroll amongst the happy, friendly people. You managed to get turned on at the zoo." Audra shook her head. "Suz would be so proud."

"Suz would be making animal-sex jokes. It's just as well she's not here," Diane noted. "I don't think I could take it, and I *know* you couldn't."

The three of them sat in silence. Hayley couldn't quite get a read on the mood. It seemed pretty glum. But it wasn't just because Suz was missing. "Did I give you enough relationship trauma to build a good paper around?" Hayley asked Diane with a smirk. Maybe Diane would perk up if they talked about her schoolwork.

"Yeah. The paper's done. I turned it in after you told us about quitting your job and confronting Grant."

"Well, I'm sure you'll do very well," Hayley said cheerfully. "You certainly worked hard on the research."

Diane smiled a little woefully. "I'm pretty sure it nailed my A. I'm not worried about it."

"Great," Hayley said.

Audra looked at Diane. "Well, I guess we won't be seeing her around much anymore," she said quietly. "We all know how it goes."

"Her? *Who* 'her'?" Hayley asked. "Are you guys talking about me? Or Suz?"

"Yeah, I know what you mean, Audra. I wish my friends would stop getting involved in committed relationships," Diane said, picking at a hangnail. "I keep losing girlfriends."

"Whoa, you're talking about *me*. Don't be ridiculous," Hayley blurted out. "First of all, it's hardly a committed relationship. I'm not saying it couldn't go in that direction, and at this point I'm hoping it does. But whatever happens with me and Grant, I'm not going to disappear. I'm not like that. You know I need my girls."

Audra looked only slightly convinced.

Suddenly Suz sprinted into the café, ran up to the table, and just stood there stiffly, breathing hard.

Audra stood up and helped Suz take a seat. "Suzy, what happened? Are you okay?"

Suz sat there, her eyes wide and staring. "Holy shit. You aren't going to *believe* what happened."

"Did somebody hurt you?" Hayley asked. "If somebody hurt you I'm going to call Grant and have him come down here and kick some ass."

"That's not it, that's not it."

Diane pushed a glass of water toward her. "Get some water in you. And take some deep breaths, Suz." She pulled some stray hair out of Suz's face. "Just catch your breath, and then when you're ready to say it, you can just say it. Whatever it is."

Suz picked up the glass of water and guzzled it down to the bottom. She slammed the empty glass down on the table and breathed in deeply a couple of times. "I think I'm having a crisis."

The three other girls looked at each other. Audra sighed heavily, but Hayley could see she wasn't the least bit upset. Neither was

Diane. In fact, they were already looking a lot perkier than they had minutes earlier. Diane took out her handheld, and Hayley just leaned back in her chair and smiled to herself.

"Okay, I'm ready. Go ahead; we're listening," Diane said.

"You see there was this guy. . . . God, I don't even know where to start. Um, there was this guy . . . and then there was my cruiser . . . and . . ." Suz trailed off, unable to articulate the exact nature of the disaster. "And I think I'm having a midlife crisis."

"You're not even thirty yet," Audra said patiently. "It can't be a midlife crisis."

"It can if I die before I'm sixty. And the way it's looking, I might be on my way out a lot sooner than I'd planned." She grabbed Hayley's water glass and added, "I'll give Fred Leary your regards."

Hayley watched Suz slam down another water. Calmly cradling her au lait mug in her hands, she produced her most comforting look and said, "Don't worry, Suz; we're here for you. So just take it from the beginning and don't leave anything out."